W9-AVC-254

THE LAKE EFFECT

THE LAKE EFFECT

ERIN McCAHAN

 Dial Books

DIAL BOOKS
An imprint of Penguin Random House LLC
375 Hudson Street
New York, NY 10014

Copyright © 2017 by Erin McCahan

Printed in the United States of America
ISBN 9780803740525

10 9 8 7 6 5 4 3 2 1

Design by Jennifer Kelly

For Tim, who gave me South Haven

1

WANTED: Strong eighteen-year-old guy with reliable means of transportation and reasonable handyman skills to work for eighty-four-year-old widow in relatively good, if controversial, health at her house on Lake Michigan. Candidate must enjoy swimming, sunsets, beach volley-ball, girls in cowboy hats, attending funerals, blue paint, things that jiggle, flamingoes, small dogs, new words, Episcopalians, noodle kugel, losing friends, losing family, and watching his life as he knows it pretty much come to an end. Knowledge of the intestinal tract, including the role of the ileum, helpful but not required. Smokers and tourists need not apply.

This wasn't the ad for the job I took last summer. But it should have been.

2

It was a couple weeks before graduation when I got the job working for Mrs. B. I'd been bussing tables, part-time, at Cascade Country Club for four years by then. I worked like a dog, but the money was good. Especially after big parties. I always went home with tips and phone numbers from women who wanted me to meet their daughters. I didn't call them, because what was I going to do? Say, "Hi, I'm the guy who schlepped your mom's dirty dishes all night. Want to go out sometime?" Plus I had a girlfriend—for a while—and, anyway, that's not how I wanted to meet someone. Still, I'd be lying if I said it wasn't a huge ego feed.

Moms loved me. Especially Taylor's mom, who called me a catch, which really pissed off Taylor, which kind of amused me. "Does she think I would go out with some-one who *isn't* a catch?" she asked me one night back in April, ten days before we broke up.

But, yeah, moms loved me, including my own, I'm not embarrassed to say. She bragged I had a million-dollar smile. Dad called it a $5,600-smile, which is what they paid for my braces in eighth grade. $5,651 to be exact.

Dad reminded me enough times and gave me all sorts of grief, a couple years later, for chewing gum, until I finally just quit. I mean, I get it. $5,651 is a ton of money. Especially for someone else's teeth.

Grandma Ruth just said chewing gum in public was common. As if *common* was a dirty word.

My smile and Grandma Ruth got me the job with Mrs. B. There wasn't an old lady in the world I couldn't charm after handling Grandma Ruth all my life. I learned to fake this kind of carefree, easygoing, unbothered smile just for her. Fake it till you make it, my dad said, and he would know. I mean, carefree, easygoing, and unbothered were three things no one ever felt around the woman. More like tense, tired, and dyspeptic, which is a word I learned at the beach. Before I got the job with Mrs. B., I just said sick to my stomach.

My smile came from playing cards with my grandmother for hours on end, watching HGTV, and force-feeding myself jars of her homemade grape jelly, which I'm pretty sure she made with toadstools and piss.

She was my babysitter—her house, after school and every weekend—from the ages of nine to eleven when Mom and Dad were swamped by life. There was no saying *no* to Grandma Ruth. Not even *no, thank you.* She was kind of a fascist, and my parents were not part of the resistance movement. Too busy to take sides. So I learned to get along. With a smile. Like you do with dictators when you really just want to be left alone.

I honed it over the years—this smile—and developed others, especially when I went to work at a country club.

I learned from going out with Taylor that every expression has meaning behind it. My Country Club Smile said, *No matter how nasty, demanding, or bat-shit crazy you are, I can get along because I'm getting paid, and one of us is leaving soon, so* [big smile] *how may I help you?*

One of the women at the club—Mrs. Conkright, overly tanned and dripping with gold—always told me after her two-martini lunches how much she liked my smile. "Oh, that smile, Briggs. The hearts you're going to break with that smile." She'd press her hands flat against her chest—jewelry clinking—and add, "Mine is already one of them." And she was, like, fifty, and married, so this was just the game, you know?

My dad always said that much of life was a game, so it was important to know the rules.

Mrs. Conkright owned an elder-care advocacy company and had recently been hired by Mrs. B. to find suitable live-in help for ten weeks over the summer. Mrs. B. owned a house on the beach in South Haven, here in Michigan, that needed some minor work. She didn't drive but wasn't ready for assisted living, and really only lived in the house from late spring through summer. She had a second place somewhere warm for the rest of the year. When Mrs. Conkright learned I'd done my senior-year service project volunteering at Bluestone Court Assisted Living Center—and smiling till my face hurt—she hired me on the spot.

"Try not to break her heart," she said to me, after telling me a little about Mrs. B., and I said, "She'll probably end up breaking mine."

Mrs. Conkright grinned at her lunch companions and said, "Ladies, what did I tell you?"

She gave me a ten-dollar tip, which I put in the tip pool. She also gave me her niece's phone number, which I put in my pocket and only threw out after she left.

3

I mastered a bunch of different Old People Smiles at Bluestone Court, which my dad called Bluehair Court, like it was the punchline to the most hilarious joke he'd ever told. I had to be careful not to say it that way when I was there. His jokes had a way of sinking into my mind, whether I wanted them to or not.

There was my:

- There's My Girl Smile
- Why, Yes, I'd Love Another Hug Smile
- All Right, *Law & Order*'s On . . . Again! Smile
- Your Granddaughters *Are* Beautiful Smile
- Yeah, You Farted and We All Heard It Smile
- No, Nixon Is Not the Current President Smile
- Yes, I Would *Love* to Hear Again How You Met Your Husband Smile
- Cards? I'll Deal Smile

And the classic . . .

- Yes, It Is a Good Day to Be Alive Smile.

At home, it was pretty much just my Yeah, Dad, You're a Hoot Smile, 24/7.

4

I met Mrs. B. a week after graduation, which came and went much faster than I thought it would. Senior year was crazy busy, crazy stressful. Then suddenly it was over. It was graduation morning, and I didn't have school, swimming, baseball, studying, volunteering, stressing, work. I had this whole day with nothing but the ceremony that evening, so I made coffee for my parents and then *had* coffee with my parents and kept thinking, *Man, this feels weird.* For the last two years, we all had mismatched schedules. First one up—that was me—made coffee. Last one to leave—that was Mom—washed the pot. We only drank coffee together on Christmas. On every other holiday or weekend, at least two of us were working. The other was sleeping in.

I was quiet until Dad said he wasn't proud of me. As only my dad could. Mom and I smiled to let him know we found him funny.

Mom listed some of my highlights from the year:
- class president
- ranked ninth academically
- captain of the baseball team

- co-captain of the swimming team
- double letter winner
- Academic All-State baseball
- Scholar Athlete of the Year
- homecoming king
- full academic scholarship to the University of Michigan
- makes coffee every morning

"And he remembers to put the toilet seat down," she said. "Our son's quite a catch, and I'm not the only one who thinks so."

Dad didn't look up from the newspaper when he said, "Are we supposed to be proud?"

"You've got to admit it's a good list," I said to him.

"It's not a bad list."

"It's a good list," Mom said. And she would know. She lives by lists.

Dad put the paper down and dropped his hands on top of it. "It's high school," he said to Mom. "I have always expected our son to do well in high school and graduate, so, no, I am not proud of him for doing what was expected." Then he reached out his long arms—I inherited his build, his height, but Mom's light coloring—and rubbed my head and said, "Ah, you need a haircut."

And since I always wore my hair super short, he found this hilarious.

Such a cut-up, my dad.

To me he said, "If you were a halfwit, then I'd be proud of you."

"If I were a halfwit, you'd have to be one too," I said. "You know. Apples and apple trees and all that."

Mom said, "If the two of you were halfwits, I'd have put whiskey in this coffee."

She put a splash in whenever Grandma Ruth dropped by. Not that she was a halfwit. She was just Grandma Ruth. And she liked to show up unannounced. Always unannounced. And she left the same way. Without warning. Coming or going, she was like the wind. The wind or diarrhea.

This was my family. The Henrys. We had expectations. We achieved. We catalogued our successes, and we never needed our hair cut. We were a riot at Thanksgiving too.

5

- cap
- gown
- speech
- wallet
- keys
- a twenty

"Got 'em, Mom," I said on my way out the door.

Mom always said good-bye with a list or schedule. Also she believed that no matter what happened, I would somehow be saved by the emergency twenty-dollar-bill in my wallet. Car crash? I slip the EMTs a twenty and they work harder to rescue me. Tornado? Sucks up my twenty, leaves me alone. Alien abduction? Totally pay off my own ransom with twenty bucks.

She was a mom. It was her job to worry about shit that was never going to happen.

6

I arrived early to graduation. The school rented one of those mega churches for it. Big modern auditorium, all beige, raised stage, comfy seats, great acoustics. There were 354 people in my class. The church sat 3,500. There was even room for all of my buddy Kennedy's relatives. Between his dad, mom, and stepdad, he had sixteen first cousins. I had three, somewhere in Indiana, who I only saw at weddings and funerals. The last funeral I went to was for Mom's mom, when I was six. This was her List of Funeral Commandments:

- Do not squirm.
- Do not wipe your nose on your sleeve.
- Do not put your hands in your pockets.
- Do not put your hands down your pants.

A list to live by, right? I should have made it my yearbook quote. Instead, it was this: *If I had a million dollars . . . I'd be rich.* From "If I Had $1000000" by Barenaked Ladies. Mom loved their music and listened to them endlessly in her car. I knew every single one of their songs. Dad listened to sports or talk radio and yelled at the players, callers, and hosts. He loved it.

Grandma Ruth never turned on the radio in her car. She told me once it might prevent her from hearing a siren, and she'd hate to be run over by a fire truck. She pushed her eyebrows as far down as they'd go and said, "I'd be livid, and that is not how I care to begin my life in eternity."

As class president, I sat on the stage during graduation, next to Mr. Bauer, the assistant principal, who bumped my arm and nodded at me whenever one of the other speakers said something interesting. I wasn't really listening. But I nodded back at Mr. Bauer and gave him a look like, *Oh, yeah, sure, got it*. Made the guy happy.

Then it was my turn to speak, and I had things to say, but my dad said if you want people to listen to you, be clear, be confident, and most of all, be brief. So I kept it short. Five minutes. Five minutes of equating life to baseball because that was my sport of choice. Mine and my dad's. Both of us good but not good enough to make a decent living at it, and making a decent living came before dreams.

"Life is all about stepping up to the plate," I said from the podium toward the end of my speech. "Stepping up to the plate and swinging for the fences.

"This is our time at bat," I said, and spied Taylor in the crowd of green and white caps and gowns just then. She gave me two thumbs-up and that V-shaped smile I loved, and I lost my place. "Uh, yeah, this is our time at bat. This is what we've been waiting for for four years. We're saying good-bye to the minor leagues tonight and stepping into the bigs. We might not hit a home run in our first at-bat. Or our second or third. There are no guarantees, but if we keep practicing, keep improving, keep getting stronger—if we keep our eye on the ball— sooner or later, we're either going to knock it out of the park or hit it farther than we ever thought we could."

I finished up. People clapped. Grandma Ruth got up to go then because she didn't like graduation ceremonies. Not a big fan of birthday parties, either. And, anyway, she expected me to graduate too.

Just before I left the podium, I caught Taylor's eyes again. Huge brown eyes under a ton of dark makeup, and she mouthed, "Perfect." Which was nice. Sure beat the hell out of the last thing she said to me, which was, "Amazing." It was my own damn fault. I never should have asked her how things were going with Nishesh.

7

At home, I tossed my cap and gown on a kitchen stool, grabbed a Coke from the fridge, and guzzled half of it by the time Dad walked in. Talking. He did that. He thought people in other rooms sat quietly waiting for him to enter. At least he had the grace to laugh at himself when he realized he interrupted a conversation. 'Course, by then, the floor was his.

"You don't get points for effort," he said.

"Sorry?"

"Your speech. You made it seem like you get points for effort. You don't. Not in the real world."

I nodded over the Coke I was drinking.

"Also, you were wrong when you said no one's promised a home run," he said.

"No one is."

"I taught you better than that, didn't I? That's just negative thinking. And negative thinking gets you where?" he asked, smiling.

"Nowhere," I said, playing along with this game he loved—finishing his favorite quotes and sayings. Which he had a thousand of. Sometimes for extra kicks, we said them together.

"Exactly," he said. "Life is what you make of it. If it's not going the way you want, who's to blame?"

"I am," I said, raising my hand.

"You bet you are. You can quit and feel sorry for yourself, or you can change your circumstances. Success—or a home run, as you called it—is guaranteed as long as you keep working hard."

"Failure is not an option," I said, summarizing the way he liked, complete with a smile and an emphasis on *not*.

"Failure is not an option," he confirmed. "But that's not what you said tonight."

"I said you have to work for your success," I said, and scratched the back of my neck.

"You said it isn't guaranteed. I'm saying it is if you work hard."

"I think we're saying the same thing."

"I think you're arguing with me," he said. "And I think you're wrong."

"Sorry about that," I said, and pressed my hand against my stomach. It was starting to ache, and that soda hadn't helped.

"Ah," he said, and rubbed my head and laughed. "You need a haircut."

8

Stomach knots were nothing new. I'd had them since I was nine, and they were worse at high stress times. Like graduation. Or Christmas morning. Mostly I ignored them. They went away. Mom tried to do the same with Grandma Ruth. But who can ignore the wind? Or diarrhea.

9

The All-Night Senior Party started at ten o'clock. It was almost nine by the time I finished showering and threw on jeans. Then a T-shirt. A faded blue one with the University of Michigan logo on the back. Taylor used to say it made her sad when I wore it because it reminded her we weren't going to the same schools in the fall. Of course, this was before she broke up with me in April and started going out with Nishesh, who was the biggest douchebag in the class. That's just by the numbers. The next guy who goes out with your ex-girlfriend is always a douchebag.

Nishesh was okay. Kind of a nice guy. He obviously made Taylor happy. She was still with him.

Douchebag.

I just sat down at my desk when I heard, "Briggs dear," in that flint-edged voice that sent me bolt upright out of my chair, slamming my knees on the underside of my desk and knocking over the Detroit Tigers mug I kept pens and pencils in.

"Hi, Grandma Ruth. How are you?" I said, giving her my best Grandma Ruth Smile as she air-kissed my cheek and ignored my question.

"Come downstairs," she ordered me. "I have something for you."

She hadn't changed clothes since graduation. She hadn't changed wardrobes since Reagan was president. She wore a standard uniform of starched white shirt, navy blazer, khakis, loafers, and she buttoned her shirts right up to the top, where they almost touched a flap of loose skin she was forever trying to smooth away with the back of her hand. When I was little, I asked her all the time if I could touch it. She let me do it once when I was four. It was the softest thing on her.

Her hair was white at the temples, gray everywhere else, and her lips were bright red from drinking the blood of small children who had the nerve to ring her doorbell on Halloween. It was a nice house and big, but dark on holidays and had stickers in every window warning trespassers that *This Property Is Under 24-Hour Surveillance.*

I started to follow her downstairs.

"Clean up your desk first," she said, and I obeyed because that's what you do with dictators. "A tidy home is the sign of a tidy mind." She started out the door. "And a tidy mind rejects untidy ideas."

Not once in my life had I ever heard this woman laugh. Given that she raised my dad, it was no wonder he found "You need a haircut" hilarious.

I followed Grandma Ruth into the kitchen, which was so much nicer than our last one. Brighter too. Even with Grandma Ruth there darkening it. Dad sat at the island. Mom leaned against the far counter, drinking coffee. Our last house was a shoebox. You couldn't have fit four people in the kitchen, and there was no island in it.

On the floor near my dad stood a box, about three and a half feet high, wrapped in brown-and-blue-striped paper with a brown-and-blue bow on top. Leave it to Grandma Ruth to find poo-colored wrapping paper.

I opened the box, at her command, and pulled out a . . . pulled out a . . .

"It's a Ficus," she said.

"A Ficus," I repeated.

"Technically it's a *Ficus benjamina* or weeping fig, but I didn't think you'd know it by either of those names."

"Yeah. No. Ficus is all I need to know."

"Well, how about that, son," Dad said in his best stand-up comic voice. "You don't already have one of those, do you?"

"No, I don't. Thanks, Grandma Ruth," I said, and didn't even have to fake enthusiasm because this was just a riot.

"I want you to take it to school with you," she said. "Put it in your dorm room and learn to care for it." She turned to my mother. "If he kills it, at least it's just a tree. And not terribly valuable. Not like jewelry."

Mom took a huge swig of coffee. Somewhere in our previous two moves, she lost a pair of earrings Grandma Ruth had given her. Since then Grandma Ruth only gave her jars of grape jelly on her birthday and at Christmas. Mom wrote thank-you notes for the "treat" and spooned the stuff into the toilet. She smiled and smiled watching it swirl around the bowl.

Grandma Ruth handed me two pieces of paper and said, "I've written the care instructions for you." Typed. With subheadings. "If you manage not to kill it, then when you graduate, I want you to plant it in the backyard so that it will remind you of me after I'm dead."

"Yeah, you are already unforgettable, Grandma Ruth," I said.

"Everyone is forgettable eventually," she said.

"Well, I promise that every time I see a Ficus—any Ficus, not just this Ficus—I will think of you."

"Is that sarcasm, Briggs? You know I don't like sarcasm. No one likes sarcasm," she said.

"I mean it sincerely," I said in that voice I reserved just for her—like *You know I'm bullshitting you, of course I'm bullshitting you, but come on, it's a game, life's a game, loosen up.* I was determined to get the woman to play a little. Just once in her life. But, man, she was work.

"You and Ficuses," I said, and held up two crossed fingers. "Inseparable in my mind from now on."

"Sarcasm is rude," she said.

"Right," I said.

My stomach started to cramp again. It had been quite a day.

"Well, take it up to your room and water it," she said. "I didn't give it to your mother, so don't make her look after it." To Mom, she said, "You over-water everything, and the beds out front show it. If it dies"—she looked at me—"I want to know whom to blame."

"You'll know, Ruth," Mom said, and polished off the coffee in her mug.

I made a mental note to nurture that damn plant into a forest, since I was fairly certain I had no smile in my repertoire that would compensate for killing it, and I would never—absolutely never—hear the end of it from Grandma Ruth. With her dying breath, she would say to me, "I was going to leave you everything, Briggs, if only you had taken care of that plant." She'd point at me. Her eyes would bug. "Ficus killer," she'd say, then leave this world for the next, mad as hell for all eternity.

10

Upstairs in my room, I took a picture of the plant and was just about to send it to Sam when I got this text from Taylor:

U have time for the party tonite right?

I texted back:

Yep

She texted back the word *good* underneath a selfie, biting her bottom lip in a smile she knew I could not interpret. As far as I could tell, she either missed me or was plotting my death.

Gorgeous.

11

We lived in Forest Hills, Michigan, a western suburb of Grand Rapids. Population 20,942; 68.7 miles from North Beach, South Haven, where my summer job was. *The beach, baby! The beach!*

I knew numbers because I was expected to know numbers. Dad used to quiz me at the dinner table. On those rare nights we ate as a family. *16 percent of 23? 3.68.* He approved with a nod when I got the answer right but preferred it when I got the answer wrong. He thrived on what he called teaching moments.

He'd scoot his chair close to mine, lean in like he was imparting the secrets of the universe, and say something like, "Remember that sixteen percent of twenty-three is also twenty-three percent of sixteen." It was completely useless, but Dad was so psyched about it that I played along. I didn't have it in me to be his buzzkill.

Mom worked bigger numbers than that in her head. Faster too. Dad made her perform at parties and always grinned ridiculously at her. After completing two impressive equations, she'd tell my dad, "That's enough, Richard." If he pressured her for a third, which he almost always did, she made their friends laugh with, "We're being bores, Richard."

So, yeah, we were all good with numbers in my family, and I'm not ashamed to admit that people were usually wowed by it. As my dad said—never deny your talents or apologize for your success. "But above all else, never sugarcoat your defeat." Every time he heard the coach of a losing team praise his players' effort or determination, he curled his lip and said, "Now there's a loser."

One talent I never had was pronouncing foreign words. I could write them, like any math equation. I just couldn't easily pronounce the sounds. I practiced like crazy just to get a B on my Spanish oral exam.

It took me, easily, six months to learn how to pronounce my best friend Sam's last name. Nguyen. No one could pronounce it. We met in third grade, and every morning during the attendance count, he'd correct the teacher until she just stopped saying it entirely. People still call him New-win or Nu-goo-in. Sometimes he gets Gwinn or Quinn.

Here's how he taught me to say it during recess one day: Put your tongue at the back of your throat like you're about to say the word *quick*. But instead of *quick*, say *ng*—like any word ending in *ing*—without making a hard *g* sound, and go straight from ng into the word "win."

Sam was laid-back even in third grade and gave me a pass with, "It's hard for most Americans." His parents were born in Vietnam and spoke English as fast as they spoke Vietnamese. Sam's mom was a pediatrician.

His dad was a tax attorney. Dr. Nguyen chatted easily in either language. Sam's dad listened patiently in both.

So I practiced saying *Nguyen*. For months. And I think that was one reason Sam and I became such good friends. That and our dads had similar expectations. Sam was ranked fifth in our class, and his dad wasn't proud of him either.

12

First thing I saw when I walked into the All-Night Senior Party was Taylor in the middle of a crowd of her friends, throwing her head back when she laughed and hanging like a cape on Nishesh. And he was exactly the kind of douchebag who would wear a cape too.

No, really, he was a good guy. Never saw him in a cape.

I kind of nodded a hello at Taylor. She waved at me, then used that same hand to twist and play with Nishesh's curls, and, man, that guy needed a haircut.

There were about seventy-five people there already. I heard two hundred were coming, which must have been why I saw about a dozen adults there. Crowd control. All standing in a group, talking, totally oblivious to the smell of beer smuggled in, and all the flasks that were tipped into our yellow plastic cups. I didn't know. Maybe they were just the neighbors, since they clearly sucked at being chaperones, which was fine by me as I grabbed a beer.

My parents never volunteered for school stuff. Too busy with work. They never even made it to any of my games. Grandma Ruth came to every one we played at home—arrived at the top of the first inning, left at the bottom of the third, and called me at night to learn the score. Last year we made her our unofficial mascot, The Ruthinator. Sam, who played shortstop, nicknamed her. I'd have told her, but I was afraid she'd think it was sarcasm and would quit coming to the games. I planned to tell her one day, *after* I got her to loosen herself up.

The senior party was at this guy's house. Jason Hirsch. I knew him the way I knew just about anyone in our class. From seeing him around. I gave him the big handshake and said, "Jason Hirsch," like it was a better way to say hi. Dad said, in business, it was important to learn a person's name and have a firm handshake. Mine was so smooth, he said I should go into politics someday.

"Graduation, man," Jason said. "We did it."

"We did it."

"Hey, we're going to set up some volleyball nets later. You wanna play?"

"Sure."

"Cool. We'll catch up later."

"Later, Jason."

That was about the longest I'd ever talked with Jason Hirsch.

He and his parents had a massive place on the third fairway of the golf course at Watermark Country Club. We Henrys used to live in a massive place on the thirteenth fairway. Then we moved to the shoebox when I was nine. By graduation, we were halfway between the shoebox and the golf course and headed in the right direction.

It was all part of our game plan, and failure was not an option.

My dad played golf like it was part of his job. Literally. He said it was great for business contacts and insisted I learn. Naturally, he taught me. I was in eighth grade, with $5,651 worth of braces, the first time we played. Since I'm left-handed, the lesson he gave me began like this: Just do everything I'm doing but backward.

It's not exactly how lefties learn and probably one reason why I hate the game. That and it's boring as hell, tied for sheer dullness with doing jigsaw puzzles at Grandma Ruth's. I had a Golf Smile that said *Please, God, get me out of this*. It wasn't one of my subtler looks, but subtlety was lost on my dad. Fortunately, by ninth grade, I was working part-time, taking honors classes, was class vice pres, made the swim team in fall, baseball in the spring, so I didn't have much time for golf. Or anything else, really.

It's been that way ever since.

"You suck, Henry!" Kennedy shouted at me, and we slapped hands over our heads and shouted, "Yeah!" He was catcher on the baseball team. All muscle, no tact. His voice and huge gestures always cleared a space. Sam was the opposite. Everything about him was long. Long arms, long legs, long hair Taylor always said she liked.

"Although competent in most other areas in life," Sam said, walking in behind Kennedy like he was some famous actor making his red-carpet entrance, "I would have to agree with our fine friend here that you do, in fact, suck."

"Hey," I said, with a slow shrug. "Life is what you make of it."

Sam and Kennedy had been saying *You suck* since I got the job with Mrs. B. I tried to downplay it when I first told them. For about ten seconds. I said she was old, couldn't get around, needed an errand boy. Still, her house was on "the beach, baby! The beach!"

You suck. We laughed.

A couple times over the next hour or so I made eye contact with Taylor, who finally let go of Nishesh. Third time I looked at her she walked over to me like I was the only guy there.

She had on skinny jeans and a gray hoodie over a tight, white T-shirt, and in the sea of skinny jeans and hoodies, she stood out. Those soft curves and intense eyes. As she walked, she pulled her hair out of a ponytail, and it fell to the point of her V-neck tee.

"Where's Nishesh?" I asked.

"You don't care."

"Yeah, I really don't."

"Then why'd you ask?"

"Why aren't you with him? And what's with the selfie?"

"Didn't you like it?" She couldn't keep a straight face asking.

"Yeah, I liked it. Why'd you send it?"

She shrugged. That was her answer.

We were outside then. The party spilled from the Hirsches' huge walk-out basement into their yard, which looked like it had been designed for a magazine shoot. Perfectly cut grass, mulched beds with some kind of sculpted shrubs Grandma Ruth could have identified, and four big flowering crabapple trees. I only knew they were crabapples because we had them at our house on the thirteenth fairway too. Bunch of houses in Watermark did. I had zero interest in botany. 'Course, that was before I owned a Ficus.

"Come talk with me," Taylor said, grabbing my wrist and walking with me to the edge of the yard where it butted up against the golf course's cart path. It was quieter there. A little more private too, courtesy of one crabapple tree with dark red blooms all over it.

"Don't you love that smell?" she asked, taking a big whiff.

"I guess," I said. All flowers smelled the same to me. I leaned toward the party and copied Taylor's big sniff. "That's the smell I love."

"What?"

"Burgers," I said, and she kind of slapped my arm.

There were two grills going. Kennedy was on his fourth burger. I'd had three and was still hungry.

"How's your stomach?" she asked.

"Good now. A little sore earlier."

"I've got antacids in the car if you need any."

"You still carry them?" I asked, trying hard not to grin too much.

"I do when I know I'm going to see you," she said. "Only because you won't."

"You're sweet."

"Sometimes. So when do you go down to South Haven?" she asked.

"In a week," I said.

"Emily and I are going to come down some weekend. Hannah and Ashley too. It'll be fun," she said. A few months earlier, Taylor discovered that she and her three best friends all had Top 10 Most Popular Baby Names from the year we were born and considered it a sign. Also predictive of all future friendships.

"What about Nishesh?" I asked her.

"He can come," she said, and shrugged again. "If he has time."

"Time? Isn't that why you broke up with me?" I asked—half seriously—just as Sam walked over to say, "Pizza's here. Grab it while it's hot."

"I'm going to go find Nishesh," Taylor said, and walked back toward the house, slowly, so I could watch her. She called over her shoulder, "It was really nice talking with you, Briggs. Maybe I'll see you in South Haven. *If* you have time."

She turned and walked back to Nishesh.

"What was that?" Sam asked.

"I don't know, but I think she's trying to kill me."

He slapped his hand onto my shoulder and said, "What a way to go."

13

Taylor's parents had a cottage on the beach in Grand Haven, thirty miles north of South Haven and much closer to Forest Hills. She loved being at the lake almost as much as I did, but for her it was all about hot sand, the right playlist, and the kind of coconut-smelling lotion that made her tan and me hungry. She had zero interest in swimming. Or boats.

Mom and Dad had berthed their boat in South Haven, a boat with two staterooms and a kitchen way nicer than the one in the shoebox. They sold it when I was nine.

Dad had named it *The DealerShip*. I guess that was funny once.

14

I left the senior party when everyone else did. Around six o'clock the next morning. Taylor and I didn't say good-bye. We just kind of locked eyes on each other through the crowd, and she shot me a little grin and a wave as she got into Nishesh's car.

"Dude, give it up," Kennedy said, walking past me.

"Yeah."

"By the way. You suck."

I didn't wave back to Taylor. I just watched her drive away the same way I watched her go the night she broke up with me. It was late, the night of her friend Emily's eighteenth birthday. I had just gotten back from work. Taylor was waiting by her car outside my house, and she looked hot in this tight red dress that hugged every curve. Her perfume smelled like incense—spicy and just a little smoky.

"How was the party?" I asked. Emily's parents had thrown her a bash.

"Briggs," she said, taking a step backward when I tried to reach for her waist. "I don't want a boyfriend who doesn't have time for me."

"All my extra time is for you."

"It's not enough."

"It's all I've got."

"It's not enough," she said, and she shrugged, and she got in her car and drove away. Cool and peace-out. That was Taylor.

My stomach ached every time I thought about her.

I didn't say good-bye to the last person I saw at the senior party. I just said, "Jason Hirsch," and shook his hand.

15

I texted my dad at work the day after Taylor broke up with me. Told him the news. This was our conversation:

Dad: You're better off without her.

Me: Knew youd say that

Dad: It's her loss.

Me: We'll stay friends

Dad: I would never stay friends with someone who dumped me.

Me: Too harsh for me. We've been friends for 4 years

Dad: Never stay where you're not wanted.

Me: We're okay as friends

Dad: Your choice. Not mine.

Me: Roger that.

16

I made our coffee the morning I left for South Haven. Extra strong, the way Mom liked it.

Dad slipped me a pre-paid credit card—a hundred bucks—later that morning, and then pretended he didn't know what I was talking about when I tried to give it back. My dad was always generous, even when he didn't have much. We were well known in the shoebox neighborhood for giving out the most candy on Halloween. Dad dropped fistfuls in kids' bags, insisting, "You need more" or "You didn't get enough."

Then he asked them this question: "What do ghosts eat for breakfast?" Pause. "Boo-berry muffins." He chuckled. Every time. "Here, you need more candy."

No kid left our house disappointed.

Grandma Ruth did not come over to see me off. She disliked good-byes more than graduation ceremonies and birthdays combined. The woman just got up and left when she wanted, without saying a word. There was something kind of admirable in that. And something kind of odd.

"South Haven population?" Dad asked.

"Four thousand three hundred seventy-eight," I said.

He, Mom, and I stood in the driveway, which I'd sealed a few days earlier. Dad tapped his toe at a spot of sealant I splashed on the cement steps leading to the back door. I pretended I didn't notice, except he knew that I did. Which was all he wanted.

"How many barbers?" he asked.

"I don't know."

"Get your hair cut down there and find out," he said.

"I'll do that."

"Now, remember," he said, putting his arm around me like we were a huddle of two, "this is a job, not a vacation. I expect you to work hard."

"I will."

"I expect you to do well."

"So do I."

"I expect you to make me proud."

"Will do."

"Ah," he said, lightening up his tone a little. A little. "I expect you'll have this lady and all of South Haven eating out of your hand by the end of summer."

He rubbed my head, and we shared a laugh because we were both thinking it.

"I got this," I said.

Mom's good-bye included:

- Call or text when you get there.
- Don't call or text while you're driving.
- Don't speed.
- Emergency $20.

"Got that too, Mom," I said, and they left for work, and I cleaned up the kitchen.

Dad owned forty percent of a company called Foam Works. Mom worked as the billing coordinator for the law firm Haan, Haas & Jaworski. Sam's dad was a partner there. He was kind of obsessive about his clients and often asked Mom to work through lunch with him or stay late to review his billable hours. Dad enjoyed teasing Sam that Mom was Mr. Nguyen's work-wife. Sam over-faked a laugh every time.

Mom worked as the accountant for Foam Works, unpaid, from the day Dad bought into the company until the second he could afford to hire a bookkeeper. He and his partner offered to keep Mom on at a salary. She declined, citing the higher divorce rate among couples who work together as her reason for leaving. Later she confided to me that she made up that statistic.

"Couples who work together," she said, and made a face like she was about to eat Grandma Ruth's grape jelly.

17

I tossed a couple duffel bags into the trunk of my car—
Grandma Ruth's thirteen-year-old Honda Civic. Gray
outside, gray inside. She gave it to me for my sixteenth
birthday, apparently on the condition that I look completely uncool in it. Sam gave it a completely random
nickname. Uncle Orville's Babe Bucket. Eventually we
all just called it the Bucket. It was awesome. The thing
was geriatric but ran almost perfectly. Kind of like
Grandma Ruth herself. I packed the Ficus last.

I was carrying it out to my car just when Kennedy and
Sam pulled into my driveway.

"Okay, what?" Kennedy asked the minute he got out.

"It's a Ficus. Got it for graduation," I said as I put it on
the floor behind the front passenger seat. "And it's all mine."

"Oh, yeah," Kennedy said. "First the job at the beach.
Now the . . . fisc . . . What was it? Whatever. You got it
all, man."

"It's my graduation present from Grandma Ruth," I
said.

"Whoa. You say that name, and my sphincter tightens,"
Sam said.

"Your what?" Kennedy asked.

"It's the Grandma Ruth Effect," Sam said.

"What the hell's a sphincter?" Kennedy asked.

"How can you be a graduate of a fine American high school like ours and not know what a sphincter is?" Sam returned.

"*I* know what it is," I said. "And I know where it is."

"*Where* it is?" Kennedy was getting hot.

"All God's children got a sphincter," Sam said. "Couple of 'em. Can't believe you don't know that, Kenn."

"Can't believe it," I repeated.

"You should have yours checked if you haven't been taking proper care," Sam added.

Kennedy pointed at Sam and said, "You're walkin' home." Then he pointed at me. "And you. Ah." He slapped my back in a loose kind of man-hug and said, "We're comin'. Every weekend we can. It'll be crazy."

"Cool," I said.

"Briggs," Sam said, shaking my hand. A little too long. "I have one word of advice for you this summer. Sunscreen."

"Got it."

Then he tried to pinch my cheek, but I batted his hand away as he was saying, "We don't want anything to happen to this baby-soft skin of yours."

He draped a long arm around Kennedy, gave a couple sniffs, and said, "Our boy is leaving the nest."

"Dude," Kennedy said, shoving Sam's arm off. "You're creepin' me out."

"Did anything in your ass just tighten?" Sam asked.

"Yeah."

"That's your sphincter," Sam and I said.

"Hey. Hey. Record this," Kennedy said. "Just do it." Sam and I pulled out our phones. "You ready? You ready?"

"Yeah. Come on," I said.

Kennedy cleared his throat, waited two seconds, flipped the bird with both hands and shouted, "You suck! You! Both! Suck!"

"I'm texting this to your parents," Sam said, and Kennedy yanked his phone away and threw it in the backyard.

Couple minutes after they left, I got a text from Sam.

Reminder: SPF 100 is a waste of $$. Just buy SPF 30

Seconds later he sent this:

SPF 1000: Sphincter Protection Factor, apply liberally & rectally before next Gma Ruth visit

Then this:

Kennedy says he'll take the job if U f it up.

I texted back: **In his dreams**

I climbed in the Bucket. No USB port. Not even a CD player. But the radio worked, so I turned it up. Put the windows down. I thought about the gorgeous house I'd be staying at all summer, the lake, the beach.

Then I laughed to myself. *I got this.*

18

Warning bells clanged. Red lights on the crossing gates flashed. The drawbridge over the Black River in South Haven was going up when I got there.

I slowed to a stop, first car at the light, turned the radio off, and opened all my windows to let the car fill with cool, slightly damp air. I could almost taste it, like sweet water. There wasn't a cloud in the sky, which—I swear—was the bluest blue I'd ever seen. Unreal blue. Like postcard blue. And the sun turned patches of the Black River silver-white.

A sloop with a twenty-eight-foot mast glided toward the lake, cutting a path through the river like the water was thick and soft. There were four people on the deck dressed in shorts and bright jackets. Sitting all loose and comfortable and looking completely right. Like they belonged there. Like we used to look and feel on our boat.

Couple minutes later the lights flashed and the bells clanged again, and the bridge's motor hummed as Dyckman Street returned to normal. I glanced down at the harbor as I drove over the bridge. Most of the boat slips—229 in all—were empty. It was early in the season yet. Ours had been number 17. I didn't look to see if it was occupied.

Sam's parents were boat people. In third grade, Sam and I thought we had this in common. We were nine and lived in the suburbs. What did we know? At the time we were just excited that this made us brothers in some way. Sam's dad explained the difference the way a teacher would. Clear and concise. He left Vietnam with nothing but the clothes on his back in 1978. He was six. He and fourteen members of his family escaped on a boat. An old wooden thing with oars and a torn sail. The only thing it had in common with our boat was the stuff it floated on.

I told my parents about Mr. Nguyen when I got home. Dad said, "Now there's a man who didn't let anything stop him. And do you know why?"

"Why?" Mom asked without looking up from her crossword puzzle.

"Because he knew failure was not an option," Dad said, and he nodded at me, and I nodded back, like, *Yeah, I got it.* But I was nine. I had no idea what he meant. I was just sad we had to sell our boat later that year. I was a wreck when we got rid of the dog.

19

We had a six-month-old Portuguese water dog named Cutlass when I was nine. We re-homed him when we re-homed the boat. Dad said the house we were moving into was too small for so big a dog. That's when Mom called the new place a shoebox.

Boater friends of my parents from Saugatuck—just north of South Haven—took Cutlass and renamed him Wesley. They sent us Christmas cards of Wesley and the whole tanned family on their boat and always wrote that Wesley was very happy.

They took excellent care of him and were total douchebags.

20

Once I turned onto North Shore Drive from Dyckman,
I ended up behind the slowest driver in the world. The
guy was going three miles an hour. In a giant blue Sub-
urban with—I swear—*God Yacht* professionally painted
in white on the hatch. And underneath was this: *Are you
ready?*

For summer at the beach? Hell, yes! Anything else, I
didn't want to know.

It would have felt like eternity inching behind this guy
anywhere but North Shore Drive. The slow pace gave
me a chance to catch more than a glimpse of the lake
between the big, expensive houses on the west side of
the street. Waterfront property. Man, some people had
it made.

That lake water. Navy blue with random stretches of
turquoise close to shore and shining like glass in the sun.
I hung my arm out the window to feel the heat of it. I'd
have cranked up some music, but South Haven was quiet
in the mornings, and I didn't want to be the douche who
wrecked it for the locals. I was practically a local myself.
Not only was I living there that summer, but South

Haven was *our* place. Mom's, Dad's, and mine. I came here as an infant. Even before that. Mom had tons of pregnant pics of herself—round, freckled, and happy—on the boat and on the beach.

The boat and the beach are the settings of my earliest memories. Dad at the wheel, grinning like he owned the lake. Mom in big, dark glasses, lounging in the sun. Me fishing or swimming. Every day at the lake was the best day ever.

The driver of the God Yacht stopped in the road across from two women—older than me, younger than Mom—walking dachshunds on matching pink leashes and shouted at them, "Ladies, are you ready?! Are you ready?!"

"What the hell?" I said quietly.

"Yeah, we're ready!" the nearer one called, and handed her leash to her friend.

"Ah, you're not ready!"

"No, I'm ready!" she called back, looking kind of jazzed and held her hands up, prepared to catch—I didn't know—something the guy threw from his car. Some bright red cloth sack or something, square and half again as big as the woman's hand. She almost dropped it—juggled it a couple times before grabbing it.

"Woo-hoo! You were! You were ready!" the God Yacht guy called, and the woman waved and showed her friend the sack. First one side, then the other, and the God Yacht crept on, and I said again to myself, "What the hell?"

Finally, I reached Mrs. B.'s and said, "No way," when

I pulled in the driveway. I knew the houses at this end of North Shore Drive were bigger than most, but this place was unreal. A huge, white Victorian, spotless, with a turret and a porch that wrapped around the south side and windows just about everywhere you could fit a window. Long, narrow windows. Arched windows. Bay windows. Wide square windows. Huge picture windows. Windows in the attached garage.

"No way," I said again as I parked my car, got out, and inhaled that perfect lake air. Cool and unspoiled and just a little mossy.

I tried calling my mom—then texting—to let her know I'd arrived, but I couldn't get a signal. Happened a lot at the lake. At least, it did to me. I had my dad's old phone, six years old with a cracked screen and a weak battery that Taylor called old-school and Kennedy said should be in a museum. But, hey, it worked—most places—and I didn't want to spring for a new one. I figured I'd use Mrs. B.'s.

I rang the bell, and a tiny, white-haired woman answered. Not five feet tall, with watery blue eyes magnified by thick glasses, and the kind of face that looked like she loved kids, not like she ate them.

"Mrs. Božić?" I asked.

"No," she said.

"You're not Mrs. Božić?" I asked.

"No," she said again, and raised her shoulders like she was about to laugh.

"Oh, man," I said, pulling my phone back out of my pocket to double-check the address. "I'm at the wrong house."

21

"Is right house," she said in a thick accent, and I remembered that Mrs. Conkright told me Mrs. B. was from Serbia.

"I thought she meant Siberia," Mrs. Conkright had told me, laughing. She'd had one and a half martinis by then. "I told her, 'No wonder you don't mind our winters here.'"

"I'm looking for Mrs. Božić," I said as this woman, the size of a hobbit, stepped out onto the porch, and I was met with the smell of lemons and cedar. "Mrs. Vesna Božić."

"Yes," she said, and scrunched her oblong face into such a smile that just about everything but her cheeks disappeared. Cheeks like shiny crabapples at our house on the thirteenth fairway.

"You *are* Mrs. Božić?"

"No."

"But this is her house?"

"It is my house."

"But you're . . . not Mrs. Božić?"

"It is not Boh-sick," she said. Then she raised her

hand like a music teacher and tapped at me through the air as she said, "Bozhitch."

"S—sorry?"

"Bozhitch," she said. Again with the air tapping. "Bozhitch. It is Serbian. I am Serbian."

"Serbian. Huh," was all I could think to say.

"You say now. Bozhitch. Bozhitch." We stared at each other for a couple seconds, until she poked me in the ribs—*oh, man*—and said through a smile, "Now you say. Boh. Boh. Boh."

"Bow, bow, bow," I said, rubbing my side.

"No, no. Not bow, bow, bow. *Boh. Boh. Boh*," she said, accentuating each *boh* with her forefinger pointed at me—long for such a small lady and gnarled like wood. Wielded correctly, she could have robbed a bank with that thing.

"Isn't that what I said?" I asked.

"Try again."

"Bow or Bow-sic?"

"You say Bosick," she said.

"Right."

"It is *not* Bosick. It is Bozh-zhitch. Like this," she said, and pushed her lips out. "Say like you are *keessink* someone."

"Bo-shish."

"Bozh-zhitch."

"Bo-jeesh," I said, and her face disappeared into itself again, and I thought of Sam, in third grade, contorting his face into all sorts of hilarious shapes as I struggled with the sounds of *Nguyen*. "Boj—wait—Boj-shish or something? Close? No?"

"Say like you *keess*," she said again, so I pushed my lips out and said, "Bohw-jush," and felt completely stupid.

"You never *keess* a girl before?"

"I've kissed a girl," I said, like *What the hell?* "A few of them."

"You are not very good at it, I think?"

"They didn't complain."

"Okay," she said, grinning some as she patted my stomach with both hands. Then she pressed that weapon of a finger against her round chin for a second before saying, "You call to me Mrs. B."

"Mrs. B. Okay. Thank you," I said, relieved. I'd be out of there long before I ever mastered it.

"And I call to you Baby."

"Or Briggs," I suggested, "because, you know, that's my name."

"Briggs. Baby. Baby Briggs. Boh, boh, boh." She tossed her hands in the air. They barely went over her head. "Everybody have the *B* names. Now. You bring with you the suit?"

"A swimsuit? Yeah. I got a couple."

"No, no, no. The suit with the coat and the tie."

"Yeah. I have a coat and tie with me."

"Good. You go put."

"Put? Put on? Sure. We're going somewhere?"

"We go to my funeral."

"Uh. S—sorry?"

"You go. Put the suit." She grasped my arm, and for a woman with little hands, she had a seriously strong grip. "I must *seet*."

"Sit? Sure. Let me help you inside."

"No. No," she said, and started to lower herself to the floor right there in the doorway. What could I do but ease her down?

"Are—are you okay?" I asked.

"Yes. Yes, I wait here. Maybe I lie down." She shrugged. "Maybe no."

"You— You— You want to lie down? *Here?*"

"Here. Yes," she said like old ladies everywhere were lying down in their doorways. "You go put the suit or we will be late for my funeral."

"Mrs. Boz—Mrs. B., I don't—I don't understand." My heart was pounding, and I was starting to sweat a little, and I was thinking, *My God, is the hearse on its way?* "You're okay, right? We're not really going to *your* funeral. Are we?"

"Yes," she said again. She closed her eyes, lying there on the polished pine floor, and she smiled.

22

I'd heard some weird stuff from the residents at Blue-stone Court, but this was a first.

"So wait. One more time," I said. "We're going where?"

"My funeral," Mrs. B. said again, from the floor. "Is the right *wood,* yes?"

"Wood?"

"Wood," she said again.

"Word?"

"This is what I say."

I was translating English to English.

"But sometimes I do not know the *wood.* I use the *wronk wood."* Wrong word. "You tell to me when I do."

"Funeral? Yeah. It's—I mean—it's the right word, I think." God, I hoped not. "But *yours? Your* funeral? I don't understand."

"Ah. No," she said, smiling. "Not yours."

I exhaled.

"Mine," she said, and my sphincter tightened.

All God's children got a sphincter. That should have been painted on the God Yacht.

"Okay. See. Here's where I'm having a problem, Mrs. B. *Your* funeral. When you say *my* funeral, I'm thinking you're the one *having* the funeral."

"Ah!" she said again, this time raising her forefinger in front of her face. "You think I am the one in the coffin."

I cringed just a little.

"How I am the one in the coffin if I am the one *lyink* here, *talkink* to you?" she asked, like I should have figured out that story problem for myself. "I think when I am the one in the coffin, I cannot be the one who tells to you to put the suit."

"On?" I asked. I mean, I was genuinely confused.

"Yes. Put. You put," she said. She sat up and mimed pulling her arm through a sleeve. "We go."

"Right. So *whose* funeral is it?"

"I already tell to you. It is mine. Not yours."

I paused. Then held up my finger just like she did, but in surrender instead of clarity. "I'll just grab my bags out of my car," I said. *And think about getting in and driving slowly away.*

It was a language problem. Or cultural. I didn't know, and by the time I hauled my bags out of the trunk, I didn't really care. For two reasons. One, I was a Henry and Henrys didn't quit. I mean, my parents could have given up years ago, and we'd still be in that crappy shoebox, but we're not. And, two, when I shut the trunk, I found a girl standing behind me—freckled with blond hair spilling out of a cowboy hat, and staring at me like it was the most normal thing for her to be doing just then.

She looked to be about my age. Maybe a little older.

Maybe younger. Who could tell with girls? She was tall and skinny like a model. I mean, no curves where there ought to be. Just straight lines and sharp angles. She held the handlebars of a pale green bike, leaving her long arms loose and exposed. I could have easily lifted her over my head if I'd gotten close enough. But something in the way she held herself—straight and serious—told me that getting close would be difficult. Still, I was willing to try.

She was pretty but not, you know, glamorous-looking. Like if she *had* modeled, it would have been for something like soap or Q-tips or cotton balls.

Grandma Ruth kept jars of cotton balls in her bathroom, but I never asked why. I think she ate them. And enjoyed shitting white fluff.

"Hi," I said, flashing her my best smile, my I'm Briggs Henry and I'm Just Happy to Be Here Smile. It didn't have that name at the time, but that's what it was.

And she said this back:

"Hi."

No smile. No nod. No edge either. No nothing. Just a tall, pretty, Q-tip model blinking at me, like she was waiting for me to say something while I was waiting for her to smile. Because, come on. *I'm Briggs Henry and I'm Just Happy to Be Here* should have worked.

After a few seconds, she wheeled her bike closer and crossed the strip of grass between Mrs. B.'s driveway and the one next door. A massive modern cottage, white with a blue tile roof. Fewer but much bigger windows than Mrs. B.'s place.

"You live there?" I asked.

"Looks like it," she said without stopping.

"I'm living here." I pointed at the house behind me. "This summer."

"I'm happy for you," she said. She looked back over her shoulder and added, "Enjoy your funeral."

23

Mrs. B. held my arm as we walked into Lakewood Lutheran Church, like I was an usher seating the grandmother of the bride. She stopped once in the narthex—fancy name for the lobby in a church—and twice in the aisle to greet people. I half expected someone to take our picture.

"So sad. So sad. She was nice lady," Mrs. B. said to a couple mourners in their pews.

They agreed that whoever was in that casket—thank God it was closed and covered with a sheet—was, in fact, a nice lady.

Her name was Pauline Ostrander, and she was seventy-seven. It was printed in script on the front of the program. Mrs. B. snagged me my own copy and handed it to me when we sat down. Middle of a middle pew, left side of the sanctuary.

The pastor began his eulogy—called "remarks" in the program—about two-thirds of the way through the service. He said something like, "Everyone who knew Pauline liked her." And the two women directly behind Mrs. B. and me agreed.

"Yes, they did."

"They did."

"You know what he should say?" came the first voice again, much deeper than her friend's, and hoarse, like maybe she had smoked her whole life.

"What?"

"Something about her chicken and biscuits."

"Chicken and biscuits."

"Didn't she make the best?"

"The best."

It took some restraint not to turn around to get a look at these two, who clearly did not appreciate the volume of their voices.

"I wonder what the family's going to do with her roaster," came the gravelly first voice.

"I wonder."

"Do you think it would be in bad taste if I asked for it? I know for a fact her daughter won't want it. She's a terrible cook."

"But terrible."

"Inherited none of her mother's cooking skills."

"Not a one."

They were quiet. Then:

"Best chicken and biscuits ever, Pauline's."

"The best."

One sighed.

Then the other one did.

I was kind of sorry when they stopped talking, since they were more entertaining than Pastor Krantz—his name was in the program—who was monotone and took weirdly long pauses between sentences. Pews creaked. People sniffed. A couple coughed.

I was bored out of my mind. If Chicken and Biscuits were allowed to have a conversation about food, I figured I could quietly flip through some pics from the senior party. I held my phone low on my right so Mrs. B. wouldn't see, and, for a few minutes, that worked. I had scrolled nearly to the end of my pics when she caught me.

"This is my funeral," she whispered. "You do not use the phone at my funeral."

"I'm just looking at pictures, Mrs. B."

"No. You do not look at the pictures either. You look at the priest or the coffin. Give. Give to me," she said as she reached over and grabbed my phone.

"Mrs. B.," I whispered, trying to pull the thing away, but the woman had some grip.

I tried not to laugh. I mean, she was a foot and a half shorter than me and sixty-six years older, and she was practically wrestling me. For a second, it was hilarious. Me and this old lady playing slap-hands over a phone while the pastor intoned, "I have always found comfort in these words of Henry Wadsworth Longfellow," and then Kennedy's voice filled the church. *"YOU SUCK!"* I lost my grip on the phone.

"What? What?" Mrs. B. spluttered, looking intently at the video.

"YOU! BOTH! SUCK!"

I grabbed at it, panicked, trying to shut off the video I'd made that morning. The one of Kennedy shouting at

Sam and me. "Mrs. B.—" I reached for the phone as she squinted at it. And, in classic old-lady style, she tapped the first button she saw, which was play, and we heard the whole thing. Again. Only louder, it seemed, because now the church was deathly quiet.

"*YOU SUCK.*

"*YOU!*

"*BOTH!*

"*SUCK!*"

And then there was silence.

And just about everyone, including monotone Pastor Krantz, was staring at me.

24

"Uh . . . sorry," I kind of mouthed and kind of whis-pered, and I felt a fiery heat in my whole head. "Sorry."

I shoved the phone back in my pocket. Pastor Krantz cleared his throat and waited an eternity before speaking.

"Henry . . . Wadsworth. . . . Longfellow," he finally said, still looking directly at me.

"Go," Mrs. B. said quietly. She pushed her eyebrows way down over her eyes. "Go. You leave. Go."

"Go?"

"You wait outside."

"Are you serious?"

"Yes, I am *series*. You make the scene. You go."

"Sorry," I said again, and stood and worked my way down the pew, excusing myself and stepping over knees and feet. Like I wasn't blistering hot enough, and Pastor Krantz wasn't mad enough.

I tried to act normal as I walked down the aisle—like, no big deal, my face is the color of a baboon's butt every day—and I tried not to make eye contact with people who were looking at me, but it seemed like everyone was. I felt sweat at my temples.

In the last pew on the left, right there on the aisle, there was this one guy with black hair hanging in his eyes—maybe my age—sitting with a bunch of friends, I guessed, who were whispering to each other. Couple girls put their hands over their mouths and laughed. This guy was staring at me with a smart-ass grin on his face, and he showed me his phone when I got close and said in a loud whisper, "Dude, there's a new feature. It's called mute."

"Yeah," I said, and tried to look like I thought it was funny. I also tried to think of something to say back but got distracted when I saw my new neighbor—the girl with the bike—at the opposite end of the pew. Staring up at the altar and smiling, not like she was posing for her senior picture but in a way she definitely did *not* smile at me a couple hours earlier.

"Hey," the guy said to me, jerking his head to the left to get his hair out of his eyes. "Show's over. Move along."

What could I do but leave and wait for Mrs. B. outside? And wonder if I had just lost the best job I never had.

I pushed open the front door and squinted into the white light of my exile.

I didn't know how I was going to explain to my friends or my parents that I got fired for ruining Pauline Ostrander's funeral. And Mrs. B.'s. Mom should have put *Do not play with your cell phone* on her List of Funeral Commandments, right after *Do not put your hands down your pants*. At least I got that one right.

25

It was twenty impossible minutes later when the service ended and a few of the guests started leaving. I was sitting in the church's side yard, in the shade of a big oak, and hopped to my feet when Mrs. B. emerged, flanked by Chicken and Biscuits. They looked to be around Grandma Ruth's age—seventy-six—with soft cheeks and big earrings. One had a fluff of yellow hair like a dandelion. The other had brown hair, flat and short like a swim cap.

They smiled pathetically at me, like Mrs. B. just told them my dog died, only I didn't know it yet.

"Hi. I'm Briggs Henry," I said, and extended my hand, which Mrs. B. pushed down.

"Come. You meet people later when I am not mad with you any *lonker*."

She took hold of my arm, and we walked just a few steps toward the Bucket when she said, "I will not stay mad *lonk,* Briggs Baby."

"You won't?" I asked. I mean, I was used to Grandma Ruth's general state of irritation, so I thought Mrs. B. would be mad pretty much all summer, if I made it that long.

"No," she said. "You make the *meestake*. I know you do not do it on the purpose."

"I'm really sorry, Mrs. B."

"Yes, I know." She squeezed my arm and smiled up at me. "But." She raised her index finger. "You do not *brink* phone to my next funeral."

"Next funeral? There's another one?"

"There is always the next one until you are the one in the coffin, and then," she said, and shrugged, "it is your last."

"Right," I said, and reminded myself—twice—I got this.

I got this.

26

I knew what a narthex was—also nave, chancel, and transept—from Grandma Ruth. She volunteered for every committee at Saints Peter and Paul Episcopal Church and hauled me to meetings and events for the three years I was in her charge.

Mom, Dad, and I used to attend Saints Peter and Paul on Christmas and Easter. Then Grandma Ruth blabbed our business at her committee meetings, and they took up a food collection, and Grandma Ruth told Mom to write a thank-you note for it. She did and then gave the food to the West Michigan Food Bank.

We switched to Trinity United Methodist Church for Christmas and Easter after that and donated bags of food to all their holiday drives. And I mean *bags*.

27

I once asked my dad what the difference was between Methodists and Episcopalians.

He said, "Episcopalians belong to better clubs."

We used to belong to three. Including Cascade, where I bussed tables for four years. By then we had quit them all.

28

I had just helped Mrs. B. into my car and shut the door when I heard some girl yell, "Abigail!" across the parking lot and turned to see my Q-tip neighbor stop by the church door and look up.

"We're all going to Nicole's! You wanna come?" the girl with the impressive set of lungs called.

Abigail shook her head and started walking across the parking lot, headed in my direction.

"Oh, come on! You never come out anymore!"

Abigail just waved and turned again and gave me a blank look to match the one from earlier. Man, this girl should play poker with that face.

"Nice show back there," she said.

"It was an accident."

"You shouldn't have had your phone on."

"Like I said. It was an accident."

"Still," she said, and pulled her keys out of her pocket. Over her shoulder I saw the girl with the loud voice, the Mute Button guy, and a couple other people getting into the same car.

"After-funeral party?" I asked.

"Just some friends," she said.

"You're not going?"

"Nope."

"You could have ridden here with us."

"I thought I might have to leave early. I'd hate to make you and Vesna miss anything."

"Yeah," I said in a tone Grandma Ruth definitely would have hated, "that would have been a real disappointment."

"It would have been to Vesna," she said evenly, walking past me to her car.

On the way home, that bizarre God Yacht thing passed Mrs. B. and me going three miles an hour in the opposite direction. In my rearview mirror I watched him stop. Abigail, half a block behind me, also stopped. And she put her window down. And the guy tossed a bright red sack into it.

29

Back at Mrs. B.'s, she held her hand out and said, "You give to me the phone now," which I did, like I was ten and being punished.

"I give back when I think it is the right times for you to use," she said as she slipped it into her purse.

"It doesn't work anyway," I said.

"I think you don't know how it *wooks,*" she said.

"I know how it works," I said, half under my breath.

"I have the *sail* phone here in my purse," she said as she pulled it out and showed me. Thing looked brand-new and expensive. She probably had no trouble getting a signal on it anywhere. "It is off. This is the way how you turn on the phone." She pressed a button. "And then," she said as she pressed the button a second time, "this is the way how you turn off the phone." She held it toward me and asked, "You want to practice?"

"I think I got it."

A tour of the house followed and lifted my crappy mood some. Like Grandma Ruth not wanting to start her afterlife all pissed off, I didn't want to start my life at the beach the same way.

Mrs. B.'s house was pretty cool. Pale blue walls that turned almost white in certain light. Sand-colored rugs over hardwood floors, navy and beige furniture. Ticking clocks in every room, very few knickknacks—mostly just books and picture frames—and watercolors of sailboats on the walls.

I had the whole third floor to myself. Two bedrooms, one bathroom. Mrs. B. led me up the stairs, which she took slowly but evenly, holding bunches of her skirt in both hands.

"So, I saw Abigail from next door," I said on the way up. "Haven't technically met her, though."

"Yes. Abigail Howe. She is nice girl, but sometimes she disappears."

"Disappears?"

"Is right *wood*?"

"Uh. That depends."

"Disappears," she said again. She made her hands into little fists and opened them as she said, "*Puff*. Sometimes I look out my window, and she is there. On the beach. Then I look again, and she is gone."

"Yeah, well, maybe she just had to go inside for a little bit. You know. Like you do."

"She is inside for three, four days. No one sees her," Mrs. B. said as we reached the third floor. "Then I see her again. I say, 'Where do you go?' She says, 'I go here. I go there.' But." She pointed to herself. "I go here and there, and she is not there. So. She does not want me to know where she goes, so I say she disappears."

We walked into the room that would be mine that

summer, and if I'd had my phone, I'd have taken a picture to show Sam and Kennedy. And my dad. It had all the standard stuff—bed, bench at the end, dresser, small desk, two nightstands, matching lamps, landline. But there was also a sliding door that opened onto a balcony, large enough for two chairs—white with navy-blue cushions—and a round table between them.

"Cool," I said, and grinned, and drifted into a hypnotic stare at the water.

"Briggs Baby," Mrs. B. said. "You are not *leesenink*."

"I'm listening, Mrs. B.," I said. "I just love being near that lake."

"Yes, yes. The lake is very nice. But now, we talk."

"Sure."

She sat on the bench. I sat on the bed and took off my coat and tie.

"You are all minc until *Owgust twelvt*," she said.

"Yes, I'm all yours until August twelfth," I confirmed.

"I fly in *Owgust* to Azirona."

"Azirona? I don't know where that is."

"It is in the south and the west."

"Of Serbia?"

"Of America."

"Oh, Arizona," I said.

"This is what I say. My *seesters* live there. The one has the birthday in *Owgust*, so I go for that, and I stay, like the birds for the *weenter*."

"Sure."

"So. Across today and *Owgust*, you paint the house." I figured she meant *between* today and August, but, *across*

70

worked too. "I am tired by this color," she said, pointing to the walls.

"Really?" I liked it. It was the kind of color you could get lost in if you stared at it for too long. Like you were floating somewhere between water and sky.

"Yes," she said. "You start in other room up here. And when you are not *paintink,* you fix *thinks*?"

"I can fix a few things. Yeah. Not like a television set."

"I do not have the television set."

"You don't own a television?"

"This is what I say."

"Right."

"It is all the junk."

Old people always complained about stuff on television. Except *Law & Order* and any movie with a nun in it.

"I don't suppose you have Internet access," I said.

"It is more of the junk," Mrs. B. said.

Great.

"So. Toilets run. *Fow-cets* drip. The drawers stick. The doors." She loosely covered her ears. *"Squick."*

"Squeak? Yeah. I can fix those."

"Then," Mrs. B. said, "when you are not *paintink* or *fixink thinks,* you drive me. I go to the groceries store. I go to the hair appointments. I go to the doctor appointments. I go to the *shursh.*"

"Church?"

"This is what I say. When I need you, I call to you. I don't shout. I call."

"Well, first of all, Mrs. B., my phone is in your purse downstairs. And, second, it doesn't work."

"No, I call to you," she insisted.

"No, I can't even get a signal on it."

"We walk and talk."

"Walk and talk?" I repeated, and tried not to sound rude, but *what?*

"Yes," she said, and pointed at the nightstand. "We walk and talk."

I reached across the bed for what I thought was the phone and then ran my hand across my head and scratched the back of my neck.

"Mrs. B.," I said, showing her the device, "this is a walkie-talkie."

"Yes. Walk and talk," she said, and pulled one out of her skirt pocket, like she was a cartoon character pulling out a fully cooked turkey or something.

She held the walkie-talkie to her mouth, pressed a button, and the one in my hand snapped and crackled to life, and I scrambled to find the volume button to turn the thing down.

"I say, 'Mrs. B. to Briggs Baby. Come in to Briggs Baby.' Or *somethink* like that." She turned hers off and pointed at me. "And then you say, 'Hello. Briggs Baby is here.'"

I scratched the back of my neck again.

"So. We practice," she said.

"I really don't think we need to practice."

"You do not know how to use the *sail* phone. Maybe you do not know how to use the walk-and-talk," she said. She got this grin on her face, mouth curling up at the corners, when she said into the walkie-talkie, "Mrs. B. to Briggs Baby. Come in to Briggs Baby."

I looked up at the ceiling and thought, *Oh my God*.

"Briggs here, Mrs. B.," I said into that stupid thing. I felt heat in my face again but forced a weak smile to my lips. "How can I help you?"

30

I learned how to fix a lot of things in the shoebox. My dad taught me. Starting in junior high, Mr. Walker, the industrial arts teacher, re-taught me without saying, "Do what I'm doing, but do it backward." He gave me my first left-handed tape measure. I still have it.

Over the years, between the shoebox and our current place, Dad and I hung doors, changed locks, plumbed sinks, installed windows, installed cabinets, finished floors. Things like that. He was unusually quiet when he worked on the house. We didn't even listen to sports on a radio.

He was quiet on the boat too. We all were.

We were better at the beach.

31

Late that afternoon, Abigail was alone on the beach next door. She sat on a green-and-white-striped beach blanket, looking out at the water. Knees drawn up to her chest, making a sharp angle of her legs. Big orange canvas bag next to her. I leaned in the doorway of my balcony, sliding glass pushed open, and watched her for a few minutes, wondering what her story was, wondering if maybe she would disappear, like Mrs. B. said. Maybe not with a *puff,* though. Or maybe. Who knew?

After Mrs. B. had gone back downstairs, I'd changed into shorts and a T-shirt and unpacked. The dresser drawers—which did stick—smelled like mothballs mixed with the scented candles Taylor kept in her bedroom. We made out there a few times when her parents weren't home. Nothing major. We only went out a couple months and never got to the I-love-you stage. Never had time. We were alone maybe six times, and in those times, she had her hands up my shirt a hell of a lot more times than I had mine up hers. Not that I didn't try. She just kept moving my hands around to her back. One thing about Taylor—she knew what she wanted. And what she didn't.

Abigail hadn't moved. I leaned over the railing and looked down at Mrs. B.'s deck. Twenty-one steps— I counted—descended about forty-five degrees into patches of beach grass that turned into thirty yards of warm sand, light brown, turning to white, and soft. And then the lake.

I settled into a deck chair, closed my eyes, and tipped my head up, enjoying the heat of the sun on my face. The muscles in my neck and shoulders and back started to relax. I think I started to fall asleep.

"What the—" I yelled, and jumped out of my chair when the walkie-talkie crackled and spit, and Mrs. B. said, "Mrs. B. to Briggs Baby. Come in to Briggs Baby."

"Briggs here, Mrs. B.," I said, and this was definitely making the list of Random Things Old People Do. "How can I help you?"

"I am on the decks." There was only one, but, whatever. I looked down. We waved. "I am just *checkink* this *wooks.*"

"It works, Mrs. B."

"Okay. Over and off," she said, which amused me enough that I said it back.

"Over and off, Mrs. B."

We waved again, and when I looked up, I found Abigail looking at me, and, spontaneously, I waved to her too. She didn't wave back. She just kept looking at me like it was the most normal thing to do at that moment.

Couple minutes later she disappeared. Got up, walked inside her house. She left her towel and bag outside. They were gone too by morning.

32

"Don't be dead, don't be dead, don't be dead," I said as I ran barefoot to my car the next morning just minutes after I woke up.

I had forgotten to bring Grandma Ruth's Ficus inside the night before and was relieved to find it had not even withered.

I hauled it out and told it, "Good. Not dead. Not dead is always good. Grandma Ruth would have . . ." I looked toward the street. ". . . killed me . . ."

Apparently Abigail hadn't disappeared. She stood next to her bike at the end of Mrs. B.'s driveway. Watching me.

"It's a Ficus," I said, and I pointed at the thing.

"I see."

"My grandmother gave it to me. For graduation."

"So it's a special Ficus."

"Yeah," I said, and laughed a little.

"My grandparents gave me *this* for graduation," she said, showing me a little silver butterfly on a chain around her neck. "It's supposed to remind me—" She lowered her chin, and with her thumb, she pulled the chain up a little higher for a better look. A couple seconds passed. Then a couple more. I took a few steps closer, still cradling the damn plant like a baby in a diaper.

She looked up at me and smiled. Lips pressed tight. Freckles blending into pinker and pinker cheeks.

"Nothing. Never mind," she said.

"No. What? It reminds you of what?"

"That change can be a good thing," she said.

"What kind of change?"

"Oh, you know," she said, and slid the butterfly back and forth across the chain a few times. "I just graduated a couple weeks ago. College in the fall. That kind of thing."

"Yeah, me too. You worried about it?"

"Not really." The pink was fading from her face now.

"Me neither. I've been through much bigger changes. Well, one, anyway."

She looked at me then like Grandma Ruth sometimes looked at me through her bifocals. Head tipped back, lips slightly parted.

"Good or bad?" she asked.

"Big."

"But good or bad?"

"Not great, but life is what you make of it," I said.

"Not always."

"Sure it is," I said. "Anything else is just negative thinking. And I'm Briggs, by the way. Briggs Henry."

"That's better than what some of my friends are calling you."

"Meaning?"

"They were at the funeral yesterday."

"Oh, great. So what am I? Captain Bonehead?"

"Something like that." She looked like she wanted to laugh just then.

"I'm Abigail Howe," she said.

"It's nice to meet you."

"Is it? How can you be sure?" She sounded genuinely curious, which surprised me enough to stutter.

"Uh—I—I—guess I can't be."

"Then you shouldn't have said it."

"You know, most people just say it back."

"Are you the kind of guy who says what most people say?"

"I'm the kind of guy who says 'nice to meet you' because I think it's nice to meet you."

"But you don't know anything about me yet," she said plainly. "You might find out that you *dis*like me."

"*Dis*like?"

"It is a word, you know."

"No, I just—" I couldn't help grinning. "I just think most people would have said 'don't like.'"

"*Most* people would have said 'nice to meet you.'"

"Most people would love to meet a guy with a special Ficus."

"I will say you're the only guy with his own Ficus I've ever met."

"And that doesn't mean it's nice to meet me?" I kind of teased.

"I don't want to say it too soon. I'd hate to regret it."

"You won't regret it."

"Since I'm trying to minimize my regrets, we'll just have to wait and see, won't we?"

"I'll bet you a million dollars that you will say 'nice to meet you' before I leave in August."

"Do you *have* a million dollars?" she asked.

"Not yet, but I will. Someday."

"So you're the kind of guy who makes plans?"

Did I make plans? I almost laughed. I'm a Henry. We always have plans.

"Undergrad in three years," I said. "Then a combined JD-MBA." Law degree and Master of Business Administration. "Get out and start making money."

"Yep. That's a plan."

She touched the tip of her tongue to the corner of her mouth for a moment. I only realized I'd taken a step toward her when she started pushing her bike down the sidewalk, saying, "I hope one of those big changes doesn't happen again and mess it up for you."

"I won't let it," I said, realizing my palms were sweaty. "Maybe I'll tell you about it sometime."

"Maybe I'll ask," she said, and she smiled over her shoulder. Well, sort of. It was a small smile, lips closed, as if she smiled like that all the time and knew exactly how to control it.

I looked at the Ficus and thought it was kind of a cool plant. But I'd still rather have a dog.

33

The Mock Awards were printed in May in the special senior edition of our school paper. I was voted Most Likely to Make a Million Dollars Before the Age of 30. I showed the paper to my dad, who nodded as he read but didn't comment.

Taylor was voted Most Likely to Have Her Own Reality Show, and she'd been trying to think of a name for it ever since.

Sam was voted Most Likely to Discover a Cure for Cancer. In a private vote—done entirely by text—he was also voted Most Likely to Still Be a Virgin by 30, which he found funny because it was probably true. His parents were so worried he would ruin his future over a girl that they said "no girlfriends" until his second year of medical school. He tried to keep secret his three dates with Ashley Hernandez in tenth grade, but his parents found out and grounded him for a full nine weeks.

Parents bitching for 8 days straight, he texted me back then. **Who knew hell was entirely in Vietnamese?**

So no more girlfriends until med school.

Sam said he was probably going to get carpal tunnel syndrome from whacking off so much before then, but his parents would pay for the surgery.

34

At the breakfast table, I found a pen and a piece of off-white stationery at my place and asked Mrs. B., "What's this for?"

"You want back your phone? You write the note *say-ink* you are sorry."

"Mrs. B., I am really sorry."

"No, the note is not for me. You write to the *pasture*."

"The pastor? Are you serious?"

"Why I am not *series*?" she asked, like it was the weirdest thing I could have asked her. "You interrupt my funeral, his funeral, everybody's funeral. You write to *heem*. He knows all of the *Ostrenders*. He knows where they *leeve*. I don't know. He calls to them on the phone. He tells to them you are sorry. He reads to them your note. Everyone is *heppy*. And." She said *and* like it was its own sentence. "I am *heppy* too."

"Yeah, well, I'll—I'll do my best to make everyone happy." Oh, my God. "Do you remember his name?"

"No. But I save the booklet."

I followed her into the living room, where she opened the top drawer of her desk and took out Pauline

Ostrander's funeral program. When she handed it to me, I glanced down at the drawer and saw another program underneath.

Celebration of the Life of Robert James Allen.

Under that was another one. *A Loving Farewell* to someone. I flipped through a *Mass of Resurrection*, couple *Homegoings*, bunch of *Loving Farewells*. There was a stack of these things. A collection.

"Mrs. B., did you go to all these funerals?"

"Yes."

"And you saved the programs?"

She smiled up at me, squinting her eyes above glowing red cheeks. "See?" She patted the pile of programs and scrunched her shoulders up when she said, "Room for more."

35

A guy named Ben Zuckerman dropped off paint and supplies mid-morning. Rain was predicted but never materialized, and the thin gray clouds broke apart, revealing the blue sky above. Cool thing about the lake effect—the temperature of the lake changes the weather along the shore. You can never fully predict how the lake will affect the day.

Turned out, Ben was only a year older than me but looked much older since his hair, which was curly black, was already receding a little. And judging from the size of his arms, the guy lifted. It surprised me how gently he greeted Mrs. B. He gave her a big grin and a loose hug, like she had invisible padding around her.

He kind of laughed through his nose when he asked, "You're the guy from the funeral?"

"You were there?"

"No, but I heard about it. Everyone's heard about it."

"Great," I said, and scratched the back of my neck.

"Don't worry about it. Everyone knows you're a tourist."

"No, I'm here for the summer."

"It's the same thing. And tourists are always pulling dumb stunts."

"Yeah, it wasn't a stunt. Thanks."

I helped him carry paint and pans into Mrs. B.'s nearly empty garage. No car. Ben said she sold it after her husband died several years ago.

"It was a 1985 Oldsmobile Cutlass," he said, laughing. "Huge. You ever seen one?"

"I have."

"Talk about retro. I mean, they don't even make the things anymore."

"Yeah. I know." I felt like saying *no kidding,* but I didn't really want to get into it.

"It was a boat. We're talking land yacht."

"So, I'm driving in here yesterday, and I get stuck behind this SUV that has *God Yacht* written on it."

Ben nodded.

"John Dumchak," he said. "Goes by Dum."

"Doom? As in, what, doomsday?"

"No, Dum as in how he pronounces his last name. Doom-chak. Guy's kind of a local celebrity."

"For what?"

"Pretty much for that car."

"Is he crazy?"

"Doubt it. He used to be some big corporate attorney and then something happened. I don't know what, but he gave it up and became one of those—whaddya call it—evangelical types who just want to talk about God."

"What does he throw at people?"

"You'll see. Just—if he ever asks if you're ready, say yes or he'll want to talk to you for hours."

"Got it," I said.

We walked back to Ben's truck, and he told me that he played volleyball with a bunch of friends down at North Beach most afternoons around five.

"You should come," he said right when we both noticed Abigail pushing her bike past Mrs. B.'s. She stopped when she saw Ben and gave him what I was coming to know as her poker face.

"Ah, great," he said under his breath. "Hang on."

He jogged down to talk with her for about a minute and did most of the talking himself. Also most of the smiling and all of the gestures. He tried to hug her, but she never let go of her bike's handlebars.

Ben jogged back to me as Abigail watched, and she nodded what I assumed was *Hello* at me. Could have been *Go away.* Or *Oh, I see you're still here.*

"What was that?" I asked.

"Nothing. Just haven't seen her since I got home a few weeks ago." He said he just finished his freshman year at Michigan State.

"Yeah," I said, and wanted to know what the story was, but didn't want to pry.

"Her parents threw her a big graduation party last week. I said I'd go, but—you know. Whatever. I messed up." He shook his head. "So volleyball. North Beach. Around five if you're interested."

"Definitely. If Mrs. B. lets me off by then."

"She'll let you off."

"How do you know?"

"Because I had your job two summers ago. Buddy of mine had it last year. Four thirty *eez the times to queet*," he said in a fake Serbian accent. Kind of funny.

He got in his truck, rolled the window down, and said, "She's pretty sweet, so don't let her get to you."

"She's not getting to me."

"You just got here."

"Hey, I am great with old ladies. They love me."

"Well," he said as he started to back out of the drive, "everyone's good at something, right?"

I walked back toward Mrs. B.'s house but slowed down to watch as Ben stopped to talk to Abigail through his window. I saw her nod at him like she was saying *Hello, Go away,* or *Oh, I see you're still here.*

36

This girl in a hot-pink bikini top and cut-off jean shorts—totally filling out both—ran up to me from outside the snack bar the minute I walked onto North Beach later that afternoon. At that end of the beach, which was about three football fields long, the place smelled like hot grease.

"Hi," she said, and tipped a paper tray of fries toward me. "Want some?"

"No, thanks," I said. She looked familiar, but at the same time I knew I had never met her. Either I looked familiar to her too, or she was just the single friendliest girl on Earth.

I kept walking down toward the volleyball courts, and she walked with me. Two of the four courts were empty. Bare poles. No nets. You rented those from the snack bar. Ben and his friends were stringing one. On the nearest court, six people about my parents' age played beanbag toss with red and lime-green beanbags. When someone scored points, they all cheered.

"You're sure you don't want some fries?" she asked, and held the fries closer to me. "They're really good. You'll be sorry if you don't."

"Yeah, I'm sure, but thanks."

"What's this?" she asked, and pressed her finger against a spot of blue paint on my arm.

"Misty Harbor Blue," I said. "I was painting all day."

"Oh my God, it matches your eyes. I'm Maddy, by the way."

"Maddy," I said back to her. "I'm Briggs."

"I knew it!" She hopped a couple times, spilled some fries, said, "Oh, snap. Oh, well." She popped one of the remaining fries in her mouth and chewed as she talked. "Ben said he had met this cute guy named Briggs and that you might be coming here today." She chewed and talked really fast. "Well, no, he didn't say you're cute. I mean, that would be weird, right? Only 'cause he's not gay." She shrugged and lost a few more fries. "I just figured with a name like Briggs you had to be cute, and you are, so I'm right."

"Uh. Thanks."

"Where'd you get it?"

"My name? Family name."

She told me the family history of her name and its various spellings and how she wished she had been named Victoria because of all the cool nicknames you can make from it. She listed them. I had to admit, I had no idea the list was that long. My mother, the Queen of Lists, would have approved.

Maddy had just finished her list and her fries when we came upon Ben and friends, and one of them looked a lot like Mute Button from yesterday. Tall, kind of skinny, longish black hair hanging in his eyes. Maddy introduced me by saying, "This is Briggs. I knew it was him, and I was right. Yay me."

"Yay you," I said, and shot her a quick smile.

"Oh, man, you're the Phone Douche," the guy with hair in his face said, and, yep, that was him.

"Brandon," Maddy said like she was scolding him, but the guy just laughed. Couple guys did.

"Seriously, you assed up on that one," he said to me.

"Yep," I said, and scratched at the back of my neck.

So that was Brandon. The others were Mike, Josh, Lauren, Nicole, Zach, and Danny. All of them tanned but for Nicole, who barely looked up to say hello from her seriously intense application of sunscreen. I found out she and Maddy just graduated high school. Abigail's class. The rest graduated a year ago.

"Brandon worked for Vesna last summer," Ben said.

"Everybody has the *B* names," I said, in my own fake Serbian accent, which was greeted with silence. "It's something Mrs. B.—never mind."

"Oh! Oh! Oh!" Maddy said, and hopped in place and waved both hands at me. "My middle name is Brittany. Brittany. With a *B*."

And she was so excited, she hugged me.

"I don't think I could do your job," Nicole said, blinking up at me against the sun. "I mean, it would be like moving in with my grandmother, and there's just no way that's happening."

"He's great with old ladies. They love him," Ben said in a way that entertained everyone but me.

"No, I've just—I volunteered at an assisted-living

center this year. Place called Bluestone Court."

"Why?" Nicole asked.

"I've got a lot of experience with that generation, I guess."

"So you're like Mr. Geriatric?" Brandon asked. He jerked his head to the side to move his hair out of his eyes. "Can we call you Geri?"

"Briggs."

"Between Geri and Phone Douche, I'd pick Geri," Brandon said. "Come on. Let's play."

I ended up on his team. He called himself captain and played like a pro, taking out some serious aggression on the ball.

"Nice!" I said after he won our third game in a row with a spike, and I went in for the high five, but he waved me off.

I played across from Maddy and completely missed the ball the first time she smiled at me. She had a huge mouth, and she stuck her tongue between her teeth in a way that should have been a lot sexier than it was.

"Trade!" Brandon called when I lost the point.

We'd been playing about forty minutes, and it was my turn to serve again when I saw Abigail Howe walking her bike toward us down the sidewalk, which ran the length of the beach, separating it from the parking lot.

"Hey, Abigail!" Maddy shouted, waving both hands as if she were signaling for help. "You wanna play?"

"The funeral," I said, nodding at Maddy. She was the girl who called to Abigail in the parking lot. "I knew you looked familiar."

"Aww," Maddy said. "Mrs. Ostrander was our fifth-grade teacher. She was so sweet."

"Come on. Let's play," Ben said as Abigail called to Maddy, "Not today, thanks."

"Tomorrow then," Maddy shouted back. "Or next week. Come next week."

"Maybe," Abigail said. She stopped walking and looked right at me and asked, "You gonna serve?"

"You gonna watch?" I asked.

"Probably not," she said, like she was happy to say it.

"You're missing all the fun," I said, flashing her my best smile one more time.

"Yet somehow I survive," she said, and started walking away.

I served the ball and stole a quick look to see if she was looking back. She wasn't. Guess I stole too long a look, since I completely missed the ball heading back my way, and we lost the point.

"Trade!"

37

There were only two fishermen on the pier the next morning, standing yards apart and leaving each other alone. It was five thirty, and the lights all the way out to the lighthouse were on, and the only sound was the slap of my running shoes on the cement. Even the lake was quiet.

I nodded to the fishermen as I ran past. They nodded back.

There are certain silences no one should disturb, and morning at the lake is one of them. I think painting houses is another.

And funerals. Obviously.

38

"Briggs Henry. Guy with the phone," I said to myself, shaking my head as I approached the small, tidy yellow house with green shutters. Mrs. B. had made me come.

There were zero residential zoning laws in this part of South Haven. Inland. South of the drawbridge. I ran through here every morning past big, modern cottages, next to old brick houses, next to white frame houses, next to shacks. And I mean shacks. Here and there. Porches propped up on cinderblocks, torn screens, dead grass.

I called one the Flamingo Shack for the eight lawn ornaments out front, arranged in pairs like Santa's reindeer in a yard that was mostly dirt. Brown crud covered the screens. The front steps were broken, and part of the doorframe had rotted away.

It was half a block and a world away from the spotless house I approached that morning. There wasn't a chip in the yellow paint, a mark on the door, or a blade of grass out of place. The bushes around the front beds were trimmed and squared, and bunches of blue and white flowers spilled out of the window boxes under every window—up and down. Still, I thought it might have been easier knocking on the Flamingo Shack's door.

I grabbed the back of my neck for a few seconds and ignored a small stomach cramp before ringing the bell. A woman about my mom's age with puffy eyes and a bright pink nose answered and tried her best to smile at me.

"Yes?"

"Hi, I'm Briggs Henry," I said, and we stared at each other a few seconds. "I'm here to help move."

"Oh. Oh, of course. Come in."

It was Pauline Ostrander's house. The woman who answered the door introduced herself as Shirley Gorski, Pauline's daughter, and apologized for crying.

"No, I'm sorry about your mom," I said.

"Were you one of her students?"

"Students? No, I'm here because Mrs. B.—Mrs. Boz—Vesna Božić sent me."

Ordered me, was more like it. "You want the job, you do what I say, and I say you are *helpink* the *Ostrender* family pack," she told me at breakfast that morning.

"Mom knew so many people," Shirley Gorski said, and wiped her nose with a crumpled tissue. "She taught fifth grade for forty-one years. Some of her former students are already here helping."

She gave me a quick tour of the house, which was twice the size of our shoebox and smelled of fresh coffee. Most of the furniture had been moved out, but tons of taped boxes remained. Upstairs in a small loft space Ben Zuckerman and that guy Brandon were hauling boxes out of a storage closet. Ben made it look easy. Between his skinny arms and hair in his face, Brandon kind of struggled.

"Boys," Shirley said. "This is—" She turned to me. "I forgot your name."

"We know Geri," Brandon said, and Ben grinned.

"It's Briggs," I said to Shirley Gorski, and snagged a box and hauled it down to a panel truck someone must have rented.

We got the loft cleared out in no time and started on the rest of the boxes on the main floor. Brandon managed to work *phone, mute button,* or *funeral* into every sentence he said when Shirley Gorski was nearby. Fortunately, she was too busy directing a bunch of women packing up the kitchen to hear him.

I headed in there once the loft was done and headed right back out again when I saw the Chicken and Biscuits ladies. Near them on a counter was a stainless steel roaster that would easily have held a twenty-pound turkey

"Jerry!" Shirley Gorski called, and Ben and Brandon busted out laughing. "Jerry!"

"Yes, Mrs. Gorski," I said, returning to the kitchen.

"Would you please carry this out to their car?" she asked.

"Happy to," I said, and grabbed the roaster, eager to show those two women my back.

"Wait a minute," the one with the gravelly voice—the blond one—said.

I paused in the doorway, and, man, this thing was heavy.

"Which car?" I asked over my shoulder.

"The little white one," her friend said.

"We know you," the first one said.

"My grandmother has a roaster like this," I said, walking toward the front door.

They followed.

"I just know we know you," the one said again.

"She never uses it. In fact, she's not really much of a cook," I said, talking a lot faster than I was walking. "She likes to can things. Well, one thing."

"So familiar," she said.

"Could someone get the door, please?" I asked, shooting a glance over at Ben and Brandon, who were practically purple trying not to laugh.

"The door," I said again to them as Shirley Gorski opened it. I couldn't even do the gentlemanly thing and let Chicken and Biscuits go first. I just hurried outside right as one of them—probably Biscuits, not that I knew which was which—snapped her fingers.

"The funeral," the one with the gravelly voice said.

"The funeral," her friend confirmed.

"The funeral?" Shirley Gorski asked.

Then there was silence.

I stopped and turned around in time to see Shirley Gorski's mouth hang open, and her red-rimmed eyes rake over me, and she said, "You're the one with the phone," before sobbing into her hands.

39

Dear Mrs. Gorski, my letter began.

I finished it at Mrs. B.'s kitchen table that afternoon and shut my eyes and felt sick—like stomach-flu sick—every time I pictured Mrs. Gorski crying.

Mrs. B. sat across from me while I wrote, and I handed it to her for her approval.

"You have the nice *hen-writink,*" Mrs. B. said as she read. "Maybe you are *goink* to be the engineer?"

"Lawyer," I said, and then downed a glass of ice water. "Rich lawyer."

"Why you want to be the lawyer?"

"Because any time any bank or business gets into trouble, the only guys who make any money out of it are the lawyers."

"Your father and your *mahther,* they are the lawyers?"

"I wish," I said, and carried my glass to the sink. "They're the people who have paid lawyers fortunes over the years."

I rinsed my glass out, and Mrs. B. said, "This is good letter. But why you sign your name Jerry?"

40

Next morning, I slowed from a run to a walk, pulled my shirt off, and dried my face. The air was warm, even that early, and quiet. My feet hitting the sidewalk and a bunch of sprinklers were the loudest sounds in town.

I was just nearing Mrs. B.'s driveway when Abigail walked out of hers, pushing her bike. She saw me and pressed the tips of three fingers against her lips when she smiled.

"What?" I asked.

"I heard you made Mrs. Gorski cry yesterday."

"Man," I said, and shut my eyes tight at the thought. "Brandon tell you that?"

"Nope," she said. "A friend of my dad's heard it at work."

"Are you serious?"

She nodded, and I scratched the back of my neck for a second or two, and she brushed her hand against my cheek. I just stared at her, like *What just happened?* and she did it a second time.

I was about to step closer when she said, "It was a bug."

"Right. Thanks."

"Anytime," she said as she pushed her bike past me, walking toward town.

"Hey, do you ever ride that thing?" I asked.

"Who says I *want* to ride it?" she answered.

41

"I just don't see why I have to go *in* with you," I told Mrs. B. I had just driven into the parking lot of Pickler Funeral Home. "I mean, can't I just drop you off and wait?"

"Taxi driver drops off. I do not hire the taxi driver," she said. "I hire you."

"I know, but—"

"You do not want the job?"

"No, I want the job."

"Good," she said, and patted my knee three times. "Then you do what I say."

"Yeah, but, Mrs. B.," I said. "Another funeral? In one week?"

"People die when they die," she said, shrugging a little, and I shuddered a little. "Oh. You do not like the *wood die?*"

"It's not my favorite word."

"No, it is nobody's favorite *wood,* Briggs Baby, but"— she tossed her hands up—"everybody dies."

"Mrs. B.," I said, hoping she'd stop because this was starting to freak me out.

"Americans do not like the *wood die*. You say pass away. You say *keeck* the farm."

"Bought the farm. Kicked the bucket." I ran my hand over my head and scratched the back of my neck. "I can't believe I'm having this conversation."

"No, you think you don't say *die,* it never happens." She grinned when she tapped my knee again.

"No, I know it happens. I just don't really want to talk about it."

"Because you are American. I am Serbian. Serbian people talk about death. Death, food, and *shursh*."

"You guys must be a riot at Christmas," I said, and a few seconds later, she put her hands on her stomach, and her shoulders started moving up and down, and she went, "Mmm-mmm-mmm."

She was laughing.

42

I'd never met anyone from Serbia, and the only things I knew about the country came from tenth grade's world history class. The death of Franz Ferdinand, and later the Bosnian War. The Black Hand. The breakup of Yugoslavia. The movement of armies but never the lives of the people. The world's always been a mess.

I can't imagine being in a war. My dad's dad fought in Vietnam. His name was Richard, like my dad. Richard Gordon Henry, Sr. Richard Gordon Henry, Jr. He died a couple years before I was born. Grandma Ruth told my dad she was tired of Richard Gordon Henrys, so I became Briggs Cooke Henry after my mother's and Grandma Ruth's maiden names.

Grandma Ruth told me when I was sixteen that she didn't like the name Briggs Cooke Henry any more than she liked Richard Gordon Henry.

"Why did you name Dad that then?" I asked her.

"It was expected," she said.

"What would you have named him if you could have chosen anything?"

She looked at me as if she didn't understand the question. That, or why I was asking it.

"I never entertained any name other than the one he has," she said.

"What if he had been a girl?"

"It is too late to wonder *what if,*" she answered.

43

"Is your phone on mute?" an usher at Pickler Funeral Home—this total stranger in a black pinstripe suit—said to me, like I should find it really, really funny.

"It's off," I said.

He held out a program and then yanked it back as he asked, "You're sure?"

"Yeah, I'm sure."

Ah, you need a haircut, I half expected him to say.

Pickler Funeral Home looked to be new, a sprawling brick ranch on the outskirts of South Haven and set among gas stations and fast-food restaurants. Good place to get a signal, I thought, so I had shoved my phone in my coat pocket to check later when I had the chance.

We were at a memorial service for eighty-two-year-old Maria Santos. She was a nurse for thirty-two years. Late in life, she volunteered at free clinics all around southwest Michigan. I learned that from the right side of the program. The left side was entirely in Spanish, which was my lowest grade sophomore year. B+. I wanted that A but couldn't master the sounds.

The director of the funeral home walked to the front

of the room, introduced himself, and said, "We're about to begin, so I'd like to ask everyone to make sure their cell phones are turned off."

And six people—seriously—six people I'd never seen before turned around and looked right at me.

I felt like saying *My phone's off, and I'm not about to shove my hands down my pants, so don't worry. I am familiar with the List of Funeral Commandments.*

44

Taylor: Thought u were mad at me when u didnt return my txts!!

Me: Not mad. No signal at beach house. Cant use my phone there

Taylor: Where r u now?

Me: U dont want to know

I was texting her from the bathroom at Pickler Funeral Home. Big bathroom. Private. In the corner was a fake palm tree in a maroon urn. Probably some dead guy's ashes were at the bottom.

I'd been in there about ten minutes, excusing myself after the service ended. Maria Santos's family served coffee and cookies in a big reception room where I left Mrs. B. talking about how nice Maria Santos was.

Taylor: R u having fun?

I typed *yes*, then deleted it. I was typing *its OK* when she texted again.

Taylor: Emily, Ashley & me r going to Grand Haven Sat.

Me: Nice. Nishesh going too?

Taylor: Dont know yet. U r SOOOOOO lucky u get to spend the WHOLE summer at the beach!

Me: Everythings better at the beach

Taylor: I KNOW!!!!!!!!!!!!!!!

I stared at the phone, not quite knowing what to text back. A few seconds passed, and someone knocked on the door.

Me: Gotta go. Will check msgs when I can

Taylor: Have fun!

I slipped my phone into my pocket and opened the door to a guy standing half a foot from it with a big, weird grin on his face—like his mouth was half a size too big for it. And he said, "Are you ready? Are you ready, man?"

"Yeah, it's all yours," I said, and got the hell out of there.

45

Next day, I drove Mrs. B. in to Kalamazoo, 38.5 miles east of South Haven. She took one look at Misty Harbor Blue in the room across from mine and said, "No. The color is all *wronk*. The *paintink* is good." She patted my arm. "But the color is *wronk*. So. We *shange* it."

I liked this about her immediately—that if something was wrong, she fixed it. We Henrys did the same thing. So did Taylor. Out with the old, in with the new.

I texted her from the parking lot of K City Creative Paints, while a store employee named Chuck with big teeth loaded my car with eight gallons of Windswept Sky.

U & my new boss lady remind me of each other. Shes 84.

She texted back: **Maybe she should b ur new girlfriend**

Me: **Jealous?**

She texted me a selfie of her and Nishesh, pressed close together in her kitchen and smiling with their mouths wide open.

Her: **Do I look jealous? Hes coming with us Sat btw**

Me: **That guy needs a haircut**

Her: **Say hi to ur girlfriend for me**

"Boh!" I said, and nearly dropped my phone as I grabbed my side where Mrs. B. had just poked me.

She smiled up at me and patted my stomach with both hands when she said, "You are too *jahmpy*, Briggs Baby. You need to relax or you will have the heart attack and die *younk*."

"I'm not going to die young, Mrs. B.," I said as I opened the door of the Bucket for her.

"I think the same *think* when I am your age," she said.

"You're eighty-four."

"You see." She grinned. "I am right."

46

I headed back down to North Beach around five o'clock and greeted Ben, standing with Brandon and a few of their buddies, like he was my new Jason Hirsch.

"Ben Zuckerman," I said, rounding my arm for a handshake.

"Hey," he said, and shook my hand briefly.

"You running for mayor or something?" Brandon asked. He jerked his head to the side but never really got his hair out of his face.

They were standing by the volleyball courts, but no net was strung, and I was disappointed not to see Maddy there yet.

"Just saying hi," I said.

"I'm ready for campaign buttons," he said. "Geri for Mayor."

"It's Briggs."

"It's Geri," he said, and took a step toward me with his chest sticking out. "Mr. Geri Atric."

Couple of the guys laughed. Brandon stood there, looking at me like it was my turn to say something.

"We gonna play?" I asked.

"You see a ball or a net?" he asked.

"Annette who?" I asked, pissed, but it backed Brandon off. Made him snort and grin sideways.

I was channeling my dad, and, of course, it worked. Everything he did worked. Well, nearly everything. Definitely his stupid puns.

Zach and Danny had backpacks with them and dropped them in the sand.

"You throw?" Danny asked as he pulled a baseball out of his bag and tossed it to me.

"Captain of the team. All-State honors," I said, tossing the ball to Zach.

"He didn't ask for your résumé," Brandon said as Danny threw me an extra glove.

He and Zach started running in opposite directions to get some yardage between them. I looked at the glove and said, "Aw, man, I'm left-handed."

"Sorry about your luck," Zach called.

Brandon told Ben something about work. I came into the conversation at ". . . have to be there at five a.m. I pull in at six, and I'm thinking I'm totally fired. I'm like five days on the job, you know? And the guy says to me, he says, I swear, 'You're not on the schedule today.'"

"No way." Ben laughed.

"So I'm like, *Dude, is it cool I showed up on my day off or bad that I got there late,* you know?"

"Where do you work?" I asked.

"Joe-Pro Janitorial," Brandon said. "We do commercial cleaning."

"You just doing it for the summer?"

"No," he said like he was really offended or like I was a serious douche for asking.

"You're not in school anywhere?" I asked.

"Nope, and I got no immediate plans to go, either. Something wrong with that?"

"It's your life, man," I said. "Make it whatever you want."

"Well, I want to make it like Kanye West's, but since I can't rap for shit, I guess I'll just clean offices for a while," Brandon said.

He grabbed the glove out of my hand and jogged off to join the other guys.

"What's his problem?" I asked Ben, who was looking at his phone.

"Don't worry about him. He's just not a big fan of tourists."

"I'm not a tourist, Ben," I said. "I live here."

"Sure, Briggs," Ben laughed as he checked an incoming text. "Ah, man, Josh and the girls aren't coming. No game!" he called to the others.

"I've always got game!" Brandon called back, and threw a high lob to Danny, who dropped it.

"We're probably just gonna hang out here for a while," Ben said to me. "You're welcome to stay."

"Yeah, I think I'll just head back to Mrs. B.'s," I said, and left while Brandon told his friends, "If I have a son, I'm going to teach him to throw and hit left-handed. I mean, think of the advantage he'll have."

I pictured him coaching the kid, "Just do what I'm doing, but do it backward."

47

I walked back to Mrs. B.'s along the shore, ankle deep in cold, smooth water. Only took about three minutes before I acclimated. If June's warm weather kept up, the lake would be bathwater by July.

A bunch more people were on the beach—public and private ones—since the day I got there. I had to step around a lot of little kids filling buckets with water. Parents and grandparents sat nearby in beach chairs or under umbrellas.

Grandma Ruth never came with us to the beach. Never came with us on the boat. I'm not sure she knew how to relax. The woman was wound so tight she could crack walnuts with her sphincter.

A chain-link fence and a sign marked the northern border of North Beach. PRIVATE BEACH signs dotted most of the landscape north. When I made my first million, I was going to have a condo here. *And* a boat.

Every now and again—maybe once every two or three years—a story makes the news that some owner refused to allow people to cross his sandy property on their walks along the shore, but the courts always side with the walkers. Ownership stops at the edge of the water.

No one owns the lake.

48

"No volleyball tonight?" someone called as I walked closer.

I looked up and squinted toward the beach.

"Oh. Yeah, no," I said. "Not tonight."

"Good," Abigail said. "Then you can sit with me." She was just a few yards back from the water, sitting on that green-and-white-striped blanket.

"Okay," I said, almost as if it were a question.

There was a little breeze in the air, and it blew strands of Abigail's hair around, making them glow pink in the sun, and flashed off her butterfly charm. Also brightened her eyes, which I'd thought were dark blue but now looked really light. I wanted to reach out, touch her face, move her hair aside, but she beat me to it. She tucked those few strands behind her ears and asked, "Yes?" when she saw me staring at her and trying not to smile too much.

"You're sure you want company? Because you haven't really seemed like you wanted to hang out," I said. "With anyone."

"I've just been"—she shrugged—"a little under the weather lately. Something I ate. It made me dyspeptic."

"Dys-what?"

"Dyspeptic. In a bad mood because of an upset stomach." I made a face like *what,* so she said, "It's a word."

"Yeah. Okay. I get it. I mean, who doesn't get dyspeptic?"

"Is that sarcasm?" she asked in a way that said she knew it was and didn't mind.

"No one likes sarcasm," I said.

"Okay, so what makes you dyspeptic?"

"One particular kind of grape jelly and needing my hair cut."

She glanced at my very short hair before I said, "Someday I'll tell you more about that."

"Someday I might ask," she said.

I rubbed my hands back and forth on the blanket, which was softer than our towels at home.

"So is it nice to meet me yet?" I asked.

"Not yet."

"You know, people have said it"—I leaned a little closer—"and not regretted it."

"As far as you know."

I flattened my hands over my heart. "Hey, I've been called a catch."

"By someone who caught you?"

"No." I laughed. "By her mom, actually."

Abigail smiled, and it was quick and full and great. "Well, at least you have that going for you. Why did she say it?"

"I never asked. I just took the compliment."

She looked back at me, still faintly smiling. I couldn't really read her expression.

"Ask me something interesting," she said.

"Is that an order?"

"Was that it?"

"Was it interesting?"

"Not really," she said, but I saw her trying not to smile this time. "Ask me something no one's ever asked me before." She waited a second before adding, "Please."

"How am I supposed to know every question you've been asked before?"

"That counts, but it's not very interesting."

"Okay, then how about this," I said. "Why are you asking me to ask you something no one's ever asked you before?"

"I'm tired of my own thoughts," she said, glancing at me for a second before looking out at the lake, squinting into the lava-colored sun. "Do you ever get tired of your own thoughts?"

"You know, I really don't."

"You're lucky."

"Or maybe I'm just not a deep thinker," which was fine with me. I shrugged. "I don't know."

"Well," she said. "This is the place to find out. No better place to just sit and think." She fiddled with her butterfly necklace. "My own private lake effect."

"But you're tired of your thoughts," I said, like, *Why the hell are you here, then?*

"I've got nowhere else to go."

"Yeah, poor you," I said. "And, yeah, that was sarcasm."

"I've been looking for a distraction and hoping you'd come out here."

"You could have just rung the doorbell."

"But that wouldn't have been very interesting, would it?"

"So I'm your interesting distraction?"

"Not yet."

"All right." I leaned back, hands in the sand. "What's seventeen times forty-five?"

"What?" She turned to look at me like she hadn't quite heard me.

"Have you ever been asked what seventeen times forty-five is?"

"No, and I'm going to need a calculator for it."

"Seven hundred sixty-five."

"Did you already know that?" she asked.

"Give me one. Two numbers, two digits each."

"Uh, fifty-eight times thirty-two."

It took me a few seconds, but I said, "One thousand eight hundred fifty-six."

"Hang on." She grabbed her phone out of her pocket.

"Seriously?" I asked as she double-checked my work on her calculator.

"Seriously," she said, and, when she got the answer, she said, "No way."

I shrugged, like, *Told you so.*

"Twenty-six times sixty-six," she said, and clicked keys.

"One thousand seven hundred sixteen."

"Huh," she said.

I did a few more, and then Abigail's phone chimed. Company had arrived, and she was needed inside.

"Do you hire out for parties?" she asked. "I should take you inside and show you off."

"You sound like my dad."

"Is that good or bad?"

"Uh. Neither, maybe. Or both." I thought for a second. Then glanced at her. At least fifty-eight times thirty-two only had one right answer. "I don't know," I said.

We stood, and I helped her fold the blanket.

"Are you going to tell me about these thoughts you're tired of?" I asked.

"They're not very interesting."

"Is that why you're tired of them?"

"I'm tired of them because they're all I've been thinking about lately. I just don't know how to think about anything else."

"Maybe," I said as I handed her my side of the blanket and brushed my fingers against hers, "it'll be helpful to tell someone about them."

"Are you a helpful kind of guy?" she asked, taking the blanket from me. "A big-plans, helpful kind of guy?"

"I got no problem admitting that I am."

"Helpful *and* a catch," she said, stuffing the blanket into her bag. "How lucky can one girl be?"

"You know where to find me."

She slung her bag over her shoulder, which tipped her off balance a second. I reached to steady her, grabbing her arm and a hip.

"Thanks," she said as she stepped backward. "But I don't need rescuing."

"Good to know," I said. "Next time I'll just let you fall."

"I'll do the same for you."

"I'm not gonna fall."

"Everyone says that before they do," she said, and walked inside.

49

Next day, Abigail Howe disappeared. It was like Mrs. B. said. I saw her on the beach, early Saturday morning. Then I looked again, and she was gone. For days.

50

"Just double-checking. I don't have to go in with you for this one, right?" I asked on the drive to St. Mark's Episcopal Church Sunday morning. Sunrise service, six a.m. Mrs. B., the priest, me, and a couple fishermen were the only people awake in town.

"Why I make you go to the *shursh* with me?"

"You make me go to funerals."

"Funerals are your job. *Shursh* is not your job. *Shursh* is your private *beezness*."

"Funerals are my job?" I asked, kind of laughing. "That was not part of the job description, Mrs. B."

"You don't like the job?"

"I like the job," I said. "I don't—you know—really like the funerals."

"I think you don't like the job. I think maybe you want to *queet*?"

"I do not want to quit. Really. I want to stay."

"You want to stay?"

"I want to stay."

I pulled up outside the church.

"Maybe I put you on the probe . . . probe . . ." Mrs. B. squinted her eyes into little slits while she searched for the word.

"Probation?" I asked, like, *Are you serious?*

"Yes. The probation."

"No, I'm good."

"You stay another week. Then." She held up her index finger in triumph. "We decide if you stay all the *sahm-mer*." She patted my knee three times and said, "You pick up in one hour. And don't be late."

I was sixteen minutes early.

51

I had weekend afternoons off, so I drove home Sunday after making sure Mrs. B. had everything she needed. I had only been gone about a week, but I missed the place, definitely missed my friends, and just kind of wanted to hang out there for a little while. Also needed to pick up my baseball glove.

I walked through the back door of my house five seconds before dad walked out of the bathroom and into the kitchen. Talking.

". . . late getting home tonight because of a— Oh, Briggs." We shook hands. "I thought you were your mother."

"She's not home?"

"No. Why are you? Everything going okay?"

"Oh, yeah, it's great. Saturday and Sunday afternoons off," I kind of bragged.

"So you're a man of leisure now. Well"—heh, heh—"don't get fat."

"You either, Dad." Heh, heh.

"I'm on my way back to the office. I don't have time to get fat."

"Who does? I got up at five today to take Mrs. B. to church."

"I'm just having a little fun with you, Briggs," Dad said. "You're too much a chip off the ol' block to ever get lazy."

"Yeah," I said again, kind of relieved and kind of pissed.

I walked with him outside.

"Job's okay?" he asked, and didn't let me answer before he laughed and said, "Hell of a lot easier than Bluehair Court, I bet."

"Yeah. Different."

He never asked me why I liked it there. 'Course, I never told him that I did.

"Boss Lady treating you well?" he asked.

"Mrs. B.," I said. "Yeah, she's great."

"Got her twisted around your little finger, I bet," he said as he got in his car, gray, like my old one, like Grandma Ruth's new one.

"Oh, yeah."

"Well, don't go breaking her heart."

"She'll probably break mine," I said through what felt like a pretty feeble smile, and I waved as he drove away. But he wasn't looking back.

52

Sam's phone rang twice.

"Hello," he said. "You have reached the humble personage of Sam Nguyen, lover of creation, doer of good deeds, champion of the downtrodden, and defender of people afraid of monkeys. Please don't leave a message. I'm live."

"What?" I asked.

"I'm thinking of making it my greeting once I'm at Stanford," where he was going in the fall. "How does it sound? Think chicks will dig it?"

"Oh, yeah. And they love being called chicks, so be sure to say that a lot."

"I know," he said, and he laughed. "I'm not going to have a girlfriend until I'm fifty."

"You're still going to need your mom's permission."

I met him at his house. Mom was there, which wasn't a surprise. She went over there on weekends sometimes to review the Nguyens' personal expenses at Mr. Nguyen's request. It was the result, he said, of literally having nothing but the clothes on his back when he came to this country.

My dad lost his shirt once, so he understood, and he told Mom, "Nguyen better be paying you overtime."

Dad pronounced it New-yin.

Mom never put in for overtime.

I hung out with Sam for an hour. We shot hoops. I told him Abigail was hot and Mrs. B. was sweet and her house was incredible. On the beach, and all.

"So, then, what?" he said, tossing me the ball.

"What?" I said, and took a shot. And missed.

"What's wrong?"

"Nothing's wrong," I said. He threw me the ball, and I took another shot and missed again.

Basketball was never my sport.

Sam held the ball under one arm and stared at me a couple seconds. Waiting.

"No, it's just new, you know?" I said. "I still have to figure out stuff."

"Stuff?"

"Stuff," I said as Kennedy walked up the drive and shouted, "Hey! You a kept man yet?"

"I'm working on it," I called back, swiping the ball from Sam and making a shot.

Later I told them the story of accidentally playing Kennedy's video at Pauline Ostrander's funeral like I was totally cool with it, and Kennedy laughed so hard, he said, "I'm gonna piss my pants. I swear I'm gonna piss my pants."

When we said good-bye, Kennedy said, "Glad you're havin' fun, man. Even though you gotta work while you're there."

"Oh, yeah," I said. "Everything's . . . everything's better at the beach."

53

My stomach made a hell of a groan, like distant thunder, as Mrs. B. and I walked up the aisle of Haven Reformed Church. The place was huge and plain. No carpet. No pew cushions. Every step, creak, cough, and sniff bounced through the whole sanctuary.

"I am not *feedink* you enough, Briggs Baby?" Mrs. B. asked, and looked at me with wide eyes.

"No, your food's great. It's more than enough."

"But your stomach. It makes the *rahmbles*."

"It does that sometimes. I'm fine," I said, but the truth was that my stomach had been a little off for two days, ever since I went home.

"You tell to me if you are *seek*."

"I'm not sick, Mrs. B.," I said as she smiled and waved at the Chicken and Biscuits ladies, who scooted over to make room for us in their pew.

They introduced themselves with big grins and gentle handshakes.

"I'm Mae Maitland," the one with the husky voice and fluff of yellow hair said. "You can call me Miss Mae. Everyone does."

"Miss Mae," I said quietly, and shot her my There's My Girl Smile.

"And I'm Connie Steiner," her brunette friend said, leaning across Miss Mae and squeezing my hand a really long time.

"That's enough, dear," Miss Mae said, and tapped the top of Connie Steiner's hand until she let go.

The funeral was for a woman named Dorothy D. Webb, and the funeral was long. Minutes into the service I noticed Miss Mae bite her bottom lip, sniff a few times, and touch the back of her fingers to her nose.

"Mrs. B.," I whispered. "Do you have a tissue?"

"Of course I have the tissue. This is my funeral. Why you don't have with you the tissue?"

"It's not for me."

"You should still have the tissue," she said as she handed me one from her purse. "The gentleman always carries the tissue."

I offered it to Miss Mae, who gave me a whole new kind of smile. It was like How to Say Thank You When You Really Just Want to Cry. I had to look away because my stomach felt weird, like driving too fast over hills. I didn't know if it was just my gut acting up or if it was also that smile and not having a clue how to respond. After a few minutes, I started to have cramps. And then the cramps got worse. Sharp, from the inside all the way out.

Judging from the length of the program, I knew we were going to be there a long time, so I whispered to Mrs. B., "I'm sorry, Mrs. B, but I have to—I have to—"

"You have to go?"

I nodded.

"You go," she said, patting my knee. She pointed to the side aisle and said, "That way, and go quietly."

"Yes, ma'am," I said, and managed to reach the side aisle without too much disruption.

One quick stabbing pain made me lose my breath for a couple seconds. I pressed my hand against my gut, hoping that would help, and I was hauling out of there, passing the last pew, when I was stopped by a hand on my arm.

"What the—?" I looked. "Oh, man."

"Gotta make a call?" Brandon asked.

"Yeah," I said, and took another step, but the guy didn't let go.

"You're being kinda rude, Geri."

"Man, I gotta go," I said, and pulled my arm free. And as I did, I cut one of those popcorn popper, repeater farts into the holy echo chamber of Mrs. Dorothy D. Webb's funeral.

54

It wasn't *that* loud. I mean, it wasn't a car backfiring. Probably not that many people even heard it. Probably. What they definitely heard was Brandon and me running out of the sanctuary, through the narthex, and into the safety of the reception hall, where we both started cracking up.

"I need to find the john," I finally said.

When I emerged an uncomfortable eight minutes later and returned to the reception hall, I saw Brandon standing like a statue, holding his breath, trying not to laugh, and Mrs. B. standing in front of him.

She pointed her finger at me and said, "Two weeks. You are on the probe—probe—"

"Probation," I said.

"Probation," she said.

"Mrs. B.," I said. "I'm really sorry, but it couldn't be helped."

"No, you are not in the *trahbles* for that. But there is no *runnink* and *laughink* at my funeral."

"Yeah, you gotta watch this guy," Brandon said, and Mrs. B. poked that knobby index finger into his side, which made him laugh out, "Oh," as she said, "I watch you too."

Then she patted his side and smiled up at him and led us back to the service. We sat in the last pew, with her in the middle, her head and our shoulders the same height, and the two of us staring straight ahead. If I looked at Brandon one more time, I was going to bust out laughing.

55

I had just popped a cube of Swiss cheese into my mouth at the reception after the funeral when the woman behind me said, "Looks good. I'm starving."

She looked to be in her thirties, wavy red-blond hair with dark roots, big eyes, and a smoking body under a stretchy black dress.

She smiled at me and said, "That's probably bad to say, isn't it? We should be talking about Dorothy, right, and not thinking about food."

"I didn't know her," I said, and moved along in the buffet line. I didn't want to get into a conversation with anyone. I wasn't sure who I had accidentally gassed earlier and didn't really want to find out.

There was a big buffet in the reception hall, similar to the Sunday brunch buffet at Cascade Country Club, where I used to work. I counted seven big covered chafing dishes along with a fruit tray, cheese platter, coffee, tea, and even wine. The hall felt like a really depressing party. People ate and drank but spoke quietly and cried.

"You look like you can eat whatever you want," this woman said, walking along with me.

"Yeah," I said.

"You're so lucky," she said, "all you guys are," and put her hand on my arm. She had silver rings on most fingers and half-inch-long maroon nails.

I put a couple more cheese cubes on a plate. Also some mini quiches. When my stomach ached like this, cheese and eggs were about the only things that didn't hurt. Then I made my way to a quiet corner of the room next to—I swear—a potted Ficus. I had just pinched one of the leaves to see if it was real—it was and needed watering, which Grandma Ruth would have done if she was there—when that rusty-blond woman walked over and asked, "Do you mind some company?"

"Nope, feel free."

"I'm one of those people who just hates seeing someone stand alone," she said with that hand against my arm again.

"I don't mind it."

"Oh, well, I can leave if you want," she said in a way that did not sound like she really wanted to. Actually, she sounded like she wanted my phone number.

"No, don't go," I said, and flashed her one of my signature smiles. "I'm Briggs Henry."

"Jennifer Zuckerman."

"Zuckerman? Any relation to Ben Zuckerman?"

"All the Zuckermans in South Haven are related," she said. "You know Ben?"

"I met him a week ago."

"You know he's here somewhere."

She stood on her toes and searched the crowd.

"There he is," she said, waving to him, but he didn't see her. He was far across the room, talking with Brandon and some other people.

"I'll go get him," she said.

"No, that's okay," I said. I was enjoying talking just with her. But it was too late. She crossed the room and sent them over, and got stuck talking with the minister on the way back.

"So," Ben said, looking across the room for a second. "This is a gas, isn't it?"

"Funny," I said. "What are you guys doing here?"

"Mrs. Webb was Brandon's grandmother," Ben said.

"No, she was my grandma's sister," Brandon said.

"Oh, man, I'm sorry," I said.

"Why? You didn't kill her."

"Yeah, that's not what I meant."

"Anyway, she was ready to go," he said, and I looked at him like *What*? "She told me she was. She had breast cancer." He shook his head. "Chemo didn't help. Just made her sicker. I used to stop by after work and make her a rum and Coke, and, like, a month ago, out of the blue she goes, 'I'm ready to die.'"

"That would have freaked me out," I said.

"Freaked the hell out of me," Brandon said. "But I guess she meant it. And get this. She left me five hundred bucks in her will." He laughed. "I guess all those rum and Cokes paid off."

"So, was that your sister I just met?" I asked Ben to change the subject.

"My sister?" he asked.

Brandon snickered and tried to toss his bangs out of his face again.

"What?" I asked. "She's not your sister?"

"Yeah, that's his sister," Brandon said. "You think she's hot?"

"Yeah, she's hot. Why? You don't think she is?"

"No, man, I do not think Ben's *sister* is hot," Brandon said like he was about to bust out laughing.

"Okay. What?" I asked.

"I don't have a sister," Ben said. "That's my mom."

"Oh, man," I said as Brandon laughed through his teeth and slapped my arm and said, "Good one, Geri," in a way that sounded very much like *You need a haircut*. If he rubbed my head, I was going to have to hit him.

56

In the car on the way back, Mrs. B. scribbled something on the funeral program, folded it up, and put it in her purse.

Little bit later, I said, "I'm sorry that you lost another friend, Mrs. B."

"She is not lost." She shrugged. "She is in the coffin. Soon she is in the ground in the cemetery. If she is lost, nobody knows where she is."

"Yeah," I said, and kind of shuddered. "I just meant—you know—it's one of those sayings." Like *Kick the farm*.

"Ah," she said, and patted my knee. "Don't worry, Briggs Baby. I do not *loose* anyone."

"No?"

"No. The Webb family. They *loose*. But me? No."

I glanced at her out of the corner of my eye, and she had this grin on her face kind of like Abigail's at Pauline Ostrander's funeral. It made my stomach ache a little again. That or too many mini quiches.

57

Abigail reappeared Wednesday evening. I saw her from my balcony, where a nice little breeze off the lake blew the wet, woody scent of beach grass through the air.

She was back on that green-and-white towel, watching the sunset. Which I was doing too. Or trying to. Mrs. B. said her friend's death wasn't a loss. I mean, how could it not be?

Around nine o'clock and still pretty light out, Abigail got up and bolted into her house. Ran. Like she or it was on fire. That girl could move when she wanted to.

I checked my watch when the last bit of sun disappeared behind the lake, leaving the horizon a pale yellow and the sky bluish gray with a few clouds.

9:20:34.

I checked my watch again when a guy—I assumed it was her dad—walked outside, picked up the towel and Abigail's beach bag, and carried them inside.

9:36:17.

They turned the floodlights over the deck off at 11:32:12. I'd been out there the whole time. Thinking.

About what? I had no idea.

58

"Mrs. B.?" I asked when I walked into the kitchen the next morning before my run. "Oh my God! Mrs. B.!"

Mrs. B. lay on the floor, on her back, eyes closed. Glasses in one hand. The material from her bright pink robe spread out all around her. Little fuzzy white slippers pointed straight up.

"Mrs. B.!" I ran to her side. Got down on my knees. *Oh my God*. "Mrs. B.!"

"What? What?" she asked, opening her eyes wide at me. "Why you are *shoutink,* Briggs Baby?"

"Oh my God," I said, and exhaled. My throat tightened. My ears rang. It felt like my heart was trying to beat itself through my chest. "I thought . . . I mean, you looked . . . you looked . . ."

"Dead?"

"Yeah."

"You see. Americans do not like the *wood*."

"We really don't."

"You worry about me?" she asked, grinning a little.

"Yeah."

"I am not dead. My *beck* hurts. So. I lie down on hard floor. Sometimes I fall asleep."

"Do you want me to help you up?"

"No. My *beck* still hurts. So. I stay here a *leettle lonker*."

"Do you want an aspirin or something? For your back?"

"No. The *peels* do *nothink*. Doctors give the *peels* for the pain. I take, and still I have the pain."

"Okay."

"But," she said, and pointed her index finger at my face, "you see this is the way how I look when I am dead. I look like I am *sleepink*. So you see. It is *nothink* to be afraid."

"No, it scared me to death, Mrs. B.," I said, and she laughed, "Mmm-mmm-mmm," and her shoulders shook.

"It's not funny," I said, trying really hard not to laugh too. Her eyes and lips were shut. Head bobbing. Body twitching. "Mmm-mmm–mmm." A little part of me wanted to be pissed off at her, but that was impossible.

"You are scared to the death *thinkink* I am dead," she said. "We are both dead on the kitchen floor. Who finds us? The *mails*-man? Mmm-mmm-mmm."

"Yeah, that's"—I ran my hand over my head, squeezed the back of my neck—"that's a riot, Mrs. B."

"Mmm-mmm-mmm."

59

My heart didn't stop pounding until I had reached the lighthouse at the end of the pier. I had just run 2.2 miles in near record time to burn off the adrenaline of thinking about Mrs. B. on the kitchen floor—you know—not—breathing, or whatever.

I ran back through the downtown. One main street, couple of side streets, lined with shops and restaurants. Could have been a college town if there were more bars and bookstores instead of fudge shops and bakeries.

The drawbridge on Dyckman was up when I rounded the corner, on my way back to Mrs. B.'s. Two sailboats were passing through to the lake. Bunch of fishing boats were farther down the river. The lake was calm, the sky was hazy white, and there was a cool breeze off the water. Perfect day for boating. If you owned a boat. I still didn't look to see if there was one in our slip.

"Hey, man," someone in an old SUV at the light said.

When I looked to my right, I saw a guy with messy yellow hair and a mouth half a size too big for the face it was in. Smiling at me.

"You work for Vesna this summer, right?" he asked.

"Yeah," I said. I was looking at the sailboats coasting through the bridge's opening, thinking, *Come on, come on.*

"She's a sweet lady."

I nodded.

"You having a good summer so far?" he asked.

"Yeah," I said, and when the bells clanged and the lights on the gates flashed and the bridge's motor hummed as it began to lower, I thought, *Thank God.*

"Hey, let me ask you something!" the guy shouted over the noise. I tried to ignore him, but he called, "You ready? *Are you ready?*"

"For . . . ?" I turned to him. *For what,* I wanted to say, but he threw me a red beanbag and hollered, "Good catch!" before he waved and drove on over the bridge.

On one side of the beanbag was this in big black letters: *Are you ready?*

On the other side was this in white: *Plan for the future . . . and beyond.*

I looked at the thing, looked at the guy's car, looked at the lake, and said, "What?" Like one of them was going to answer me.

60

Ben was just getting out of his truck in front of a house on North Shore Drive when I rounded the corner.

The truck had this on the side:

ZHIS

Zuckerman Home Improvement Specialists
Improving homes since 1967

"Beats the hell out of God Yacht," I said, and wiped my face with my shirt.

"Hey, you finally got one," Ben said, pointing to the beanbag in my hand.

"What *is* this?"

Ben shrugged. "It's this thing he does."

"What am I supposed to do with it?"

"I'll take it," he said, and I tossed it to him. "We play Toss with these. He's got bright green ones too. Three of each makes a set."

"I'll try to remember that," I said, and looked over at the truck again. "Family business?"

"Yep."

"Nice. Is this what you want to go into?"

"Uh, I think I'm already in it."

"No, I mean after you graduate."

"Probably. For a while anyway."

"You got a major?"

"Construction management," he said.

He hauled a huge toolbox out of the truck bed.

"What about you?" he asked.

"JD-MBA," I said. "It's a dual program."

"You must be good with numbers as well as old ladies."

"And he's a catch," Abigail said from behind me.

She walked her bike to a stop.

"Is that right?" Ben asked.

"Yeah, just ask him," she said, looking sideways at me, kind of like she was joking and kind of like she wasn't.

I started protesting. It was said *about* me, and never deny your talents, and, yeah, I thought it would impress her, and I don't know. My dad would have said it. And wouldn't have apologized. I just—whatever—I was trying to put together some kind of explanation when Ben cut the biggest fart I had ever smelled. My little pop-pop-pop at the funeral was like a jingle compared to this.

Abigail couldn't get away fast enough. She just said, "See you guys," and hurried home, still pushing her bike.

"Dude!" I said, trying to wave the stink away.

"Wasn't me, man," Ben said. "Besides, you're one to talk."

"Oh, come on."

"It was you."

"Hey, I claim my farts," I said.

"I would if it were mine."

"You're telling me it was Abigail?"

"Well, if it wasn't you and it wasn't me, then, yeah, it had to be her."

"No way that smell came out of that girl."

"Believe what you want," he said, and walked toward a couple guys standing by the vans in the driveway.

I jogged back to Mrs. B.'s wondering what kind of guy doesn't fess up to his own farts. Or tries to blame them on a girl?

61

"That was not me this morning," I said to Abigail later that night. It was cool, almost chilly, and we were both in sweatshirts. Mine was an old blue Detroit Tigers thing. Hers was white and said *South Haven HS Volleyball* in purple and yellow. She had spread her blanket a few yards back from the water to watch the sunset. I saw her from my balcony and wandered out.

"Looked like you," she said.

"No, I mean— Never mind."

She tipped her head toward her blanket, and I sat next to her, close enough to notice that she smelled like soap. Fancy soap—heavy on the perfume—like the decorative soaps Grandma Ruth had in her half bath and got mad at me for using.

Abigail's and my shoulders nearly touched a couple times. She seemed to be aware of that—very aware of the space she occupied—and expertly avoided contact with me the few times I tried to make it happen.

"Tired of your thoughts today?" I asked.

"I won't be if we talk about something interesting," she said.

"Where've you been lately? I haven't seen you around."

"That's not interesting."

"It is to me."

"I've been here."

"Not here, specifically," I said, pointing down. "I'd have noticed."

"A, creepy much? And B, you want an accounting of every place I've been in the last few days?"

"Yeah," I said in the same tone I hoped would get Grandma Ruth to loosen up. "I do."

"Well, you're not getting one."

"Why not?"

"Because it's not interesting. I've been around. Just because you haven't seen me doesn't mean I wasn't here," she said, sounding just a little icy.

"You might've been out of town," I said.

"Might've been," she said. "Wasn't, though."

"Jury duty?"

"No," she said, warming up.

"Some weird church thing?"

"No."

"Locked in the basement?"

"I figured out how to escape after last time," she said, and, see, this was what I wanted Grandma Ruth to do just once. Just play a little.

"Is it a secret?" I asked.

"There's no secret. I wasn't gone just because you didn't see me. I mean, I could ask you the same thing. Where've you been the last few days?"

"Oh, I've been places. Been to another funeral," I said, like, *Lucky me*.

"Whose?"

"Dorothy D. Webb's. I have no idea what the *D* stands for."

"Another mystery," she said, and looked almost like she was about to smile. "How was it?"

"The funeral? It was a *funeral*."

She looked at the lake when she said, "I don't mind funerals."

"What?"

"I don't."

"You and Mrs. B.," I said. "But I guess when you've lost as many friends as she has, you kind of get used to them."

"I doubt anyone gets used to losing friends."

"So that's another thing. Mrs. B. doesn't even consider it *losing* friends. She said so."

"Hmm," Abigail said. "For me, funerals seem like they're going to be impossible to get through. Like the sadness and the heartache will replace everything I've ever felt or will ever be able to feel."

"But you don't mind them?"

"Yeah, but then I get there, and I find that there *is* sadness, and there *is* heartache, but there are other feelings too. Good ones. Love. Respect." The faint trace of a smile appeared on her lips. "And a little contempt for the guy who plays with his phone during the service."

"Am I ever going to live that down?"

"Not here," she said. "Anyway, funerals are never really as morose as I think they're going to be."

"Morose?"

"It's a word."

"Yeah, I know." I nearly laughed and tried to bump her shoulder. "It's just not one I hear that often. Outside of school."

"People at your school say *morose* a lot?" she asked, leaning just beyond bumping range.

"No. I mean it sounds like something I'd learn for a test. And then never use again."

"So you're the kind of guy who just wants the A," she said.

"I want an A, yeah. I don't think that's a bad thing. My grades got me a full scholarship to U of M. And what's this 'kind of guy' thing? You keep saying it like I'm one particular kind of guy."

"No," she said plainly. "Not *one* kind but *a* kind."

"And what kind is that?"

"Right now I'd say the kind who works hard to get ahead. For the sake of getting ahead."

"Something wrong with that?"

"Nothing at all," she said unconvincingly. "If that's what you want."

"Please do not give me the 'money isn't everything' spiel while you're sitting in front of a million-dollar house."

"It's not a million dollars."

"It's close," I said, and she shrugged.

"Is money that important to you?" she asked, and there was nothing rude in her voice. It wasn't a challenge, but I still didn't like the question. It wasn't interesting.

"It's important to everyone," I said. "And don't tell me about priorities, because I love my parents. I've got good friends. I work hard, and I'm honest." I pointed to Mrs. B.'s house. "I'm the guy you want taking care of your grandmother or whoever. I also happen to have plans for my life that include making a hell of a lot of money. Because I'd rather have it than not have it."

"What if one of life's big changes happens again, and you can't do what you want to do?" she asked, tipping her head to the right when she looked at me and scrunching her eyebrows until the skin between them looked like a little accordion.

"I'll figure out a way."

"What if you can't? What if you find out tomorrow that you only have six months to live?"

"That's not going to happen."

"Somewhere it is. Someone tomorrow is going to get that news. More than one person."

"It's not going to be me," I said, laughing. "Wait. You're not waiting for test results, are you?"

"No," she said, smiling like she was completely amused by me.

"Did you already get them and only have six months to live?"

"No."

"You're not on a heart transplant list or something like that?"

"No."

"Parents doing okay?"

"Brother and grandparents too," she said. "They all

live near Chicago, but I'm sure I'd have heard if anything happened."

"Good," I said as I ran my hands over my head and scratched the back of my neck. "For a minute I thought I was in one of those movies my girlfriend loves where people drop like flies."

"You have a girlfriend?"

"Ex-girlfriend."

"You said girlfriend."

"Well, I meant ex."

"The one whose mom called you a catch?"

"That's her. Taylor."

"Maybe you should have gone out with the mom," she said, which made me chuckle.

"I do have a way with older women," I said. "What about you? Got a boyfriend?"

"Ex."

"Ben?"

"Yes," she said, like she wasn't surprised I figured it out, but it really wasn't that hard.

"I got dumped," I said.

"So did I."

"No way."

She nodded.

"Wait. He broke up with you? What was that guy thinking?" I asked, and she looked like she didn't know how to respond, at first. She looked like she was about to say something. Something nice. But instead she smoothed one palm over the blanket for a couple seconds and looked down. I really wanted to reach for her hand.

"It was last summer," she finally said. "He was going away to school and didn't want a long-distance relationship. He said they only work if you really love someone. And we didn't."

"That's harsh."

"But honest. Which I respect."

"So will you honestly tell me where you've been for a few days?"

"Well, we ruled out jury duty, church, and my basement," she said, and we both smiled.

A few seconds passed while she looked at me like she was studying my face. Then she turned toward the lake again and drew her knees up to her chest and wrapped her arms around them. For warmth, I guessed.

The air around us smelled like wet slate. Smelled good.

"So how come Taylor broke up with you?" she asked.

"I didn't have enough time for her."

"That doesn't surprise me," she said. "Guys like you never have enough time for relationships."

"Again with the guys like me?"

"Yeah. Driven. Ambitious." She sighed like she was sorry for me or something. "You tell yourself there'll be time for relationships later when the truth is that they're just not that important to you."

"They are important, and there will be time later."

"Not if you find out you only have six months left to live."

"Okay," I conceded. "If I find out I'm about to kick off in a few months, I promise I will get myself a girlfriend."

She tipped her head at me again before asking, "What would you do? For real?"

"Uh . . ." I thought a second. "I don't know." I looked at the lake and squinted into the sun, looking like liquid itself, spilling across the water as it sank below the horizon. "Whatever I'd do I'd definitely do it here."

"So this is the place you'd like to die?"

"This is the place I'd like to live," I said, and a smile slowly spread across her face. She tried to keep her lips from parting but couldn't. She turned to face the half circle of sun on the horizon, bumped her shoulder against mine, and said, "Good answer."

A few seconds later I tried to bump her shoulder, but she moved just beyond my reach.

62

Couple rainy days later I found Mrs. B. on her back on the kitchen floor again, which freaked me out, but at least I didn't panic this time.

"Mrs. B.?" I called out.

She waved at me with the hand that held her glasses.

I knelt beside her and asked, "Back hurts again?"

"*Everythink* hurts in the rains."

I ended up running in it when it didn't let up. It felt kind of good—big cool drops on my face and arms.

I ran past the Flamingo Shack on the south side of town. Man, not even three days of rain washed the dirt off that place.

63

On another morning run I caught up with Abigail, pushing her bike along Dyckman toward town. The rain had just stopped but still dripped from the trees, and the air in my lungs was damp. I walked with Abigail across the drawbridge, and we stopped to watch three fishing boats putter through the no wake zone. Couple of the guys waved to us. We waved back.

People on boats always wave to people on shore. We were like the Waving Idiot Family on ours, just stupidly excited to see anyone and everyone on land. That was about the most expressive I'd ever seen my mother. Waving to strangers.

"I'm going to head back," Abigail said.

"You've only been out—what—ten minutes."

"I'll see you later," she said, and started pushing her bike back toward her house.

"I'm starting to think you don't know how to ride that thing," I called, and stood there waiting for her comeback. Something spiky, and a quick look over her shoulder. That completely controlled smile. But she didn't say anything. And she didn't look back. She just double-timed it down the street.

Would have been faster on the bike.

64

Early in my third week there, I returned from a run and headed upstairs to shower when the walkie-talkie on my waistband—no other way to carry it—cracked and whistled.

"Mrs. B. to Briggs Baby. Come in to Briggs Baby."

"Mrs. B.," I called as I walked into the kitchen. "I'm here."

She stood at her stove on a wooden block, worn shiny from use, wielding what she called a *spaTOOla* over a pan of something sizzling that smelled like sausage, butter, and spices. Not a jar of grape jelly in sight.

"Ah, Briggs Baby. I will have the breakfast ready when you come down from the shower."

"Thanks, Mrs. B."

"You want to stay?"

"I do. I want to stay," I said.

"You do what I say? No *complainink*?"

"No complaining."

"Okay," she said, and smiled at me until her eyes disappeared behind shiny pink cheeks. "You are off the probe . . . the probe—"

"Probation."

"The probation. And tomorrow, no run."

"No?"

"No. We go to *Grahnd Rahpids* early, and I want for you to be, to be—*restink*."

"Rested?"

"This is what I say."

"Why rested?" I asked.

"So that you can enjoy."

"Your funeral?" I asked, and—on the spot—made up a Your Funeral Smile.

"My funeral," she said, returning it to me.

"Sure thing, Mrs. B.," I said, and told myself, *I got this,* like eight times on my way upstairs. I didn't believe it the eighth time any more than I did the first. But I figured funerals would be my new grape jelly. I'd get through the things with a smile, lie to Mrs. B. that I actually enjoyed them, and even write her a thank-you note if she took me to one for Christmas.

65

I'd have turned right around and walked out of Beckenbauer-Stutz Funeral Home the minute I saw poor, dead Jonathan Carroll in the open casket if I thought Mrs. B. wouldn't fire me on the spot. It was the first dead body I'd seen, and it was seriously disturbing. The guy looked like a cheap wax dummy, no offense to him. He was kind of purple-blue under a ton of makeup that didn't come close to matching any skin tone on earth.

I didn't know why anyone would want *that* to be their last image of someone they loved.

Speaking of keeping my job, I double-checked my phone to make sure it was off. Then I excused myself for a preemptive trip to the men's room and proudly told Mrs. B., "I'm good to go," when I returned to my seat.

"You will enjoy this one," she said.

"Was that part of the deal?"

She just grinned and patted my knee, like we were in a theater, excited for a really good movie to start.

There were about thirty people in attendance, and no one but me under fifty. The thick, moss-green carpet absorbed sounds, and someone dimmed the lights.

The funeral home director introduced an elderly minister with a soothing voice, and that was the last thing I remembered until I felt a series of sharp taps on my shoulder, and I jerked my head up.

I looked quickly at Mrs. B., on my right, who was making notes in her program. She hadn't noticed I had dozed off. No one was on my left, so the taps came from someone behind me. I'd turn when the service ended.

The elderly minister read a bio of Jonathan Carroll. Born in Grand Rapids, attended junior college, something about the Korean War. I felt so relaxed there—the quiet of the room, the lull of the minister's voice, no one waiting for me to make a fool of myself again—that I thought I might nod off a second time. That's when the person behind me got up and left.

Since it was Grandma Ruth, I thought I'd better follow.

66

"Grandma Ruth," I called in the hall, and she turned calmly and said "Shh," with a finger at her lips.

She used that same finger to direct me outside, where we air-kissed.

"What are you doing here?" I asked.

"Briggs, dear, what does anyone do at a funeral? Anyone who can stay awake, that is."

"Sorry about that. I just dozed off for a couple seconds."

"It was terribly rude."

"Won't happen again."

"See that it doesn't."

I told her about Mrs. B. and offered to introduce her.

"No thank you, my dear. I don't attend funerals to make new acquaintances. It is not the place."

"I've met a bunch of people at funerals lately," I said.

"Is that sarcasm?"

"I'm serious."

"Sounds perfectly morbid."

"Not really," I said, which, actually, surprised me the moment the words came out of my mouth. "How did you know—who is it?" I said, glancing down at the program.

"Jonathan Carroll. He was a friend of your grandfather's and mine."

"Did you and Grandpa Richard—"

"Briggs dear, I also didn't come here to chat or reminisce. I came to pay my respects. Having paid them, I wish to leave. Now go back inside. You're not being paid to stand out here talking with me."

"Yes, Grandma Ruth."

She left without looking back.

67

Sleeping on the job? Didn't I raise you better than that?

I was in the men's room at Beckenbauer-Stutz Funeral Home, checking my texts after the service. That one made me shake my head. Made my stomach cramp up.

Me: It was 5 min. Tops! & it was at a funeral!

Dad: Doesn't matter where it was. It was 5 minutes too long.

All I could think was—is he seriously pissed at me?

Couple seconds later, he wrote:

Your grandmother says you need a haircut.

Then this:

LOL!

Me, after thinking about how to respond for half a minute: lol

68

"Don't screw this up, Geri," Brandon said, his head tipped far back, watching the ball. "Do not screw this up."

He set up a perfect lob. I spiked it. Ben dived but missed the return, and we won the game.

Maddy was on our team and celebrated by wrapping Brandon and me into a bouncy hug and shouting, "We won! We won! Yay us!"

We dropped onto a mess of mismatched towels and battered bags. Maddy's was hot-pink, like her suit. Flamingo-pink. Must have been her only one. Or her favorite one. I never saw her in anything else.

By then, the beach was filling up. Warm sunny days brought tons of cottagers and day-trippers out. A couple of the volleyball courts were almost always in use. The scent of coconut and bananas from so many different kinds of sunscreen blew in and out over the whole place. Seagulls hopped around, squawking for chips or other snacks.

"Who's goin' in?" Zach asked.

He and Nicole and a few of the others raced into the

water, navy-blue with small whitecaps that day, leaving Maddy, Ben, Brandon, and me behind.

"You should bring Abigail with you next time," Maddy said. "I haven't seen her just to hang out with in, like, forever."

"Why is that?" I asked.

"No one sees her anymore," Brandon said as he lay on his back and made a pillow out of someone's shirt.

"Dude," Ben said, like he was telling Brandon to shut up.

"What? It's true."

"How come?" I asked.

"I gotta take a leak," Ben said, and walked off.

"She just, kind of, stopped hanging out with us," Maddy said, shrugging. "I'm sure she has her reasons. Like maybe something's going on at home."

"Or like maybe she thinks she's too good for us," Brandon said.

"She doesn't think that," Maddy said.

"Right. Ever since she got into all those fancy colleges, she's been a total stuck-up snob. She's worse than the tourists," Brandon said.

"Why do you hate tourists?" I asked.

"Are you kidding me?" He held a hand over his eyes, blocking the sun. "They come in here for three months and act like they're so perfect, and we're just the lowly townies."

"Boaters are worse," Maddy said.

"Seriously?" I asked.

"They're seriously annoying," she said as Brandon

said, "Oh, hell yes. Man, they think they own this place. Like literally own it."

I looked at the water when I said, "No one owns the lake."

"Geri," Brandon said, "that is the smartest thing you've said yet."

69

I walked back to Mrs. B.'s along the shore in the still air of dusk. It was quiet except for the low waves tumbling over themselves and my feet. Quiet except for that and Abigail Howe's laugh.

I heard it before I realized it was her, sitting on that green-and-white blanket, laughing and bumping shoulders with a guy too old to be her brother and too young to be her dad. He had on a faded blue South Haven baseball cap and aviator frames a little too small for his face. Big face. Big mouth too.

Abigail gave me a friendly "Hi" and held a half-empty bag of Oreos out.

"Want one?" she asked.

"No, thanks."

"How was the game?" she asked, and the guy she was with gave me such a genuine smile—huge over huge, perfect teeth—that I found myself spontaneously grinning back. Like I couldn't help it somehow.

"Good," I said. "Fun. You should have come."

The guy stood up as Abigail asked, "Have you two met yet?"

We both said no.

"Briggs Henry," I said, and shook the guy's hand.

"John Dumchak," he said. "Everyone calls me Dum."

"Dum. Short for Dumchak," I said, like a local. "Not doomsday."

"Not doomsday," he said. The guy's smile never dimmed. "But if doomsday comes, will you be ready?"

70

It was late when I walked outside, out to the water's edge, and sat down. The sand was cold. The sky was too. Dark. Moonless.

Earlier, I laughed off that guy Dum's question with, "Yeah, I'm not really worried about doomsday."

He didn't seem to mind. Just said, "No, me neither, but you gotta be prepared for the future."

"Briggs has a plan," Abigail said, and shot me a quick, kind of teasing smile.

"I hope it's a good one," he said. "For the future and beyond."

"Uh-huh," I said, and went inside for dinner.

Out by the lake, in the cool sand and black night, I pulled my knees up and rested my arms on them. It was impossible to tell the difference between the night sky and the black water except for the bit of it that washed up a few feet from where I sat. It sloshed up, spread out, trickled back. Sloshed up, spread out, trickled back.

"The future and beyond," I said to myself. I mean, I thought about the future. All the time. We all did. We

Henrys. That's how we got out of the shoebox. Hard work and eyes on the prize. Once we had it, that was it. *That* was the future. After that, I guessed, we'd just maintain.

71

I fell asleep on the beach and woke in the chilly morning underneath a green-and-white-striped blanket. I ended up leaving it on the Howes' deck. Big, elevated deck, white and spotless, with staircases at each corner and bright blue cushions, same color as the roof, on the chairs.

I'd have handed the blanket back to Abigail herself, but she wasn't home. No one was. Looked like the whole family had disappeared this time.

72

Couple days later, Mrs. B. and I returned to K City Creative Paints, where Chuck with the big teeth exchanged eight gallons of Windswept Sky—*Too cold,* Mrs. B. had said—for eight gallons of Cadet Blue. Then we swung by the Howard F. DeLong Heart Center for Mrs. B.'s one o'clock appointment with a cardiologist.

"Just a routine appointment?" I asked on the way there.

"No. There are no routine appointments when you are my age, Briggs Baby."

"Well, I'm sure they're not going to find anything wrong with you."

"Oh," she said, and crossed herself. I didn't know Episcopalians did that. "Don't say."

"You *want* them to find something wrong with you?" I asked for clarification.

"I want them to tell me the way how I am *goink* to die."

"Yeah, I don't really think there's a test for that, Mrs. B."

"They should make the test," she said, like it should

be as easy as peeing in a cup. "So that you know. Lju-bomir dies of the stroke. I wish the doctors tell to us the way how he is *goink* to die before he has the stroke, so it is not the terrible surprise when it happens."

"Sorry—Leeyewbo—Leeyewboh—"

"Ljubomir." She patted my leg. "You don't say this name. You say Mr. B. My husband."

"When did he pass away? If you don't mind my asking."

"I don't mind," she said through a little bit of a smile.

I didn't think she would. Widows at Bluestone Court loved it when I asked about their husbands. Seemed everyone but Grandma Ruth liked to talk about the past. Grandma Ruth and my dad. He liked to talk about the future. Grandma Ruth just didn't like to talk. Unless it was about plants.

"He dies seven years ago," Mrs. B. said.

"I'm sorry," I said, and she patted my leg again. A couple seconds later she beamed when she asked, "You can guess how old I am when I marry *heem*?"

"How old?"

"Eighteen."

"Eighteen?" I nearly yelled that. "I'm eighteen."

"Maybe you get married soon, yes?" She winked.

"I don't think so, Mrs. B."

"You have the girlfriend?"

"I don't have time for a girlfriend right now."

"Oh, no, no, no. You must to make the times for the *imported thinks*."

"Yeah, well, school and work are pretty important, and they take up a lot of my time."

"School and job will always be there. You don't want to go through the life alone, Briggs Baby. You find the right person. Like I do. You take the times for her."

"What did Mr. B. do?" I asked as I pulled into a parking space.

"He was the engineer for Ford Company."

"Yeah? Was he from here or from Serbia? I mean, with a name like Lew—"

"No, don't say," she said, wagging her index finger at me. "Mr. B. is from here. His parents move from Serbia, and he is born here. But they come *beck* in the *sahmmers*, and that is the way how we meet. Because I am not too busy for *heem,* and he is not too busy for me. You see?"

"I see. But I think, maybe, life is a little more complicated these days."

"No," she said. "Life is the way how you make it."

"Yeah," I said, partly laughing, partly sighing at one of my dad's favorite sayings. His and mine, now with a Serbian-to-English spin on it.

Mrs. B. took my arm and said as we walked inside the heart center, "And sometimes life is not the way how you make it. It is just the way how it goes. But." She shrugged. "That is the way how life is. You never know."

"Yeah," I said, and really preferred my dad's *Life is what you make it* to Mrs. B.'s *You never know.*

73

The Howes—the Way-Howes, I wanted to call them—
were home when we got back, unpacking suitcases and
boxes from a spotless blue BMW X3. After I helped Mrs.
B. inside, I ran next door and called out "Hi" to Abigail.

"Can I help?" I asked as her mom struggled with a
box marked *Storage*.

"Oh, you're an angel," she said as I took the box,
which weighed a ton.

"Mom, this is Briggs," Abigail said, walking past me
with a duffel bag. "He's a catch."

"Seriously?" I said as Abigail laughed a little, and
her mom raised one eyebrow into a sharp point over
her left eye, directing a seriously penetrating stare at her
daughter.

"Briggs, it's nice to meet you. I'm Elizabeth Howe.
Follow me. I'll show you where that goes."

It went in the basement, which was bigger than our
old shoebox. Probably cost more too, with that home
theater system and built-in bar.

Elizabeth Howe talked the whole way to the basement
and the whole way back. They had been in Chicago for a

few days, helping her son pack. He just graduated from Northwestern. He was going to U of M law school in the fall.

"I'm going—" I began.

"And, of course," Mrs. Howe said, "he has an internship this summer and no time to pack, so we're all pitching in, and aren't you a dear to help. Vesna said she was having someone new, and I can tell you're just perfect for her. I don't suppose you'd mind grabbing that one too." She pointed to another box. "You can put it right next to the other one."

I carried four boxes and two suitcases to the basement and refused the twenty Mrs. Howe tried to give me. She introduced me to Abigail's dad, Matt, who looked like he still probably got carded at bars.

Abigail called to me from the kitchen. A huge space with white cabinets, gray walls, and dark wood floors. She stood at the island eating almond butter—*Wheatly Farms Organic Almond Butter,* it said on the label—out of the jar with a spoon.

"This house is incredible," I said.

"Thanks," Abigail said. "Dad designed it."

"He's an architect?"

"He's a lawyer who took a bunch of drafting classes in undergrad. Mom's a lawyer too."

I nodded, slowly, like *Oh, yeah, I get it, I totally get it,* as I surveyed the kitchen a second time.

"Wuh?" Abigail asked with a huge glob of almond butter in her mouth. She pressed her fingers to her lips and hurried to finish the bite when she realized that sounded kind of funny.

"What was that look for?" she asked.

"What look?"

"That look just now? When I said my parents are lawyers."

"Nothing. It just—" I shrugged.

"Let's hear it."

"It just . . . figures."

"It figures?"

"Come on," I said. "Lawyers are always rich."

"A, stereotype much? And B, my mom was a legal aid attorney. They're not exactly in it for the big bucks."

"Was?"

"She's on a leave of absence right now. We'll all be happy when she goes back." She tipped the jar of almond butter toward me and asked, "Want some?"

"Seriously?" I asked, curling my lip a little.

"No, this is my jar," she said, turning it toward me so that I could see her name on a piece of masking tape across the front. She pulled a second jar from the cupboard behind her. "Everyone else uses this one."

"You have your own jar of almond butter?"

"Peanut butter and cashew butter too," she said, and licked the spoon, which was kind of sexy and kind of gross too.

"No, thanks," I said. "But, hey, thanks for the blanket the other night. I'm assuming it was you."

"I'd have stayed out there, but you were snoring."

"Oh, man," I laughed. "Sorry about that."

"No, it's okay. You can't always control what your body does, right?"

"Right," I said, trying not to laugh at my popcorn-popper fart from Dorothy D. Webb's funeral.

She ate another huge bite of almond butter. Took her a while to finish it. I just stared until she asked, again, "What?"

"You really like almond butter," I said.

"She likes almond butter on these," her mom said, dropping a bag of Oreo cookies on the counter. "You left them in the car."

"Thank you," Abigail said, and promptly smeared almond butter on a cookie.

"Want one?" she asked.

"Give it a try," her dad said, slapping me on the back as he walked in. "Some of her concoctions aren't half-bad."

He swiped the cookie from her. She protested with a playful "Hey," but it was too late, and he popped the whole thing into his mouth.

"Those have my germs on them, you know," she said, and her dad grabbed his throat with both hands and pretended to choke.

"I'm not calling 911 for you," Abigail said as she prepared another cookie.

"Your mother will save me with mouth-to-mouth resuscitation," her dad said with his mouth full.

"Not until you brush your teeth," Mrs. Howe said as her husband flashed her a cookie-crumb smile. Abigail did the same before quickly covering her mouth with both hands and laughing into them.

Mrs. Howe arched that eyebrow at both of them—she

could probably stop traffic with that thing—before snagging a cookie, taking a bite, and joining the slightly gross fun. Black spotted teeth all around.

I took a cookie, said good-bye, and thought, on my way back to Mrs. B.'s, everything's better with Oreos.

74

She was out on the sand that night. Abigail. On the green-and-white blanket. Hot, sunny days gave the lake a spongy kind of scent—like wet wood and seaweed—that drifted into the warm evenings and mixed with the smell of beach grass and the lingering whiff of sunscreen that never quite washed away.

Abigail had on a blue T-shirt with the long sleeves pulled down over her hands.

"Want company?" I asked.

"Sunset's over. You missed the best part," she said without turning around.

"It's all good at the beach."

"It is for tourists."

"It is for everyone," I said.

"Some of us live here," she said.

"I live here," I said, and she glanced sideways at me. "I do for now."

"Mm-hmm."

"So how do you know that guy Dum?"

"He worked at my dad's firm for a while. Now he's the

director of some community center in Kalamazoo. Plays in a church band on weekends."

"That's a gear-shift."

She shrugged when she said, "His choice."

"And all that God Yacht stuff doesn't weird you out? And the 'future and beyond.' I don't even know what that means."

"No. It's his thing. It's not mine," she said, scrunching her eyebrows down, like it was wrong of me to ask somehow. "Why? Are you the kind of guy who can only hang out with people just like you?"

"No," I said, a little pissed at the "kind of guy" thing again. "Buddy of mine's Buddhist. Another one's nothing, as far as I know. We just don't sit around talking about God or this life and the next all the time."

"He's all about the future. I thought you'd love that since you're the one who has his whole future planned."

"You say that like it's a bad thing."

She shrugged.

"Are you telling me you don't think about the future?" I asked.

She slid her butterfly charm back and forth across her chain a couple times and said, "Let's talk about yours."

"What do you want to know?"

"Why is it so important to be rich?"

"This again?"

"You never said why it's important to you."

"It's important to everyone."

"But it's not everyone's impetus like it is yours."

"Impetus?"

"It's a word."

"Yeah."

"So why the drive?"

"Because I've been poor, and I didn't like it. None of us liked it," I said, trying to make it sound like it was no big deal. It *was* a big deal, but my answer was true.

"How poor?"

"Not exactly food-from-the-church poor, even though my grandmother thought we were. But we lost just about everything."

"Seriously?"

"Seriously," I said, and picked a small black stick—a piece of wet driftwood—out of the sand and tossed it in the lake.

"What happened?"

"Ever see an Oldsmobile?"

"I don't think so. If I have, I don't remember."

"Exactly," I said. "My dad owned the largest Oldsmobile dealership in Southwest Michigan. My grandfather started it in 1961. So it was nice for a while, you know?"

"Must have been."

"Yeah, we had a huge house. A boat and a slip here. A dog. Cars. Oldsmobiles, obviously," I said, forcing myself to smile.

"Obviously."

"So in 2004, GM stopped making the Oldsmobile, and my dad took it as a sign to get out of the industry. Don't ask me why. So he took the buyout offer, sold the repair side of the business to a buddy, and sank all the money into real estate." I leaned a little closer when I said, "All of it."

"Uh-oh."

I nodded.

"Lost everything in the crash."

"I'm sorry," Abigail said, and put her hand on my arm for a second.

"Your fingers are like ice."

"Sorry," she said, and moved her hand just as I said, "I don't mind."

"What happened then?" she asked, and tucked her hands underneath her legs.

Girls can make sitting on their hands look completely normal.

"My dad lost his shirt," I said, and it came out weird, like, with a little resentment. "He lost my mom's shirt. He would have lost mine if I'd had one to lose."

"No college fund?"

"He never started one. There was always money. Until it was all gone."

"So what'd you do?"

"Downsized. Big-time. We sold the house." I tipped my head toward her house. "Big house. Sold the boat. Mom sold her jewelry. Sold the cars."

"How'd you get around?"

"Walk, bus, bike, or Grandma Ruth," I said. "And let me tell you, walk, bus, and bike were better."

"Is she mean?"

"No. She's just difficult. Angry, I guess."

"Why?"

That stopped me for a second.

"I have no idea," I said.

"So then what happened?"

"My parents sold just about everything to pay off creditors, and with a loan from my grandmother and sweat equity, my dad bought into this business." I told her about Foam Works. "He paid my grandmother back, with interest, because he works like a fiend. And he never declared bankruptcy. Which I respect."

"Sure," she said, and the confirmation was nice.

"But, man, we had nothing. I mean, compared to what we used to have. I get that we weren't, like, destitute. But it was . . . it was a serious gear-shift. We rented a dinky house on cinderblocks for a couple years. Now Dad wants to buy out his partner, but that's years off. He doesn't have the money for that right now."

"Does he have to buy him out?"

"No." I threw another stick into the water. "But he likes to be the guy in charge. It's his"—I leaned closer—"impetus."

Abigail poked my shoulder, and for a few seconds then, we watched a cabin cruiser leave the channel and slowly travel across the horizon. Dad used to take Mom and me for evening cruises up or down the coast, all of us tired from the day and quiet in the night air. Until Dad broke the silence when we docked with "Not a scratch on her." He said it every time. There were some scratches, but Mom and I ignored them for his sake.

"And?" Abigail said, tipping her head so that her hair fell out from behind her left ear. When I reached to tuck it back, she didn't stop me.

"And what?" I asked.

"Well, what was happening during all that? What was going on in your head?"

"I was nine," I said, and brushed my hand against her cheek. "So, you know, I was a little-kid-mess."

She put a hand on my arm. Her fingers were warmer then, and I put my hand on top of them.

"What was that like?" she asked.

"I don't know. I felt"—I shrugged—"bad. You know."

"Bad?"

"Bad. Awful. Miserable," I said, like, *How many ways could I say bad?*

She was quiet.

"I don't know," I said again. "I was—" I looked at her eyes, her mouth, and then at the lake until it blurred into dark blue nothingness. I remembered Dad bitching, Grandma Ruth lecturing, Mom packing. I remembered lawyers at the house and Dad swearing and Mom squinting at piles of papers. I remembered the day I came home to no dog. I remembered the day I came home to the shoebox. I remembered it smelled like wet dirt. I remembered Dad looking bloated and Mom looking pale. I remembered peanut butter and grape jelly sandwiches for lunch and dinner. I remembered thinking my parents looked old and tired. I remembered worrying about them like I never had before, and I looked back at Abigail and I told her, "I was scared."

Her eyes didn't move from my face. And I turned back to the lake and exhaled like I was breathing out more than just air. "And I was mad."

When I looked at her again, Abigail Howe smiled at me. And nodded.

"I'm glad you said that," she said, which was weird, but I didn't really care. I was just glad she got it.

I shifted toward her, and when she didn't move away, I lifted both hands and held her face. Her eyes were open and intent, and I kissed her. Gently. She smelled fresh and flowery, like lake water and soap. I breathed as much of her into me as I could. She deepened the kiss and leaned into me. I felt it in every part of my body, like a stone dropped in water. I slid my hands into her hair, then back to her face, cool like the air. We parted once. Her eyelashes grazing my cheekbone for a second, two, three . . . then she tilted her chin up and we came together again. And again. And again.

75

We kissed until the sky was a darker blue. She pressed close to me and I pressed back, and I felt her soft skin and sharp edges. I felt her cool hands on my face. On my neck. Everywhere she touched it was like a current—of electricity or water—streaming through me. I tasted her. Sweet and spicy, and I wanted more.

But she pulled back, and we lay on our backs, me looking at her, her looking at the stars.

"That was nice," she said.

"Very nice," I said.

"Too bad neither of us has time for a relationship right now."

"Yeah," I said, and turned to look at the sky without really seeing it. "Too bad."

76

We fell asleep under the stars, and in the morning she was gone.

She called "Good morning" to me from her deck, where she sat having her breakfast, so at least I knew she hadn't disappeared.

I waved before I walked into Mrs. B.'s through the sliding door from the deck. Something with cinnamon must have been in the oven.

"Morning, Mrs. B.," I said to her as I walked through the kitchen.

"Good *mornink,* Briggs Baby," she said to me from the floor.

77

"Whoa, man!" I shouted, coming up out of the fabulously cold lake seconds after I dived in. I'd been working outside all day, fixing some of the broken steps on the walk from Mrs. B.'s deck to the beach. The sun was pounding, and there was no breeze.

"You coming in?" I called to Abigail, who was on the beach with her mom and a couple of her mom's friends.

"Maybe later!" she called back.

Mrs. Howe rocked a red-and-black bikini. Abigail rocked her cowboy hat with her hair tucked up underneath and those aviator sunglasses on. She wore a white T-shirt over her bikini, and I could see that the straps were orange. I didn't much notice the other ladies. For all I knew, they were Miss Mae and Mrs. Steiner in big hats and sunglasses.

I walked out of the lake and used my shirt as a towel. As I dried off, I watched Mrs. Howe unpack a truckload of food—bananas, bagels, pretzels, probably almond butter, something green in a container, tortilla chips, and a bag of Oreos.

"All right, what would you like?" she asked Abigail.

Voices carry on the beach. I could hear them perfectly.

"What? No salmon with mango salsa?" Abigail asked.

"Would you *like* salmon with mango salsa?" her mom asked, sounding exactly like Abigail when she asked me the day we met, "Do you *have* a million dollars?"

"I'd like a vat of buttered popcorn," she said.

"Can't help you there. Now eat some of this. You need to put a little weight on or you're going to end up back in the hospital."

"Mom," Abigail said in a tone that let me know she understood beach acoustics all too well.

I got back to work and noticed, throughout the rest of the day, that Abigail Howe ate like a horse.

78

"Mrs. B., do you know anything about Abigail being in the hospital?"

We were in my car on our way back to K City Creative Paints. Cadet Blue was "too *series*" (serious), Mrs. B. said after I'd painted the entire bedroom across from mine.

"Yes," Mrs. B. said. "She goes to hospital in April. For the *hayernia*. She has the operation to fix."

"Hernia?"

"This is what I say."

I didn't really know what a hernia was beyond some seriously torn muscle—or something like that—that you needed surgery to fix.

"Is that why she's so skinny?" I asked.

"Oh," Mrs. B. said, cupping her hands against her cheeks. "She is so *theen*. No. She is always *theen,* but now, oh. *Theener*. Mama *hoh-vers* day and night. I try to tell to her don't worry. Worry *shanges nothink*. Worry will make you *seek*. But she does not *leesen*."

"Doesn't listen? Yeah, I saw her hovering earlier today."

"Always with the food, yes?"

"Yeah. I guess she's trying to fatten Abigail up," I said.

"Like the *Thanksgivink* turkey," Mrs. B. said with her forefinger pointed straight up.

"Exactly. Girls . . . I mean, I like when girls have curves, and the curves, you know, move." *Why was I still talking?*

"Move?"

"Like when they walk or laugh, and they just kind of . . ."

Mrs. B. looked at me. *"Jeegle?"*

"Jeegle? Jiggle. Yes," I almost laughed.

"Yes, *jeegle*. Here." She grabbed her hips. "And here." Her belly. "And the *ahther* places."

"Yes. Other places," I said. "You don't need to point them out for me."

"You like the women who *jeegle*," she said, grinning almost wildly at me. "Even you like my *jeegle*, maybe?"

"Mrs. B., I like every jiggle," I said.

Man, I wished I could talk to Grandma Ruth this way. But the only thing that jiggled on her was that flap of skin underneath her chin, and I had agreed to ignore it when I was four.

The memory of it, then, there in the car with Mrs. B. showing me her *jeegle*, made my stomach ache, like I felt sorry for myself or for Grandma Ruth. I couldn't tell. And didn't really know why.

79

I had just run up to my room after dinner to grab my laptop. I planned on zipping down to the library to use their
Wi-Fi. There was only one coffee shop in town, which
was always packed, and a couple restaurants had signs
in the windows reading *WIFI is for Customers Only*. I
wanted to check texts and e-mail and Google hernias,
when Mrs. B. called me on the walkie-talkie.

"Mrs. B. to Briggs Baby. Come in to Briggs Baby."

"Briggs here, Mrs. B. How can I help you?"

"Hey, it's Abigail. I'm on the deck with Vesna."

I walked out on my balcony. Leaned over.

"I'm feeling restless and entombed," Abigail said.

"Entombed?"

"It's a word."

"Yeah, but what?"

"I'm up for a walk. Want to come?" she asked.

I was halfway down the stairs when my walkie-talkie
crackled, and Mrs. B. said, "Over and off."

80

Abigail set her flip-flops on Mrs. B.'s deck and suggested a walk along the shore. North.

"Not too far," she said. "Maybe ten, fifteen minutes."

"Sure."

The evening air was getting heavier and stickier. July was around the corner, and a lot more cottagers had come to town. We passed a bunch of people sitting on towels or in beach chairs, paperback books and plastic drink bottles lying around. Lots of little kids bounced up and down in the water.

"Your turn to tell me something interesting about yourself," I said.

"Like what?"

"Like what is this about a hernia operation?"

"What hernia operation?"

"Yours?"

"Mine?" She sounded totally confused.

"Mrs. B. said you had a hernia operation."

"Oh," she said, and grinned a little. "No. She misunderstands things sometimes."

"Yeah, but I heard your mom say today that you were in the hospital."

She turned her head so quickly toward me that a few strands of hair flew out at the sides. From around her wrist, in one swift movement, she took a rubber band of some sort and twisted her hair into something that looked like a figure 8. I hadn't noticed until then that her ears were kind of pointed, like an elf's.

"So it wasn't for a hernia operation?" I asked.

"No."

"But you *were* in the hospital?"

"Yes," she said after a couple seconds, like she was thinking about how to answer or if to answer at all.

"When and why?" I asked.

"Nosy much?"

"I'm asking interesting questions."

"You're asking personal questions."

"You never said they couldn't be personal," I said. "And, anyway, I'd tell you if I'd been in the hospital."

"Which you weren't."

"Nope. Never." I bumped my elbow against hers. "Come on. Tell me. Why were you there?"

She stopped walking and deadpanned, "Bariatric surgery." She spread her arms open. "Look. I'm a success."

"Come on," I nearly laughed. "I told you my story last night. Now you tell me yours."

"Let's head back," she said.

I checked my watch.

"We've only been gone six minutes," I said.

"Making it twelve by the time we get back, which falls right into the time frame you agreed to."

"That was literal?"

"Yes. Literally."

"It's such a nice night," I said, and pointed ahead of us. "You don't want to keep going?"

"You can. I'm heading back."

"No, I'll come." I jogged a couple steps to catch up. "You're not mad, are you?"

"No, I just want to head back."

"You seem mad."

"Well, if you must know, I have to powder my nose."

"Powder your nose?" I repeated.

"It is a phrase, you know."

"It's a phrase my grandmother says."

"You'd prefer it, maybe, if I said *pee*?"

"No, you can say it however you want."

"I'd rather not say it at all, thank you," she snapped.

She marched along the shoreline and kicked water forward and back with each step. A few splattered the left side of my T-shirt.

"You want to rethink that answer to being mad?" I asked.

"I'm mad," she said, and slowed down enough that she stopped splashing water up to her knees. "I'm mad because I have to say it at all. I'm mad because it *is* a nice night, and I'd like to keep walking, but I can't."

"Well, maybe next time," I said, laughing a little because it was funny—it was like talking to a five-year-old—"you should pee before the walk."

"Yeah? Thanks for the tip," she said in a tone that could have cut glass.

We didn't talk the remaining couple of minutes back to Mrs. B.'s. Abigail grabbed her shoes off the deck and hurried home while I called out, "We have bathrooms here, you know!"

I was pretty sure they heard me two doors north and south.

81

I knocked on the Howes' front door about twenty minutes later. Mrs. Howe answered like she had been expecting me.

"Briggs," she said with a big, warm smile on her face. "Abigail thought you might come by."

"Yeah, I just wanted to make sure she was okay."

"She's fine. She's on the phone to her grandmother, and"—she laughed—"once my mother starts talking, she is going to finish her thoughts."

"Yeah, I get that."

"I'll tell her you stopped by."

"Thanks," I said. "Uh, could I ask a huge favor? See, Mrs. B. doesn't have Internet."

"You'd like our Wi-Fi password?"

"Or I could just hop on one of your computers, maybe, and check my stuff if you'd rather not give it out."

"I'll write it down for you."

82

NETWORK NAME: North Shore Howes

PASSWORD: Ileum

I was at the small desk in my room at Mrs. B.'s. First thing I did online was google *ileum*.

The lowest portion of the small intestine, between the jejunum and the cecum.

Second thing I did was google *jejunum*.

Third thing I googled should be easy to figure out.

83

I had a ton of texts and tweets. Most of them random. Sam was working at his mom's office that summer. Last week he texted:

Dr. Mom nice. Real mom evil. I continue observing subject to ascertain mysterious transition between office and home

Taylor sent me a long text yesterday:

Hi Briggs. Hope u get this in time. Em Ash & me r coming to SH tomorrow for the day. North Beach. Nishesh can't come. Love to c u. Come to North Beach or txt me ur address so I can c u

I had just sent a quick text back—I'll stop down at NB tomorrow afternoon, look for me by vball courts— when I smelled perfumy soap and heard a voice, two inches from my ear, ask, "You busy?" I bolted out of my chair, slamming my knees on the underside of the desk on my way.

"Oh, man!"

I ran both hands over my head and squeezed the back of my neck.

"Sorry," Abigail said, laughing a little.

"Man." I tried to catch my breath and laugh too. It came out as this weird wheeze.

"I seem to have startled you," she said, amused.

"You think?"

"You know, if I were a serial killer, you'd be dead by now."

"You'd have to get past Mrs. B."

"Maybe she and I are a team," she said, her eyes brightening at the thought. "She lures the victims here by promising them a job at the beach. Then I befriend them and—" She grabbed her neck and made a gurgling sound.

"This is completely creeping me out."

"Am I interrupting anything?"

"Not really."

"Let's sit outside," she said, walking onto the balcony without waiting for me to say okay. It was getting darker, and we turned the lights off to see the few faint stars that were just popping out.

Abigail sat and stretched her long legs out onto the railing. I didn't get quite as comfortable. You know, in case she really was a serial killer and I needed to run.

"Sorry about earlier," she said.

"No, when you gotta go, you gotta go."

"I don't want to talk about it. I just wanted to apologize for getting upset."

"No problem," I said as she crossed her legs at her ankles and tipped her head back against the chair.

"So why were you in the hospital?" I asked.

"I don't want to talk about that, either."

"Well, that's where you and I are different." I shot her a good Briggs Henry Smile. "Eating disorder?"

"Excuse me?" She sat up, put her feet on the floor.

"You *are* pretty thin."

"So all skinny girls have eating disorders?"

"I'm just guessing here, since you won't say."

"I do not have an eating disorder," she said, stretching her legs to the railing again. "And if you do guess it, I will personally give you a million dollars."

"Do you *have* a million dollars?" It was fun to give her back her own words.

"No, and I have no plans to become a millionaire, either, so it'll have to be in installments." She tucked her hair behind her ears and said, "Not everyone is motivated by money, you know."

"Yeah, well, that's easy to say when you have it," I said.

"Maybe," she said. "But it's still true."

"Well, maybe I'll say the same thing after I make my first million."

"What happens if you don't make it?"

"Failure is not an option," I said, and was about to get comfortable—feet on the railing—when she said, "That's ridiculous. Failure's always an option."

"Not if you work hard enough."

"Even then," she said. "Failure means you're either doing something wrong or you're just not good at it and need to be doing something else. Or maybe you were in the wrong place at the wrong time." She leaned back in her chair and looked at the sky. "Please tell me you're not the kind of guy who believes the platitudes you read on bumper stickers."

"Platitudes?" I tried to tease but didn't know if I sounded convincing.

"It's a word."

"Yeah," I said. "I mean, no. I just think if you work hard enough—most of the time—you're going to succeed."

"'Most of the time' being the operative phrase."

"Yeah," I said, and thought for a minute. I must have made a seriously strange face, because Abigail looked over at me and asked, "What?"

"I was just wondering what my dad would say to that."

"What would he say?"

"That I'm wrong. And that you are too." I ran my hand over my head. "It would be an argument."

"Tell him to argue with me," she said. "I won't lose."

"You speaking from experience?"

"Maybe."

"What happened?"

She exhaled a long, slow breath that dropped her shoulders a little.

"Life threw me a curveball," she said.

"Funny you should say that."

"It's not funny."

"It's a little funny," I said, and told her about baseball and my graduation speech.

"What position did you play?" she asked.

"Nice try," I said, calling her out for trying to change the subject. She rolled her eyes a little. "You were saying something about being in the hospital."

"I think I've said enough about it."

We sat quietly for a few minutes. Small white lights on distant yachts flickered near the horizon and traveled slowly toward the channel.

Finally I leaned over and asked, "Mono? Was it mono? 'Cause if it was mono, I'm in big trouble after last night."

She smiled, spontaneously it seemed. Too fast to keep her lips closed.

"It wasn't mono," she said.

"Broken foot?"

"No."

"Leg?"

"No."

"Wrist?"

"No."

"Coccyx?"

"Coccyx?" she asked.

"It's a word," I said.

"No."

"How about that weird gluten allergy?"

"No," she said again, and stood up and straddled her legs over mine and sat on my lap and kissed me, and I laughed.

"I'm only doing this so you'll shut up," she said through a smile.

"Then I'm never going to shut up."

She held my face in her hands. I held her hips. Her back. I pulled her closer. She arched her neck, and I kissed that. We locked eyes a second. I slid my hand around the back of her head. She grabbed my shirt with both hands, and my mouth found hers. She gently pulled at my lips with her teeth. We wanted more. We were tender—soft lips brushing against each other. We were demanding—mouths and bodies pressed closer and closer until we lost our breath and found it again.

And then she stopped. I placed my hand against her cheek, and she smiled, and held my wrist, and kissed my palm and said in a way that almost sounded sad, "I need to run."

"Not yet," I said, but she stood.

"I have to." She squeezed my hand and said, "Do me a favor and don't ask why."

"Okay," I said, like it was a question that I hoped she'd answer. But she didn't. She just hurried inside and left.

Like Grandma Ruth, she didn't say good-bye.

Minutes passed. Or hours. I remained on the deck, legs on the railing, head tipped back against the chair. And I thought, if Abigail was a serial killer, kissing and then leaving must be her weapon of choice.

84

At 7:25, the next morning, I escorted Mrs. B. into K City Creative Paints the way I escorted her into churches and doctors' appointments. On my arm and with a purpose. Coastal Water, it turned out, reminded her of the *sweemmink* pool, and she cannot "live under the waters of the *sweemmink* pool."

I checked texts and e-mail on my phone while Mrs. B. looked at color options, and I found this from my dad, written just minutes earlier:

Since you're a man of leisure now and today is Saturday, I expect you to come in this afternoon and help your grandmother. She's setting up for the church's rummage sale. You know what that means. But it'll keep you from getting fat. You're welcome.

I ran a hand over my head and scratched my neck.

I needed a haircut. And some antacid. Mom kept bottles of the stuff in the house and used it about as often as I did. Dad claimed never to be sick. *No time,* he always said. *No time to be sick.*

He went to work with colds and the flu and shared his bugs with the whole office.

"No time to be sick," I said under my breath, and rolled my eyes.

I texted him: I can b there by noon

Mrs. B. and I went home with eight gallons of a color called Tranquility. Chuck with the huge teeth and I tried to persuade her to take a small sample jar, but she said, "No, I do not want the *leetle* sample," and I wasn't going to argue. "How I am *goink* to know if I like it if I do not see it on the walls?"

"See you next week," Chuck said to me.

I almost just said, "Chuck." And I almost shook his hand. But enough people I'd recently met thought that was kind of a douchey way to say hello or good-bye. So I just said, "See ya," like you do when you're not running for office.

85

Grandma Ruth had a peanut butter and jelly sandwich waiting for me when I got to her house, a 3,200-square-foot brick colonial on a street called Drumlin. A cul-de-sac. One way in. No way out.

"It amazes me how much you and your mother love my grape jelly," she told me as I choked down the sandwich in as few bites as possible. "I don't know why your mother never bothered to learn to make it."

"No one can make it like you do, Grandma Ruth," I said, and struggled to swallow the last, huge bite. As I did, I thought, *I'd really rather be at another funeral.*

86

I tried to talk Sam and Kennedy into helping move stuff for the rummage sale. But Kennedy had plans and Sam wimped out.

Me: ur afraid of Gma Ruth

Sam: Yes. I am. Is it possible shes a robot?

Me: How can I tell?

Sam: Have u ever heard the woman laugh or fart?

Me: Thats the test?

Sam: Yes. Thats the test

Me: Then yes, its possible shes a robot

That would have explained a lot. I could see her being assembled from a kit and later assembling my dad the same way. She wouldn't have installed the optional sense of humor software. She would have donated it and her own to the rummage sale. Or swapped them for a spiffy new pair of loafers. Robots like loafers. Just ask Grandma Ruth.

87

"What's the woman like?" Grandma Ruth asked.

"I know for a fact she's not a robot," I said, shooting my grandmother a quick grin.

We were in my car on the way back to her house, and she wanted to know about my job. I was sweating buckets from moving stuff at the church, but the AC was off. Grandma Ruth felt chilled.

"Am I supposed to understand what you mean by that?" she asked.

"No, I'm just kidding," I said instead of what I wanted to say, which was, *Come on, Grandma Ruth. Loosen up. Just once. It won't kill you.* "She's short, and she's sweet, and"—I wasn't going to say it, but Mrs. B. got a kick out of it, so what the hell—"she jiggles when she laughs."

"Oh, for heaven's sake, Briggs," Grandma Ruth said, pinching up her face as if she'd just eaten her own grape jelly. "That's hardly an appropriate way to describe a woman of any age, let alone one in her eighties."

"It's true," I said. "She even said it herself."

Grandma Ruth pinched up her face a second time.

"But she pronounces it *jeegle*."

"Please."

"She wanted to know if I liked her jiggle," I said, completely amused.

"Enough."

"You want to know what I told her?"

"I do not."

"I told her," I said, but Grandma Ruth blew her Assistant Coordinator's whistle, and I winced.

"I will not listen to any more of this conversation. Is that understood?"

"It is," I said, but I was on a roll, so I asked her, "Don't you want to know what I think about your jiggle?"

"I do *not* jiggle," she said as she smoothed the one and only thing that did jiggle with the back of her hand. That flap of skin underneath her neck hadn't changed in fifteen years. Of course, neither had Grandma Ruth.

88

After I walked Grandma Ruth up to her house, I sat in my car, cranked the air conditioner, and checked my texts. There were three from Taylor:

(when she got to North Beach) We r here

(an hour later) Where r u?

(about an hour ago) Looks like we wont see each other

I texted back: Sorry. Had to help Gma Ruth today

She texted right back: U still dont make time for me

Me: couldnt b helped

Her: U shouldve texted me to tell me u werent coming.

Me: I totally forgot. Dont b pissed

Her: Im seriously pissed. No one wants to b forgotten!!!

Me: Everyone is forgettable eventually

I didn't send that. I typed it and looked up at Grandma Ruth's dark house and remembered her saying those words the day she gave me the Ficus. It was just a classic Grandma Ruth line at the time, but now I felt it in my stomach. And that is not where my good memories lived.

Taylor: Thats like saying its not worth ur time or effort to even think of me and that is NOT COOL.

I jumped when my phone rang and answered it quickly.

"Hello?"

"Why are you in my driveway still?" Grandma Ruth wanted to know. "Is something wrong with your car?"

"No, I'm just checking texts."

"Well, be quick about it or come inside before the neighbors think something's wrong and call the police."

"I'm going, Grandma Ruth," I said. "Sorry I made you worry," and I got out of there and ended up, next morning, with a mild case of diarrhea, which, like Grandma Ruth, was impossible to ignore.

89

For the next few days I sanded—by hand—the steps I had repaired leading from Mrs. B.'s deck down to the beach. I baked in the sun and found relief only in the shade of passing clouds or running into the lake for quick dips.

Late one afternoon under a hazy blue-white sky, I swam a little. Out to a sandbar ten yards from the shore. Sat there on my knees a few seconds, separating the glossy water with big sweeps of my arms. Then floated on my back, arms and legs spread like a star. Deep, slow breaths. The lake cool and thick and gentle around my body, my head, my face. Totally relaxed except for the thought I could not ignore:

How could I come from such a long line of robots?

90

Abigail and her mom—and sometimes some other lady friends who looked a lot like Mrs. Howe—set up their daily beach camp with umbrellas and coolers and beach chairs and books. Mrs. Howe spent her days talking with friends and handing Abigail food. And Abigail ate.

Once I wandered over—dripping wet from a quick swim—and said, "Moderate to severe plaque psoriasis." I didn't even know what it was, but some hot model advertised a treatment for it on television.

"No," she said, lips pressed into a smile, the kind that keeps a laugh just inside.

"Any form of cancer, including skin?"

"No."

"Heat stroke?"

"No, but you're getting warm."

"Hypothermia?"

"Now you're cold."

"Cute," I said, and returned to sanding the steps.

91

Sam: Will u b here on the 4th?

Me: Don't know

Sam: When u coming home next?

Me: Why?

Sam: Text me. Want to run something past u

Me: Can't u tell me now?

Sam: I'm more impressive live and in person

Me: Ur really not

Sam: True. Still

Me: OK

I checked my messages from the lobby of West Michigan Ortho Institute in Kalamazoo while Mrs. B. had her appointment.

Taylor: Just checking in to c how u r

Me: Thought u were mad at me

Taylor: Nope. u okay?

Me: Yep. u?

Taylor: I am if u r

Me: Did I miss something? U & Nishesh break up?

Taylor: Nope. Got to run. Bye!

Mrs. B. emerged, marching, a few minutes later, eyebrows furrowed, her fist gripping a yellow sheet of paper.

"You know this is what?" she said, shoving the paper at me.

"What is it, Mrs. B.?"

"This is doctor's report. It says I am fine. I say to the doctor, if I am fine, why my knees stick and *squick*? Doctor says old knees stick and *squick*, and *nothink* is *wronk*. I have the arthritis, but that is all."

"Well, yeah, I can see why you're upset." I raised my eyebrows at her.

We walked outside to my car.

"Of course I am upset," Mrs. B. said. "They say to take the *peels*, for the aches, and I do, and still I have the knees that stick and *squick*."

"Some of the people at the assisted living center where I worked like yoga. Have you ever thought about yoga, Mrs. B.?"

She pinched up her face like she smelled dog poo.

"I have tried the yoga, and I do not like," she said. "It gives to me the *cremps*."

"Muscle cramps? You should start with a—"

"No, not the *mahssels cremps*. The *cremps* in the stomach."

"Yoga gives you stomach cramps?"

"Bad, bad *cremps*. Plus." She made the dog poo face again. "I do not like American yoga. It is too sour."

"American yoga is sour and gives you cramps," I said.

"This is what I say."

I helped her into my car.

"Mrs. B.," I said when I got in, "by any chance do you mean yogurt?"

"Yes. Yoga."

"Yoga," I said, trying not to laugh, "is very different from yogurt."

"This is *wronk wood*?"

"This is the wrong word, yes."

She brightened up then. Grinned a little and raised her shoulders when she asked me, "You know who teaches to me the English?"

"Who?"

"My husband. Mr. B."

"He spoke Serbian?"

"No. I teach to *heem* the Serbian."

"Wait," I said, glancing over at her quickly. "You guys didn't speak the same language when you got married."

"Very *leetle*."

"How did you know you wanted to marry him, then?"

"Love is the *knowink*, Briggs Baby. It is not the *woods*." She patted both hands against her chest, over her heart, and smiled when she said, "*Knowink* is in here."

"You think about him a lot?"

"All of the times."

"So you won't forget him?"

"How I can forget?" she asked like it wasn't actually a question.

"You don't think everyone's forgettable at some point?"

"You forget the *unimported* people," she said, and she shrugged.

"The unimportant ones?"

"This is what I say. But. The *imported* ones, you cannot forget, because"—she tossed her hands up—"they are *imported*."

92

I dragged myself out of the water one blistering after-noon and jogged, dripping wet and with sand stuck to my shins, up to Abigail.

"Some kind of female thing?" I asked.

"Like tampons or Barbie dolls?"

"Yeah. Like that."

"You're such a guy," she said, and ate a huge bite of guacamole from a spoon.

"Come on. This is fun."

"Oh, yeah. This has *game show* written all over it."

"Really—was it some kind of—you know—woman thing?"

"Can you *name* a woman thing?"

"You know, I really don't think I can."

"Yeah, well, it wasn't." She tipped the container of guacamole toward me. "Want some?"

"Thanks," I said, and she handed me a slice of untoasted bagel.

"No tortilla chips?"

"This is all I've got."

I was about to dip a piece of bagel when I asked, "It wasn't contagious, was it?"

"No."

Then, with a mouthful of bagel and guacamole, I asked, "Intestinal parasites?"

"No."

"Oh. Hey. Diabetes," I said, sure I'd gotten it right.

"No."

"Cirrhosis?"

"No."

"Jaundice?"

"Do I look yellow?"

"You look great," I said, and I made her blush, which was cool.

I scooped up some more guacamole and popped the whole piece of bagel in my mouth.

"I gotta get back to work," I said.

"Wish I did," she said. "I'd love to have something to do other than just sit here."

"Man, I'd love to have nothing to do but sit at the beach all day."

"That's the difference between living here and being a tourist," she said.

"Why no job?"

"Plans fell through."

"Well, if you want something to do, I can help with that," I said, and tipped my head toward Mrs. B.'s.

93

Abigail followed me up the stairs.

"I had a job lined up at New Hope Animal Shelter," she said. "Washing dogs. Maddy works there."

"What happened?"

"No heavy lifting."

"But it wasn't muscular?"

"Not muscular."

"You didn't have a baby, did you?" I asked, and she slapped my shoulder.

Hard.

I laughed, but it hurt.

"It's just taping trim," I said as we stepped into the third-floor hall. "Here and maybe in the bathroom too. If you feel like it."

"Sure," she said.

"Let me grab the tape," I said, and opened the door to the bedroom across from mine, where Mrs. B. stood with her fists on her hips. Next to her were Miss Mae and Connie Steiner.

"There is the problem, Briggs Baby," Mrs. B. said. "*Beeg* problem."

Miss Mae and Mrs. Steiner smiled sympathetically at me, kind of like they did after my cell phone spectacular at Pauline Ostrander's funeral. My stomach began to cramp, so I pressed my hand against the pain and saw, peripherally, that Abigail noticed.

"We do not like the color," Mrs. B. said, and I exhaled, relieved. "But. There is no time to *shange* it today."

"No?"

"No," she said. "Howard Levy died, and his funeral is this afternoon. You will take us, Briggs Baby."

"Of course."

She turned to Abigail and asked, "You come?"

"Sure," she said.

"You know him? Or knew him?" I asked.

"No, but the more the merrier, right?" Abigail said, and Mrs. B.'s apple cheeks shined bright red in a smile that reached all the way up to her eyes.

"You see?" she said, pointing at Abigail. "She enjoys my funeral."

94

I was beginning to think that everyone in South Haven was slightly bat-shit crazy. Good thing I had a smile for that.

95

"The funeral," Mrs. B. said, "is entirely at the grave-side."

I was driving. Mrs. B. sat in the front. Abigail sat between Miss Mae and Mrs. Steiner.

"Now, he was married three times, Howard Levy was," Miss Mae said to Abigail in that voice that sounded even raspier than usual.

"Three times," Mrs. Steiner confirmed.

"Lost all three wives to cancer."

"Cancer," Mrs. Steiner said, and sighed.

"Poor man."

"Yes, poor man."

"Now, his second wife, Hava, made the best beef bris-ket I have ever had."

"Wasn't it just the best?"

"It was in the rub."

"The rub is the secret."

I grinned at Abigail via the rearview mirror.

"Now," Miss Mae said to Abigail, "Hava Levy was like you. All her life. She was thin, and she could eat any-thing she wanted."

Mrs. Steiner reached across Abigail and touched Miss Mae's leg.

"You're thin, Mae," she said.

"I'm not at all. I just hide it well."

"You have a lovely figure."

"So do you," Mrs. Steiner said as Abigail looked at the floor and pressed her fingertips against her lips to keep from smiling too much.

"Some Jewish funerals take place in the *syngock*," Mrs. B. said to me.

"Synagogue?"

"This is what I say. Some of the funerals are only at the graveside. The graveside is better. Turn left."

"Why better?"

"It is less *depressink*."

"A cemetery is less depressing than a synagogue?"

"Less morose," Abigail added cheerfully.

"Yes," Mrs. B. said. "You are outside. The sky is blue. The day is pretty."

"Good day for a funeral, eh, Mrs. B.?" I teased.

"Good day for a funeral," she said.

"Good day for a funeral," Miss Mae said.

"Good day," Mrs. Steiner confirmed.

"Good day," Abigail said.

96

Mrs. B. held my left arm, Miss Mae my right, as we walked across the uneven ground and thick grass of the cemetery. Abigail and Mrs. Steiner held hands.

A large crowd had already gathered. Every chair underneath a white tent, by the grave, was occupied. The rest of us stood in a deep semi-circle behind the tent.

"Family," Mrs. B. said. "*Beeg* family."

"Do you have a big family, Mrs. B.?" I asked her.

"Two brothers, two *seesters*. *Theerteen* nieces and nephews. They *leeve* all over the *woold*. Two brothers are dead. One dies in the war."

"World War II?" I asked. She nodded. *Man.* "I'm sorry."

"Yes. But my other brother dies old. So. It is the *way how* life goes. Women *leeve lonker*. You should marry the older woman if you don't want her to be the *lonk* widow."

"I'll keep that in mind, Mrs. B.," I said, and filed it under Random Advice from the Elderly. "You and Mr. B. never had kids?"

She stopped, so, of course, I did the same. Miss Mae let go of my arm and stepped aside to talk to Mrs. Steiner.

With her free hand Mrs. B. sort of waved at her belly and asked, "Where I am *goink* to put the baby?"

"Yeah, that's an image I could have lived without, Mrs. B."

"Baby needs room to grow. There is no room. So. There is no baby."

"See, the more you talk about it, the more I'm picturing it."

"No, you do not *peekture* this," she said, wagging that index finger at me.

"Yeah, it's a little late for that," I said.

"Did you want children, Vesna?" Abigail asked, coming up on the other side of Mrs. B.

"Yes, of course. But." She shrugged. "We do not always get what we want. Sometimes yes. Sometimes no. Sometimes there is *nothink* you can do, but say okay." She shrugged. "And then you go on."

"Make the best of a bad situation. Right, Mrs. B.?"

She patted my arm and smiled like she approved and then turned to the woman next to her and said of Mr. Levy, "He was the nice man."

"See?" I said to Abigail. "Failure is not an option."

She looked at me like I was the biggest idiot in the world and said, "She still doesn't have kids, though, Briggs."

"Yeah," I said, and glanced at Howard Levy's family gathered underneath the tent. *Beeg* family. "Yeah."

97

Just before the service started, a man with thick white hair and a gray mustache handed me and a few other men nearby black yarmulkes. I put mine on, and, without a word, Abigail adjusted it.

A few minutes later, I helped Mrs. B. to the side of the tent, where we had, in her words, *the better view of the coffin.*

"Yeah, that's important," I said.

It was plain, like something I could have made in shop class, and a huge pile of dirt sat next to it, a huge pile of dirt with two shovels sticking out.

The whole thing felt earthy and real.

The service—the rabbi's part of it—was twenty-two minutes long. He stood next to the coffin, read some prayers, and gave a brief eulogy. He said nice things about Howard Levy, who was ninety-seven—*man, that's old*—and owned one of the first hotels in South Haven when they were called resorts. The family made muffled laughing sounds when the rabbi mentioned a particular Yorkie named Noodles and also a favorite brown suit.

"The rabbi should have mentioned how much he loved Hava's brisket," Miss Mae said.

"But didn't he just love it," Mrs. Steiner said.

"It was that rub she made."

"It's all in the rub."

Abigail and I made eye contact, sideways, and we had to look away before we both erupted.

The crowd—about sixty people, not including the family—recited the twenty-third psalm from memory. Even Abigail and Mrs. B. knew it. I'd heard part of it a bunch of times—something about walking through the valley of the shadow of death—but never knew it was a psalm or its actual number until the rabbi said so.

I spied Ben Zuckerman standing across the way, near the opposite corner of the tent. We nodded hello at each other. And then he got this look like he was about to laugh, and tipped his head to his left, where his mom stood. He pointed me out to her. She waved. I waved back, and Ben widened his eyes at me like it was the funniest thing in the world.

I'd have done the same to Sam or Kennedy.

Some minutes later, the casket was lowered into the ground, and the family started heaving sobs, like some of them couldn't catch their breath. Heaving and tipping their heads onto each other's shoulders. Young and old. They heaved and tipped, and it didn't matter who heard or saw them.

I looked away, at the ground, and cleared my throat a

couple times to clear the tight, sharp lump forming there. I didn't even know the guy.

The rabbi asked us—all of us, every person there—to come place two shovelfuls of dirt on the coffin, which, somehow, felt both right and terrifying. Like, yeah, this is what you do when someone dies. You bury the body. You literally bury the body. You don't let strangers do it while you're on your way home. *You* do it. But, my God, you're literally burying the body. Howard Levy's body.

I tried to get my head around this when Mrs. B. tugged at my arm and said, "Come, Briggs Baby. You make sure I don't fall in."

"I've got you, Mrs. B.," I said.

"I am *goink* there one day, but not today."

"No, not today."

I had one arm around her waist and helped her hold the shovel with the other as she scooped her few dirt crumbs onto the coffin. Then it was my turn. After, as the rabbi instructed, I thrust the shovel back into the pile of dirt for the next person.

On our slow walk back to my car, her hand on my elbow, Mrs. B. asked, "You like this one?"

Abigail followed with Miss Mae and Mrs. Steiner.

"I don't know, Mrs. B.," I said. "I think, of the five I've been to with you"—I held up five fingers for emphasis— "I like this one best."

And then I shook my head a little, because—my God—I just said that.

"Yes, maybe I will have the Jewish funeral when I die."

"I'm pretty sure you have to be Jewish for that," I said.

"Yes, well not whole funeral. But I like some of the parts. I will write down and give to priest."

"Now there's a plan if I ever heard one," Abigail said.

98

The big, white frame house on Monroe Boulevard was packed with people dressed in black, and loud with conversation. Almost like a party except a lot of the guests had been crying and held crumpled tissues in their hands.

All of us had been invited back to the house for a meal, and "meal" did not begin to describe the spread. The dining room table was fully extended and covered with platters and bowls of food. There were mounds of bagels and toppings, sliced vegetables, pans of roasted meat, and baked noodle dishes Ben's mom told me were kugel.

"Briggs wants to know what all the different dishes are," Ben told his mom, and found himself really funny.

She pointed with a long maroon fingernail and named them as we made our way along. And she told me to call her Jennifer.

"Jews don't send flowers when someone dies," she said. "We send food."

"Food makes much more sense," I said with a huge bite of kugel in my mouth. The kugel was rich and creamy with little bits of apple in it. It was a little sweet and a little savory and just about the best thing I had ever eaten.

Jennifer Zuckerman excused herself to talk with a group of women she knew, including Miss Mae and Mrs. Steiner.

"So," Ben said. "You're here with Abigail."

"And Mrs. B. and Miss Mae and Mrs. Steiner," I said, and took another bite of kugel.

"Which one of the four is your girlfriend?" he asked, looking at the food on his plate.

"All of them. None of them. I don't know," I said.

"I'd be happier if it were Mrs. B.," he said.

"I hear you're the one who broke up with Abigail."

"Yeah, I know. It's just—" He shrugged. "I don't know."

"Man, I get it," I said. "You think I'm happy my ex-girlfriend is going out with another guy? Biggest douche-bag in our class."

"I just don't want to see her get hurt."

"I'm not going to hurt her."

"You're a tourist. You're going to be gone before fall," he said. "Long-distance relationships do not work. You're going to forget her."

"I am not going to forget her," I said. "And, anyway, I think Abigail can take care of herself."

"She seems different to me. I don't know what's going on with her."

"Have you asked her?"

"I asked her about you," he said. "She told me she likes you."

"Really?" I asked. "I'm still waiting for her to say 'nice to meet you.'"

"Yeah, that's a thing of hers I don't get. Something about not having any regrets."

"No, it's impossible to have no regrets," I said. "She's just trying to minimize hers. Or something like that."

"You don't get it either."

"Yeah, I really don't."

We looked across the living room where Abigail stood talking with Mrs. B. and some of the Levys. Abigail stared straight at us. Like trained dogs, we waved, and she smiled like she alone got the joke.

"Hey," Ben said as he tapped my shoulder with the back of his hand. "She was looking at *me*."

"In your dreams, man."

"She misses me."

"She came here with *me*."

"Yeah, this is a hell of a place to bring a date."

Couple seconds later she walked over, and Ben asked, "Okay, so who were you looking at? Me or him?"

"Neither of you," she said, and pointed over our shoulders to a grandfather clock a few feet away. "I just wondered what time it was."

99

At the door, Mrs. B. introduced me to Carole Sachs, who had orange fingernails and red-rimmed eyes. She was old Howard Levy's daughter. And heiress to the Levy fortune, according to Miss Mae.

"She's worth millions now," she told me earlier as I was on my fourth plate of kugel.

"Millions," Mrs. Steiner confirmed.

I knew better than to be happy for Carole Sachs about that. I could see, even at her age—she must have been in her sixties—that already she wanted her father back and would have traded any money for him.

"I'm sorry about your father," I told Carole Sachs, who gripped my hand, up to my wrist, in both of hers.

Mrs. B. had just introduced us. Carole Sachs seemed in no hurry to let go of me.

"Thank you," she said. "You didn't know him?"

"No, I'm just here with Mrs. B."

"But now. We go," Mrs. B. said.

"I wish you could have known him," Carole Sachs said, and finally let go and dabbed at her eyes with a knuckle. I handed her a tissue from my pocket. Mrs. B. noticed and approved with a nod.

"He was the nice man," Mrs. B. said.

"He was," Carole agreed.

I kind of nodded a good-bye to Ben and his mom on the way out and noticed the grandfather clock behind them was stuck at 7:10.

100

We were all quiet on the drive home. Miss Mae and Mrs. Steiner lived on the west side of the river, like Abigail and Mrs. B., and in equally huge, gorgeous houses but not lakeside. Mrs. Steiner's was a new, modern ranch set far back from the street and surrounded by tons of pine trees and humidity. Miss Mae's was a spotless Victorian. Pale yellow with bright yellow flowers, the color of her hair, everywhere.

At their front doors, each lady invited me to "stop by anytime," and told me, "My door is always open."

"You be sure to lock it after I go," I told each of them, and gave them my There's My Girl Smile.

I was wearing it in combination with what I knew about the grandfather clock when I got back in the car with Abigail and Mrs. B.

"What?" Abigail demanded to know.

"Nothing," I said, unwilling to wipe the grin off my face.

Mrs. B. turned to face Abigail to explain.

"He likes my funeral," she said. "He does not want to say. But he likes it."

101

I came to a stop in Mrs. B.'s driveway, and Abigail hopped out after thanking Mrs. B. for letting her come along.

"Come talk with me tonight," Abigail said to me through the open back door.

"Seven ten?" I asked.

"Seven ten?" she repeated, frowning, before remembering the grandfather clock and twisting her lips in this guilty but sort of pleased way that made me laugh. "Yeah. No," she said, smiling. "Sunset. Nine thirty–ish."

"You bringing Oreos?"

"Of course."

"See you then," I said, and she shut the door.

"She likes you," Mrs. B. said. "You like her?"

"She's nice."

I turned the car off.

"You want her to be your girlfriend?"

"I wouldn't mind. But I don't see how it'll work out."

"You want the relationship to last, to be good, you make it like the job."

"A job?"

"Yes. Like the job. You. Me. Your parents. My parents. Everyone should treat the relationships like the job. Then." She raised an index finger. "Relationships are good. And everyone is *heppy*."

"I thought relationships weren't supposed to be work."

"Oh," she said, and tossed her hands in the air. "No. This is all *wronk*. You want to be good at *anythink,* you must to *wook*. To be good cook, good husband, good son, good teacher, good doctor, good friend, you must to *wook*."

"Yeah," I said, and unhooked my seat belt, thinking about what I worked hard at.

Was good at. Bussing tables, school, numbers, baseball, Grandma Ruth. Yeah, Grandma Ruth.

"Speaking of friends," I said, "I'm sorry you lost— uh—I'm sorry another one of yours . . . died. That must be hard."

"No. It is not hard," she said with a shrug for emphasis.

"No?"

"No. He is not my friend."

"Okay, your acquaintance."

"No, he is not the *aquatense,* either. I do not know *heem*."

"You don't *know* him?"

"No."

"Howard Levy?"

"No."

"The man whose funeral we just went to?"

"No, I never meet *heem*."

"You never met him?"

"This is what I say," she said, sounding a little exasperated. "Why you are *askink* over and again? I do not know *heem*. I never meet *heem*." Again, a shrug.

"Mrs. B. We just went to the funeral of a guy you don't even know?"

"Yes."

"Why would we . . . Wait," I said like I was watching a movie and just figured out who the murderer was. And it was Mrs. B. "How well did you know the others? Mrs. Ostrander. Maria Santos. Dorothy Webb. Jonathan—whoever—the guy in Grand Rapids."

"I don't know them either."

"Any of them?"

"No, I don't know them," she said, pinching up her little face at me. "Why you are *shoutink*?"

"Mrs. B.! We're crashing funerals!"

"What means *crashink*?"

"Going to an event you're not invited to and don't know anyone at."

"Okay. Then. Yes." Those little shoulders went up and down again. "We are *crashink* the funerals."

"People do not crash funerals!"

"You do not shout," she said, wagging her finger at me. "You will go back on the probe . . . the probe—"

"Probation."

"Yes, the probation if you keep *shoutink*. The family is always *heppy* for *beeg* crowd at funeral. You say to them, 'he was nice man, she was nice lady.' They say always yes, and they are *heppy* you come."

"Mrs. B., this is not normal. Is this some weird Serbian custom?"

"Eh. It is not Serbian custom. It is not weird."

"Okay, in this country, this is not what people do."

"How else I am *goink* to see the way how I want my funeral?"

"What?" I practically bounced in my seat. "You're window-shopping funerals?"

She thought about that for a second or two before her shoulders moved up and down.

"Mmm-mmm-mmm. Window-*shoppink*. Yes. Is like *shoppink* for the shoes. You just look. You don't buy. Mmm-mmm-mmm."

Couple seconds later—couple seconds I spent staring at her with my mouth hanging open—she said, "That reminds me," and she took a piece of paper and a pen from her purse. "You like the noodle kugel?"

"Noodle kugel? Yeah," I said, like, *What the hell?*

She wrote as she said, "We will have the noodle kugel at my funeral. Just for you. See? You will like my funeral."

"Yeah. Kugel. Thanks, Mrs. B.," I said, and I dropped my head onto the steering wheel.

102

There was a buzz down at North Beach, and not just because the place was packed. July Fourth was just four days away, and the beach, the town, the harbor were full. Bright swimsuits, bright umbrellas, tanned bodies everywhere. Sailboats, fishing boats, and luxury yachts streamed and zipped across the lake. The whir of Jet Skis mixed with the cries of seagulls and music from radios and the thump and shout of volleyball games.

All the courts were full.

"Briggs!" Maddy shouted as she came running along the sidewalk to me. She grabbed my hand, hauling me down the beach, and said, "Come meet Dez!"

"Dez?"

"He's famous! Well, he will be!"

"What? Who is he?" I asked, and had to walk faster or lose my fingers.

"He's like a friend," she said. "Not a close friend, but we know him."

Eddie DeZwaan, Maddy said, was twenty years old and born and raised in South Haven. After high school, he moved to LA to become an actor and was cast in eight commercials and had small parts in three sitcoms.

She pointed him out. He was playing volleyball on what looked like a team of Vikings to me. All of them tall and blond. Like crazy white-blond. Eddie DeZwaan had shaggy hair and *believe* tattooed in black down one arm. A huge crowd cheered every single move he made, and he laughed at the attention.

"He's going to be super famous someday," Maddy said, and waved over my shoulder at him. He waved back and called out, "How ya doin', Maddy?"

"You'll meet him later," she said to me, sort of vaguely, still looking at Dez.

I met him when a bunch of us challenged him and his friends to a game of volleyball. They trounced us. Maddy could not concentrate. She kept staring at him and clapped every time he scored.

After our games, we ran like maniacs into the water to cool off. We ran out the same way and dropped onto our towels.

"Hey, Geri," Brandon said, and swatted my arm with the back of his hand. "There's a volleyball tournament this weekend. It's the best. Two days, and the winning team splits five hundred bucks. You in?"

"Yeah. I'm in," I said.

The team would be Brandon and me, Ben, Zach, Maddy, and Nicole.

"Too bad Abigail quit playing," Maddy said to me. "She was captain of the team in high school."

"Really? Why'd she quit?" I asked.

"She quit a lot of things. Who cares," Brandon said. "Wait, what's five hundred divided six ways?"

"Eighty-three thirty-three," I said. "And there'll be two cents left over." They stared. I shrugged. "Runs in the family."

"Dude!" Brandon kind of laughed. "Oh, man, I should have paid you to do my algebra homework."

"Yeah, I charge eighty-three thirty-three an hour."

He laughed.

"So who gets the extra two cents?" Maddy wanted to know.

I suggested Brandon should get it as team captain, and he said, "Thanks, Geri."

"Hey," I said. "Does Abigail not playing volleyball have anything to do with her being in the hospital?"

For a few seconds no one said anything. They all just looked at me like I was a tourist.

"When was she in the hospital?" Ben asked. "And why?"

103

I'd been sitting by the lake, in the increasing dark, for almost fifteen minutes before Abigail showed up. Taking her time. A bag of Oreo cookies swinging in one hand with each slow step.

She sat down hard and offered me a cookie without saying a word. She looked at me like she wished she could raise one eyebrow like her mom did. Both of hers went up into sharp peaks, and I figured she was waiting for me to say something.

"What?" I asked with a mouthful of Oreo.

"You know I'm mad at you. Or should be, except you didn't know, but you should've known, so, yes, I'm a little mad at you. Sort of. Not really." She pushed at a small pile of sand. "I don't know."

"Again, I ask—what?"

"You told my friends I was in the hospital."

"Two things," I said, and snagged another cookie. "First of all, I didn't tell them. I asked them if they knew *why* you were."

"Yeah. I never told them I was."

"That was going to be my second point."

She looked like she was about to say something but just blew out a long breath and dropped her shoulders.

"Yeah," she said. "Ben and Maddy called me tonight. I just said I didn't want to talk about it."

"Why not tell them?"

"I don't even know how."

"No offense, but I don't believe that," I said, and those eyebrows shot up like arrowheads again, which almost made me laugh. "I don't," I said. "Miss It's-a-Word."

"Okay, then I don't *want* to tell them."

"Well, that's different," I said, looking at her. "So why don't you want to?"

"You are persistent."

"You can't solve a problem by ignoring it."

"Is that one of your dad's sayings?"

"Probably."

"Yeah," she said, and pushed again at the sand. "Actually, that one's true."

"Some are better than others," I conceded.

She stared out over the water, which was a little rougher than usual that night. Three-foot waves broke over sandbars. Patches of gray-white clouds covered most of the sky. It was getting dark.

"Abigail," I said, and pushed her hair behind her elf ear, tracing its slight point with my finger.

"That tickles," she said.

I stopped and looked at her, waiting.

She fixed her eyes back on the lake, kind of like, somewhere between it and the sky, she'd find whatever words she was looking for.

Finally she took a deep breath, looked straight at me, and said, "I have something called Crohn's disease. I found out in March. My immune system attacks itself, and the fight takes place in my . . ." She cleared her throat and then said, quickly, "intestines."

I didn't say anything for a second. Then: "That's why you were in the hospital?"

"I had to have a little piece of the inflammation removed before it became a full blockage."

"What does that mean?"

"The disease causes scar tissue, and scar tissue can create a block." She looked at me—eyebrows only slightly arched—like I was supposed to figure out the rest myself. "So nothing can get through," she added.

"Oh." *Man.* "Got it."

"My doctor actually cut out eighteen inches of my intestines."

"Abigail," I said, "that doesn't sound like a little piece."

"Well, we've got several feet, which in my case is good. And bad. Lots more room for future inflammation."

"I never really imagined having a conversation with you about intestines," I said, and pushed my shoulder against hers.

"You would not believe how much my family and I have talked about intestines in the last four months."

"Well, yeah." I smiled slowly. "Whose family hasn't? Oh. Hey. Ileum."

"Yeah?"

"Part of the intestines."

"You know your anatomy."

"No," I kind of laughed. "Your mom gave me your family's Wi-Fi password."

"Oh, that," Abigail said, nodding. "Well, it's not one you'd guess, is it?"

"It really isn't."

"There's more if you want to hear it," she said.

"Lay it on me," I said, and leaned back, propped up on my elbows.

"There are tons of foods I can't eat," she said. "Like shellfish, sodas, French fries, milk, or much dairy. Popcorn's like eating glass. Ice cream's a nightmare. I can't gain weight. I even drink those meal replacement shakes *with* dinner and still—nothing.

"If I eat the wrong thing, I'm literally bent over in pain. *Literally.* The cramps are so bad. And this is when I'm not having a flare-up."

"What's a flare-up like?"

"It's like someone reaches up under your rib cage, grabs your stomach and everything below it, and shoves a knife into it, and the pain lasts for days or weeks at a time."

"Oh my God."

"And for added fun, they're completely random, so"—she hesitated, even rolled her eyes kind of at herself, like she didn't want to say this but had come this far—"I live my life around . . . bathrooms." She puffed out a little breath. Shook her head. "I literally can never be far from one."

"The walk," I said, sitting up. "And then up on my balcony."

"Yeah. Sometimes I just need to leave in a hurry."

"Oh, man, I am so sorry I gave you a hard time about that," I said, squeezing the back of my neck.

"It would have been funny if—you know—things were different. And for your information"—she looked at me—"my grandmother is the one who taught me to say 'powder my nose.'"

"Mine taught me how to care for a Ficus."

"Doing well, is it?"

"Thriving. I think. I don't know. It's green, and it's not dead, so I guess that's good. So, back to—what's it called—Crohn's disease?"

"Yes, back to that."

"I've got questions. I don't know if they're interesting or not."

She kind of bobbed her head side to side and said, "Let's hear them."

"Does this have anything to do with your mysterious disappearances?"

"Yeah, but they're not mysterious."

"They are to Mrs. B.," I said. "And me. Where do you go?"

"Inside," she said, nodding once toward her house. "Sometimes I'm just down for a couple days, and I don't want this whole town to know why."

"Your friends don't deserve to know?"

"Maybe, but then it gets around. And can you imagine the jokes Brandon is going to make?"

"I'd say they're going to be epic," I said, and she nearly smiled. "Maybe don't tell him all the details."

"There are more. You still want to hear them?" she asked.

"I do," I said.

"I'm on a bunch of different meds. My doctor keeps adjusting them, and until she gets them right and I stop having flare-ups"—she sighed—"I can't go away to school."

"That surgery didn't cure it?"

"There's no cure. Just treatment. You manage it—hopefully—but it never goes away. Like diabetes."

I pointed at her sweatshirt—Boston College in maroon and yellow, hard to make out now in the darkness—and asked, "Is that where you were going to go?"

She nodded. "And I was going to teach English abroad once I graduated."

"Where?"

"Everywhere," she said, like *everywhere* was the coolest word she'd ever said. "Spain first. Then maybe somewhere in Asia."

"What's Spanish for *dyspeptic*?"

"Yeah," she said, and nearly laughed. "The first sentences I'll teach my class: 'I am feeling dyspeptic today. Where is the nearest bathroom?'"

"Can't you still do that?" I asked, and watched as her smile slowly disappeared.

"Not until I'm in remission," she said. "And even then, the disease is one big cycle of remission and relapses. And you never know when it's going to hit." Her eyes got glassy and she blinked several times.

I sat up, pulled a tissue from my pocket and handed it to her.

"Thanks," she said, and wiped kind of savagely at her eyes. Then she wiped them again. "I'm fine," she said. "I'm just . . ."

I used my thumb to dry off a spot on her cheek.

". . . a little mad and a lot scared," she said.

"I've been there."

"At least your big change was temporary."

I shrugged when I said, "It might not have been. And I didn't know it would be at the time, which is part of why I was scared."

"But it *was* temporary. This one isn't."

"You know what I think?" I touched her butterfly necklace for a second and then traced my fingers along her neck. "Good or bad, all change sucks."

"Yeah, well, I'd rather have the good kind."

"Me too," I said, and I kissed her.

I eased back in the sand and Abigail came with me. We moved together. She had her legs on either side of me, and I pressed her hips gently into mine. I groaned and she laughed quietly against my mouth, doing that thing with her teeth and my lip. I slid my hands under the back of her sweatshirt and felt warm smooth skin and the sharpness of her shoulder blades and the silkiness of her bra strap. She made a sound in my ear, a quick breath, a good breath, and I had just slipped my fingers under the silky strap when Abigail Howe farted.

She pulled up, hair hanging down at both sides, eyes wide in the darkness.

We stared at each other.

Her mouth moved but no words came out. I was frozen.

And then we both lost it. We laughed, gulping huge breaths. We laughed so hard, we spit. I reached up to wipe a fleck of it off her cheek.

"Oh, my God," Abigail said, rolling off me onto her back. She covered her face with both hands and shook.

"I could die," she said through her hands, still laughing.

"So you farted," I said, and she slapped my chest.

"Will it make you feel better if I fart too?" I asked.

"No."

"'Cause I can do it."

"No!"

"Everybody does it."

"Not while they're kissing their boyfriends."

"Oh, come on. It's not like this is the first time you've done it in front of me."

"Yes, it is," she said before remembering. "Oh, wait. By Ben's truck. Oh my God." And she covered her face again.

"Yeah," I said. "I thought it was him."

"I wish it had been," she said, and she breathed out the last of her laughter and sat up. "I've got to go in."

"No, don't go," I said, and reached for her arm, but she stood.

"No, I *really* need to go in."

"You coming back?"

"Not tonight," she said, jogging toward her house.

I stood and brushed sand off my shorts and then called after her, "Did you just call me your boyfriend?"

She didn't answer. But I knew she heard me.

104

"Morning, Mrs. B.," I said to her as I walked into the kitchen the next morning.

She was lying on the floor. Eyes closed. Glasses crooked on her face.

"Mrs. B.?"

105

The squad arrived in minutes that felt like hours. The 911 operator had me check to make sure Mrs. B. was breathing. She was. And that she wasn't choking. She wasn't. Or bleeding. She wasn't.

Abigail and her parents ran in behind the four EMTs. Two cops came behind them.

Mrs. B. started to open her eyes just as the EMTs got to work, putting electrodes on her chest, taking her blood pressure. One guy opened an orange gear box that looked like a cross between a fishing tackle box and a chemistry set. A fourth guy started asking me questions.

"No, I just found her like this. No, it hasn't happened before. Vesna. Her name is Vesna."

I rattled off the answers. I pinched and pulled at my bottom lip. Abigail took my hand and squeezed it and said, "She's going to be okay."

"Vesna!" an EMT—the one who seemed to be in charge—said loudly. He was on his knees, leaning over her. "Vesna, can you hear me?"

"I can hear. Why you are *shoutink*?"

The EMT looked back at me. "Her speech always like that?"

"She's from Serbia," I said.

Another EMT asked if I knew what meds she was taking. I had the list ready on the counter. Mrs. B. kept it in her purse.

"Any changes in meds recently?" he asked.

"Yeah. Yeah, from her cardiologist."

"Pressure's coming up," a third EMT said while the one in charge asked, "Vesna, are you having any chest pain?"

"No."

"Shortness of breath?"

"No, I am *deezy*. So. I lie down. Then I open my eyes, and you are here. *Shoutink* to me."

He asked her a bunch more questions including who are you, where are you, and what is the day today. She nailed them all, and I started to relax a little. Abigail rubbed my arm and smiled at me like she knew some secret. About me. Or her. Or Vesna. I didn't know. I was just so relieved when Mrs. B. sat up in a chair and refused—*no, I do not go*—to go to the hospital when the EMTs offered a ride.

The one in charge told me to take her to her doctor that day.

"Which one? She's got like twenty."

"Her cardiologist," he said. "She didn't have a heart attack. She didn't have a stroke. EKG's normal. It's probably the meds, but you need to get that checked out. Today."

"Yeah, I will. Hey, thanks," I said.

"Sure," he said.

As the crew packed up their things, I knelt by Mrs. B.'s side. She took my hand and grinned at me. And Abigail's smile grew even more curious.

106

On our way home from the cardiologist in Kalamazoo, we stopped at K City Creative Paints to exchange Tranquility— "too *borink*"—for Dusk and Dawn.

Mrs. B. wanted me in the exam room with her at the cardiologist's, to make sure she heard everything correctly. She told the doctor I was her grandson, adding, "He has the height from his grandfather's side."

"Grandpa B.," I said, and Mrs. B. squinted a grin up at me, and the cardiologist looked completely bored with us and our inside joke. She said the dizziness was caused by Mrs. B.'s meds and made some adjustments, and Mrs. B. said to me, dully, "They never find *anythink*."

While Chuck loaded the cans into my car and Mrs. B. waited in the front seat, I checked my messages.

Taylor: **Everything still OK?**

Me: **Rough morning but alls good**

Taylor: **Im here if u need me**

Me (squinting at my phone): **What's going on T?**

Taylor: **Nothing just saying**

There were a bunch of group texts from Sam and Kennedy. This from my dad:

Since you're not working Saturdays, I expect you to come in again to help your grandmother.

I texted my dad: **Cant do it. Have plans tomorrow.**

My phone rang in seconds.

"Hey, Dad."

"Briggs?"

"Yeah, Dad."

"What's this about not helping your grandmother?"

"I have plans."

"Work?"

"Sort of. I'm committed to playing in a volleyball tournament. And—"

"That's not what I'd call work."

"No, but I need to stay around here. Mrs. B. was sick today, and I just"—I ran my hand over my head—"I have to be close by. Just in case she needs me."

"Your grandmother needs you."

"She's got, like, thirty volunteers."

"She's your grandmother."

"Dad, I can't do it."

"Family comes first."

"No. Work comes first. You taught me that. And this is my job."

"Well," he said, and even in that one word I heard his disapproval, and my stomach burned. "How convenient for you that your job allows you time to play volleyball."

"Dad, it's not just that. Mrs. B.—"

"As long as you have your priorities straight. Good luck in your tournament."

"Dad."

"Good-bye."

107

In the car, I called my grandmother. Mrs. B. had been asleep for thirty minutes.

"Hi, Grandma Ruth. How are you?"

"I'm fine, Briggs. Why are you calling?"

"To let you know I can't get in tomorrow to help with the rummage sale."

"I wasn't expecting you to come in."

"Dad asked me to."

"Did he ask you to come in to help the first time?"

"Yeah, but I also wanted to."

"Did you, indeed?"

"I did. Indeed."

A couple seconds passed.

"Is there anything else?" she asked.

"No, Grandma Ruth. That's all."

We hung up.

I put my phone back in the cup holder, looked over at Mrs. B., C-shaped with her chin resting on her chest.

"Mrs. B.," I said. When she didn't respond, I said it a little louder and gently squeezed her arm.

"Mrs. B.?"

"Hmm?" she asked, opening her eyes and raising her head.

"Oh, sorry, Mrs. B., I was just, uh, just—"

"You check to make sure I am not dead?"

"No, I . . . Yeah. I did."

"Mmm-mmm-mmm." She patted my leg. "Mmm-mmm-mmm."

108

Abigail walked over as I pulled into Mrs. B.'s drive.

"Everything okay?" she called.

"It was the meds," I said, and helped Mrs. B. out of the car. "We've got it all straightened out now. Right, Mrs. B.?"

She pointed at me and said to Abigail, "Yes, he straightens me out."

I walked Mrs. B. inside. Abigail followed. In the front hall, she said, "I just wanted to let you know that my parents and I are going to Chicago for a few days. We'll be back on the Fourth. I didn't want you to think we had disappeared."

"Mrs. B., I want you to rest today. Anything you need, I'll do it."

"You are the good baby," she said as she walked into the kitchen.

"Give me two seconds, Mrs. B., and I'll be in to cut those pills for you. Don't try it yourself."

"No, I wait for you," she said, and when I turned to look at Abigail, she was giving me that weird smile again. Thin on the lips but bright in the eyes.

"Okay. What?" I asked.

"You know what you've got here, don't you?"

"What?"

She pointed toward the kitchen and said, "You've got yourself a girlfriend."

"I thought *you* were my girlfriend," I said, slipping my arm around her waist.

"Why would you think that?"

"You called me your boyfriend last night."

"Did I?" She shrugged. "I don't date guys who are already taken."

"I'm not taken," I said as the walkie-talkie I left on the table just inside the door crackled and popped.

"Mrs. B. to Briggs Baby. Come in to Briggs Baby."

"Mrs. B., I'm right here!" I called.

"You come," she said into the walkie-talkie. "I make for you the lunch. You ask Abigail she wants to stay."

"I will make my own lunch, Mrs. B.! Yours too!" I called. To Abigail, I said, "I'm still not taken."

"I still don't have time for a boyfriend."

"You're talking to the king of not-having-time. And from where I'm standing, it looks like you've got plenty."

"Maybe," she said as she stepped out the front door. "But it's not the right time."

"Briggs, you are *comink*? It is time for the lunch," Mrs. B. said into the walkie-talkie, and Abigail pressed her lips into a smile.

"I'll see you on the Fourth," she said. "And you *are* taken."

266

"I'm really not."

The walkie-talkie crackled again.

Abigail pulled the door shut behind her with a smile.

"Over and off," Mrs. B. said.

"Yeah, over and off," I said to absolutely no one.

109

North Beach was jammed on Saturday. Tons of sails on the water. Crowds at the snack bar. A city of beach umbrellas and masses of people. Frisbees and footballs tossed around. Kites overhead. And everything in the distance looked just a little wavy in the heat and the sun.

Our team rocked the volleyball tournament until about four o'clock, when we were getting tired and went up against a phenomenal team. Of Vikings. Eddie—Dez—DeZwaan was among them.

We got clobbered in the last two games of the match. The few points we scored came from Maddy distracting Dez by smiling at him with that tongue between her teeth.

"Damn," Brandon said, and kicked the sand. Then he nearly laughed and said to me, "Man, Geri, we weren't even close."

Ben flopped down on our towels and dug through our pile of bags, looking for something. He ended up pulling my walkie-talkie out and making a face at me, like, *Mrs. B.'s?* I just nodded, and he tossed it down on my towel.

"Hey, we'll beat 'em next year, right?" I said.

He looked at me like he had no idea who I was when he said, "Who knows where any of us is going to be next year?"

"Oh, me! Me! I'll be here!" Maddy said.

"Yeah?" I asked.

"Yeah. I'm going to South Valley Community. Going to be a vet tech."

"Why not a vet?" I asked.

"I can't be a vet," she said. "They do, like, surgery. And it takes, like, twelve years to become one."

"You could do it," I said.

"You payin'?" Brandon asked.

"Student loans."

"And be in debt forever," Brandon said. "Pass."

"I'm not saying it'd be easy, but you want to be good at anything, you got to work hard," I said.

"You guys are not listening." Maddy slapped both hands against her chest in rhythm to, "I want"—*slap*—"to be"—*slap*—"a tech"—*slap*.

"All I'm saying is that you'd make more money as a vet."

"Eh," Maddy said just as Dez and a buddy of his walked over carrying a huge cooler between them.

"Thought you guys could use this," he said. He set the thing down and opened it. It was filled with sodas and water and ice, and we helped ourselves and thanked the guy.

"You all played great," he said, and in one way he reminded me of that guy Dum. He just looked happy to be there. "Maddy," he said. "Excellent technique. Dis-tract the opposition with that gorgeous smile of yours."

"You are so sweet," she said, and hugged him.

Couple minutes later Brandon and I headed for the snack bar when I heard, "Briggs!"

I turned and saw Ben pushing through the crowd and dodging sunbathers. In his hand, he had my walkie-talkie, which I grabbed from him.

"Briggs here, Mrs. B. Everything okay?"

"No. No. *Everythink* is not okay. Your father calls. Your grandma *Root* is in hospital."

"Anybody got a phone?" I asked, and Ben pulled his from his back pocket.

"Thanks," I said, and dialed my dad's number as Brandon asked Ben, "His grandma's name is Root?"

110

At the hospital waiting room, in downtown Grand Rapids, I greeted Mom with a kiss on the cheek. Dad waved to me from the Patient Information Desk, then returned to tapping his fingers on the counter and annoying the hell out of the hospital staff.

On the phone, Dad told me that Grandma Ruth had fallen at home but was "awake and talking." I took time to shower at Mrs. B.'s. This was Grandma Ruth, after all. I couldn't go there stinking from the day.

"Son, it's been forty-seven minutes since you said we'd know something soon," Dad said to the tech behind the desk. Young guy. Didn't look much older than me, but the casual way he looked at my dad told me he'd had this job for a long time.

"Forty-seven minutes," Dad said. "Is there someone else I can talk to who might actually know something about my mother?"

The tech smiled at him, and I knew that expression. It was so similar to how we looked at the club members when they demanded to know where their dinner was. It said, *Sir, I deal with people like you all day long. I'm not withholding information just to annoy you, but since you and I have to share this space until my shift ends or you go home* (big smile) *how may I help you?*

"One moment, please, sir," he said.

"One moment," he repeated when he joined Mom and me in the blue-gray seating area—a color very close to Cadet Blue, and Mrs. B. was right. It was *too series* for her house.

"If I don't hear something in five minutes, I'm calling Sam's mother," Dad said.

"You are not," Mom said as she wrote a list of errands to run if Grandma Ruth needed to stay here long.

Then it finally occurred to my dad that we hadn't seen each other in a few weeks, and he smiled at me and rubbed my head and said, "You really do need a haircut."

About fifteen minutes later, when we saw Grandma Ruth sitting up on a bed in the ER, arms crossed tight against her chest, navy blazer and khakis as crisp as her face, we all felt relieved.

"Briggs," she demanded. "Why are you here?"

"Dad called."

"Well, he shouldn't have bothered you." She pointed at my mother and said, "Or you."

"We were all worried, Grandma Ruth," I said, and she tossed one hand in the air and puffed out, "Eh. What good does that do?"

A doctor with black-rimmed eyeglasses and a streaky blond ponytail introduced herself to us as Tricia Clarke. Dad told her she had "one heck of a good handshake. You could be in politics with that grip."

"Um. Thank you," she said.

Grandma Ruth had a short air boot on her left foot. A removable brace secured by three wide strips of Velcro. Every year, at least one guy on the team had to wear one. On Grandma Ruth's lap was her loafer.

"Mrs. Henry is fine," Dr. Clarke said. "She strained her ankle."

"Not even sprained," Grandma Ruth said directly to my dad. "I could have stayed home and applied ice and taken aspirin."

"Well, now, no aspirin," Dr. Clarke said, and began to explain about something called stomach bleeds, but Grandma Ruth cut her off.

"My stomach is fine, and I don't take prescription pain killers. Don't even bother sending any home with me."

"I've written one for—"

"I won't fill it. You shouldn't have wasted the paper."

"I do think your blood pressure's a little high," Dr. Clarke said.

"Of course it's high," Grandma Ruth said. "I'm furious. I was brought here against my will. I do not need to be here, and this has been a waste of everyone's time." She pointed at Dad. "Send him the bill."

"Well, it's something I'd like you to follow up on with your primary care doc," Dr. Clarke said.

"Fine. I would like to go home now," Grandma Ruth said. "Briggs, dear."

"Yes?"

"I'd like you to take me since I do not have my car here, and I am not currently speaking to your father. I certainly don't wish to enjoy his company on a thirty-minute drive."

"Sure thing, Grandma Ruth," I said as Dad laughed.

Grandma Ruth tried to refuse the wheelchair brought for her by an orderly but relented with, "Oh, for God's sake," when told it was hospital policy.

"My policy, Briggs dear," she said on our way out, "is to stay away from hospitals. Nothing good ever happens in them." She directed her eyes briefly up at Dad and said, "It's where I had him."

"Heh-heh," Dad laughed.

They were comics, these two.

111

"I twisted my ankle getting out of the car," Grandma Ruth explained on the ride back to her house, "and I fell and had a little trouble getting up."

I waited for more details. I waited twelve seconds before asking, "And?"

"That's it. I made the mistake of calling your father from the garage, and before I knew it, a squad had arrived, and they wheeled me out on a gurney with your father there directing the whole thing—or trying to—despite my insistence that I was fine." She tightened every muscle in her face when she said, "Oh, the spectacle."

"I'm sorry I wasn't there to help."

"Well, if you must know, so was I," she said, and my stomach twisted around itself. "You probably couldn't do much in an emergency, but since this wasn't one, you'd have been more useful than your father was."

"Well, I could've helped you into the house. Gotten you that ice and aspirin."

"I could have gotten my own ice and aspirin, thank you very much. I am not a helpless old woman, Briggs. Eh," she puffed.

We were quiet for about five or six more minutes. Quiet—as in no radio, no talking. Just the sounds of traffic, and there was surprisingly little, considering it was a holiday weekend.

Finally, Grandma Ruth spoke. She didn't look at me, though. She looked directly ahead when she said, "I don't want to be a helpless old woman."

"I don't think you'll ever be that, Grandma Ruth."

"This woman you work for."

"Mrs. B."

"She's in good health?"

"Yeah," I said, nearly laughing. "Pretty good. She had a dizzy spell yesterday, but she's okay. She goes to doctors' appointments all the time, but there's nothing majorly wrong with her."

"I'm glad to hear it. I think being an invalid would be . . ."

I waited, but she never finished the sentence.

At her house, she refused my arm when I offered it to her and hobbled inside on her own.

In the driveway, I texted my dad.

Me: **Got Gma Ruth home safely**

Dad: **I expected nothing less.**

Me: **She's still mad at u**

Dad: **She'll get over it.**

Me: **She's not an invalid**

I deleted that, and wrote, instead, **Doubt that**

Dad: **LOL!**

We Henrys were a laugh a minute.

My phone rang.

"Yes, Grandma Ruth," I said.

"If you're going to sit in my driveway all night, please do it with the lights off," she said. "The neighbors have had enough intrigue at my expense for one evening."

"Yes, Grandma Ruth," I laughed. "Hey, Grandma Ruth."

"Yes?"

"Good-bye."

"Eh."

112

I was soaking wet when I woke up. Soaking wet after a run. Soaking wet an hour after my shower.

"Mrs. B.," I said to her in the kitchen. "Something is wrong with your air conditioner. I'm pretty sure it's broken, and I don't know anything about fixing it."

"It is not broken," she said. She sat at the kitchen table and opened Monday's newspaper to the obituaries. "It is not on. Heat is on."

"Heat?"

"This is what I say."

"You know it's going up to ninety-two today. It's already seventy-nine."

"Yes."

"But you have your heat on?"

"Yes, it dries the house. When it is too hot outside, house feels *demp*."

"Damp?"

"This is what I say. You will see, Briggs Baby. You will feel better in the dry house."

"I'm pretty sure the AC will dry it out."

"No. The cold air just makes things cold. Heat dries.

Cold does not dry." She looked down at the paper and shined her apple cheeks into a smile. "Ah!"

"You find a good one?" I asked, because why not?

"Friday. We go. One o'clock. To *Sowgatuck*."

Saugatuck was a little village, kind of like an artists' colony, with tons of shops, cool galleries, and restaurants nineteen miles straight north of South Haven. There were usually bigger boats in Saugatuck's harbor than in South Haven's, but South Haven had better beaches. More of them too.

"Anyone we know?" I asked, in the spirit of funeral crashing.

"No. The person is *Shinese*. From *Pekink*."

"Peking, huh? Or Beijing, I think it's been called for a while now. I've never been to a Chinese funeral," I said, and guzzled a huge glass of ice water.

"No. I never go also. This one we will both like." She pressed that forefinger against her chin and said, "I wonder if the *Shinese* people believe in the heaven."

"I don't know, Mrs. B., but if they believe in hell, I'm pretty sure it's about as hot as your house."

"Mmm-mmm-mmm," she laughed as those little shoulders moved up and down.

Filed the whole morning under Random Things Old People Do. Then kind of laughed about it myself later that morning.

Mmm-mmm-mmm.

113

"Hello?" I heard a guy's voice call when I was in Mrs. B.'s garage the next morning, looking for more sandpaper.

"In here!" I called back, and Dez stepped in, looking like he was dressed for a car commercial on the beach. Orange-and-blue surf shorts, white button-down shirt with the sleeves rolled up, river sandals, big rope bracelet on his wrist.

"Hey, man," he said.

"Hey."

We shook hands.

"I wondered who Vesna's new help was," he said.

"Word gets around, huh?"

"It's a small town."

"You probably heard about—"

"Pauline Ostrander's funeral?" He nearly laughed while I shut my eyes tight at the memory and scratched the back of my neck.

"I'm sorry I missed that," he said.

"Yeah, that's too bad."

"But, hey, I just came by to make sure everything was

okay with your grandmother," Dez said. "I saw you take off the other day. Your friends said she was in the hospital in Grand Rapids. Is that right?"

"Oh. Hey. Thanks. Yeah, she's good. False alarm, really."

"Glad to hear it. I didn't know if I could help in any way, but I thought I'd offer. In case you or she needed anything. I'm at my folks' place"—he tipped his head to the left—"just that way."

"Thanks a lot, but, yeah, we're both okay."

"Cool," he said. "So I'm sure I'll see you around the neighborhood, or back at North Beach. Maybe we'll get up an unofficial rematch."

"Sounds good."

We shook hands again, and he left just as the God Yacht inched by.

"Dum!" Dez yelled.

Dum stopped, rolled down his window, and called out, "Dez, are you ready? *Are you ready?*"

"Ready as I'll ever be," he said, spreading his arms wide and laughing.

114

I floated star-shaped on my back, with arms and legs spread, up and down with the rhythm of the lake and its low, slow waves. The world and I felt weightless and silent, just for a few minutes, drifting somewhere between the blue-green water and blue-haze sky.

The wake of a Jet Ski washed over my face, and I stood, chest-deep, and spit but couldn't feel too pissed at the Jet Skier. After all, it was his lake too.

I walked ashore, my body returning to its normal weight with each step out of the lightness of the water. Abigail was home. She set her bag and towel on the beach, tucked her hair underneath that cowboy hat, and waved.

It was so damn hot, I didn't bother toweling off. Abigail walked over looking happy and bright and gave no signal at all that I should kiss her. Her parents were on their deck with a few people. Mrs. B. was on hers. Maybe she didn't want an audience.

She walked with me up to Mrs. B.'s deck and sat with us at the table there. I'd scrubbed all the furniture last week, and that stuff gleamed like new in the sun.

"I got a text from Maddy," Abigail said. "Everyone's meeting down at North Beach around nine for Light up the Lake."

"*Fires-works*," Mrs. B. explained. She raised her fists, then opened both hands quickly. "Boom."

"It's pretty crowded," Abigail said. "I was thinking we could watch from here."

"You go up to his *bellcony*," Mrs. B. said, pointing up. "Mr. B. and I watch from there when we are *younker*. Sometimes, we watch the storms come above the lake. He always holds my hand when we hear the *thahnder*."

"Aw, Vesna," Abigail said, reaching out to squeeze Mrs. B.'s hand. "You're a romantic."

"I don't know if I am romantic person, but Mr. B. and I had the nice life together. I am *lookink* forward to *seeink heem* again when I die. If I ever do." She shrugged and looked a little annoyed.

"You know, Mrs. B.," I said. "Most people are happy to know that nothing is wrong with them."

"Most people are not eighty-four with *everythink* in order," she said with another shrug. "I am ready to go anytime. But. I am still here. So. I wait."

"So in other words, you're ready for the future," Abigail said, glancing over at me, "and beyond."

I kind of laughed an "Oh my God" under my breath.

115

Abigail and I sat in comfy lounge chairs on the deck just off the kitchen listening to bursts of laughter coming from her parents' deck and watching eight or nine little kids play with sparklers one cottage over. Mrs. B. went to bed around 8:30, as usual, and wished me *the sweet dreams*. When I was little, Grandma Ruth sent me to bed with *sleep well, young man*. I always did. I was too afraid to disobey her orders.

Far over the lake, dark clouds spread themselves into thick sheets. A storm was coming, but the sky overhead, so far, remained clear.

"How was Chicago?" I asked Abigail.

"Enjoyable if sweltering," she said.

"You don't know sweltering until you've slept here with the heat on. Like I did. Last night."

"Oh, yeah," Abigail said. "Dries out the house. My grandmother does that sometimes. Does yours?"

"No. The woman is dry as dust already. Inside and out."

"You say these things about her, and they just make me wonder why she's like that."

"Yeah, me too."

"Why don't you ask her? You're good at asking nosy questions," she said.

"Interesting questions," I said. "I'm getting really good at asking interesting questions."

"Give me an example."

"Okay," I said, and pointed toward the beach. "I'm sleeping out there tonight. Want to join me?"

"That's an interesting invitation," she said. "But I probably shouldn't. I don't want you to get the wrong idea."

"What idea's that?"

"That I'm ready to be someone's girlfriend."

"You did call me your boyfriend."

"I slipped up."

"You don't strike me as the kind of person who slips up."

"Everyone slips up," she said.

"I'm not talking commitment here," I said. "Or anything . . . else. I just thought it would be nice to get close. And sleep under the stars."

"Too many clouds tonight," she said without looking up. She dropped her hand on my arm. I put my hand on top of hers. "And we probably shouldn't get *too* close, you know, given that we have way too much going on right now."

"Big changes," I said, and she nodded, and, man, I hated big changes.

"Okay, so, no pressure or anything, but how about same time, same place *next* year," I said, grinning at my own plan.

"Briggs," she said quietly, "I don't know. If I have it my way, I'll be a world away from here next summer."

"But you'll come back. Sometime, right?"

"I don't know. I really don't."

"Are you serious? How can you *not* want to live here? Forever?"

"I've lived here forever."

"Yeah, but this is the beach. Everything's . . ."

I ran my hand over my head and grabbed my neck and scratched it. Looked at Abigail. Looked at the water.

When I turned back to her, she was smiling at me like she did before, saying Mrs. B. was my girlfriend, and like I was finally in on the joke. Except it wasn't a joke to me.

"Everything's supposed to be better at the beach," I said.

I really thought we were better at the beach, because the beach was so damn perfect.

It never occurred to me we were just tourists.

Tourists on break from our lives.

116

By ten that night, Abigail and I were up on my balcony. Up and down the beach, we heard small pops and crackles and whistles and laughter. Then everything grew quiet, and all we heard was the sound of the waves washing up on shore.

Right at the edge of the horizon, we saw several flashes of lightning that appeared small and red, but overhead, the sky was clear.

We got comfortable. Stretched our legs out onto the railing. Crossed our ankles. Leaned our heads back in the chairs.

"So, are we just going to be platonic now?" I asked lightly.

"Platonic?"

"It's a word," I said, and Abigail puffed out a little laugh just as we heard the thump of the first shell fired.

"Be quiet or you'll spoil the fireworks," she said, and a trio of red, white, and blue starbursts opened the show.

"That's fires-works to you," I said, and I copied Mrs. B.'s little game of charades, making fists, then opening them. "Boom."

117

We sat listening to random bangs, random crackles and whistles, random voices on the beach for a few minutes. Then we listened to it all trail off with only the odd little firecracker popping every now and then and echoing up and down the shore.

Smoke from the show's finale hung heavy over North Beach, and the storm at the horizon slowly moved our way.

"I'm going to head back," Abigail said.

"I'll walk you home."

"I think I can manage."

We started downstairs.

"Yeah," I said, "but I want to. Also, you never answered my question."

"What question was that?"

We tiptoed across the second-floor landing and past Mrs. B.'s room, where she snored like a bulldog.

"Are we just going to be friends?" I asked, grinning at her like I already knew the answer.

"Hmm," she said, and thought about it until we were

back on the sand. "What's between friend and boyfriend-slash-girlfriend?"

"Us, at the moment."

We heard a long, low growl of thunder.

"Then let's just enjoy the moment," she said.

I was silent for a sec. "Okay, I can do that."

We walked through cool sand to the steps up to her deck, where her parents and their friends sat talking.

"Good," she said, and started up the stairs. "Because I can't handle anything more serious than that at the moment."

"Yeah," I said, "okay," and walked back to Mrs. B.'s wondering if Abigail was watching me as I went, but not willing to risk turning around and seeing she wasn't.

118

That night, I didn't sleep much. Part of it was the storm, which came late—so much for sleeping outside—and which I watched, one shoulder pressed against the sliding door frame. Some cracks of thunder shook the house. Mrs. B. slept through it all.

Part of it was Abigail, of course. The best part.

And the part that kept me awake between thunder claps and Abigail was my parents.

I spent a good chunk of that night trying to remember what life was like before Dad sold his dealership. How it was different. How *we* were different. But here's the thing. It wasn't. We weren't. We just had a bigger house.

And a dog.

119

Mrs. B. lay on the kitchen floor the next morning. Since it was raining, I expected it, but my heart still beat a little faster at the sight of her there.

"Morning, Mrs. B.," I said.

"I am not dead, Briggs Baby."

"Neither am I, Mrs. B."

"Mmm-mmm-mmm."

120

Couple days later, Mrs. B. and I exchanged Dusk and Dawn for Blue Hydrangea. On Friday, we attended the Chinese funeral. Abigail came along, because who doesn't enjoy a Chinese funeral? On Saturday my life fell apart.

On Sunday I drove Mrs. B. to church. So it was a full week. Also, the house was dried out. Hot as a furnace. But dry.

121

So, last Friday morning:

I ran past the bank of newspaper boxes in town, and doubled back when a picture in the *South Haven Tribune* caught my eye. It was Eddie DeZwaan, and the headline read *Hometown man hits "Big Time" in Hollywood.* Turned out, Dez had landed a co-starring role in the next Matt Damon flick and was home for a couple weeks to celebrate the news with family and friends.

I'd have bought a copy of the paper for Maddy, but the only cash I had was Mom's emergency twenty, and I didn't want to break it just for that.

122

Later that same morning, Abigail walked through Mrs. B.'s front door wearing a short white dress and black heels that brought her close to my height.

"It's a tradition," she said, pointing at her dress. "I looked it up last night. At a Chinese funeral, only the family wears black because their grief is the profoundest. Everyone else wears any color except red, which is the color of joy and happiness. And if you don't know the decedent very well—"

"Decedent," I repeated.

"It's a word," she said, and then continued, "You should wear white."

"We should've been wearing white all summer, Mrs. B.," I said quietly to her.

"Do we have time for one quick detour?" Abigail asked, and pulled the *South Haven Tribune* from her purse. "I want to drop this off at Maddy's."

"We have the times," Mrs. B. said.

"Right," I said, looking at the paper. "Is it far?"

"No. I'm sure you've passed it a dozen times on your runs."

And she was right. I had. Within six minutes, Mrs. B. and I were sitting in my car, watching Abigail ring the doorbell at a grubby shack of a house with eight plastic flamingoes stuck in the dirt that passed for a front yard.

123

A bunch of mourners at Li-Li Young's memorial service wore black. None looked Chinese. They obviously hadn't done their homework like Abigail.

We sat on an aisle at the funeral home behind two balding men with a large tote bag between them that had this printed in red on the side: *Never Trust a Person Who Doesn't Love Dogs.*

At the front of the room there must have been thirty bouquets of flowers in clear or black vases. Most of the flowers were red and white, and they were displayed in groups on different-sized tables. Like they were going to be judged and awarded ribbons after the service.

Not six seconds after we sat, a tiny dog that looked to be made entirely of cotton and static stuck its head out of the bag and yipped at us.

"Shush," Mrs. B. told it, while Abigail reached to pet it, and I remembered a couple old ladies at Bluestone Court who carried their little dogs in big bags too. I just didn't know anyone would take them to a funeral. But I had seen some odd stuff that summer. This was just more of it.

The cotton-and-static dog yipped again. One of the

men mouthed "Sorry" at us and cradled the shaking fuzzball on his lap.

"You know, I got sent out of the church for making noise at a funeral," I said quietly to Mrs. B., who patted my knee and said, "You shush too." It made me laugh a little while I double-checked that my phone was off.

Abigail signaled me with a nod to her right. Across the aisle from us, I saw another woman with another small dog on her lap. Two rows up, a young man and woman fed treats to some kind of little terrier with a blue scarf around its neck, and minutes later, two more men walked in, each holding a Chihuahua.

"Mrs. B.," I said. "Are we in the wrong place?"

"No, this is where the *obit-wary* says to go."

"You're sure?" I asked, and, oh my God, a second dog popped its head out of the *Never Trust a Person, etc.,* tote bag. And it pointed its bulging eyes right at Mrs. B. and blinked nervously.

"I have with me the *noosepaper*," Mrs. B. said as she began searching through her purse, which she called her *pocketsbook*.

As she dug, an older man, with a rim of white hair and deep creases from his nose to the corners of his mouth, walked to the front of the room and thanked everyone for coming and for "bringing your darling babies with you. My Li-Li loved dogs. All dogs." He pressed both hands over his heart and said through a cracking voice, "It would have meant so much to her to see this turnout and to know how important she was not just to me but to you too."

"Mrs. B.?" I whispered.

"I am *lookink*," she whispered back.

"Check your skirt pockets," I suggested.

"Li-Li was the center of my life," the man continued. "Which is exactly how she liked it." That got some quiet laughs, including from Abigail.

"Ah. Here," Mrs. B. said, handing me the neatly clipped and folded obituary.

"Li-Li loved . . ." the man said and stopped, swallowed, trying to regain his voice, as I quickly scanned the obit. ". . . three things."

"Mrs. B.," I said, keeping my voice low.

"She loved me, of course," the man said to audible sighing.

"We are not at a Chinese funeral," I said, and Abigail leaned close.

"*Pekink*," Mrs. B. said, pointing at the obit. "She is from *Pekink*. She is Chinese."

"She loved her friends," the man said.

"That doesn't say *Peking*," I said.

"And she loved a good game of fetch," he said.

"It says *Pekingese*," I said.

"Yes. *Pekink-ese*. From *Pekink*."

"Mrs. B., we're at a dog funeral."

"From the moment I rescued her at ten weeks old, she was my life," the man said, and his voice cracked, and he pressed the bottoms of his palms into both eyes for a second. "She was part of me for sixteen years. You know what it's like when you love and lose an animal. You're never the same again." He cleared his throat.

"You're never the same because part of you is missing. It's that little piece of your heart they take with them, but it's also that little piece that connects you, I think." His eyes filled. "No matter where Li-Li is right now, my heart is with her too." He cleared his throat again and showed us a red rubber crab. "She loved this," he said. He squeezed it. It squeaked. And all the dogs in the room started yapping like crazy.

The man laughed. I did too. He wiped away tears, even as fresh ones fell down his face.

Around me, everyone was wiping their eyes and laughing. The cotton-and-static dog licked its owner's face.

Abigail pressed both hands over her lips, her eyes watering, her mouth smiling. On the other side of me, I heard *mmm-mmm-mmm*, *mmm-mmm-mmm*, *mmm-mmm-mmm* and saw Mrs. B.'s shoulders moving up and down as she lifted her glasses and brushed away tears.

I felt a tap on my shoulder.

I turned, expecting someone to hand me a tissue, but saw a vaguely familiar woman, with deep lines in her forehead, like an accordion, holding the leash of an entirely familiar dog. A Portuguese water dog, a little gray around his snout. With a collar that read *Wesley*.

124

"Briggs?" the woman whispered, and shot me a really warm smile.

"Yes," I said.

"I thought that was you. Susie Gray," she said, pointing at herself.

All I could do was nod.

She tugged a little on the leash and seemed so proud of herself when she asked, "You know who this is, don't you?"

"Yes," I said again, looking between her and the dog. My dog. Cutlass.

He had no idea who I was and was far more interested in the little dogs in front of me. Because he wasn't my dog. He was Wesley. And like Abigail did sometimes but for a very different reason, I had to leave. Fast.

125

"Are you okay?" Abigail asked me after I helped Mrs. B. into the front passenger seat of my car.

"Fine. Yeah. Why?"

"You look upset, and you sound upset. Did the funeral get to you?"

"I'll tell you later."

"Tell me now," she said, so I did, and her face softened, and the tension disappeared from her mouth and eyes, and her shoulders fell a little, and I snapped at her, "Please don't give me that look."

"What look?"

"Pity."

"It's not—"

"It is. Do you want people looking at you like that when they find out you've got Crohn's?"

She tipped her chin up a little when she said, "No. I don't."

We climbed into the car then.

Mrs. B. was still laughing, still rubbing one eye.

It was kind of hard to stay pissed.

126

Mrs. B. asked me to take the *seen-it* route home from Saugatuck.

"Scenic?" I asked.

"This is what I say."

"This is actually not what you said, Mrs. B., but I'm happy to take you any way you want to go."

The route was a little over twenty miles on a two-lane road that took us past blueberry farms and undeveloped land of sandy scrub or stands of white birch trees. There were a couple of farm markets along the way. A few shabby old houses. And four or five antiques shops.

The sun lasered its rays at the road, shining like water in spots, and turned the horizon silver and wavy. Even with the windows up and the AC on, you could smell the hot asphalt.

We had just passed a shop called Aunt Fanny's Attic when Abigail said, "Can we stop there, please?"

"You like the antiques shops?" Mrs. B. asked as I glanced at Abigail in the rearview mirror and made a sharp left turn into the place.

Her entire face was tight and red.

"Mrs. B., we'll be right back," I said as Abigail and I hurried inside.

"You all right?" I asked.

"I'll be fine," she said, clutching her gut with one hand and taking short, quick breaths.

A little bell above the door rang and a gray-haired guy with a shaggy mustache said, "'Lo," from behind a counter covered with dolls and china figurines.

"She needs a bathroom," I said, and this douche pointed to a sign on a post behind him and didn't say anything.

Restroom Is for Customers ONLY.

"Mister, this is an emergency," I said as Abigail bent forward in pain.

"Gas station's nine miles that way," he said. Again, pointing.

"You gotta be kidding me," I said as Abigail said, "I'm not going to make that."

"Man, come on," I said, but the guy just stared at me. I thought about decking him but instead grabbed the nearest figurine—about six inches high, a little girl in a red hat and dumb shoes with a butterfly on her finger—and said, "This. I'm buying this. Where's the bathroom?"

"Right there," he said pointing to his left, and Abigail hurried in.

"That'll be eight fifty," he said to me.

"Ridiculous," I muttered, pulling that pre-paid credit card Dad gave me about a month ago out of my wallet.

That's when the guy pointed to another sign, just below the one about the restroom.

NO Checks
NO Credit
CASH ONLY

I gave him my emergency twenty.

Abigail emerged from the bathroom a full sixteen minutes later. She made a weak smile when I gave her the figurine but didn't say anything. Back home, she disappeared for a few days.

127

Zipping home Sat. afternoon, I IM-ed Sam from my laptop.

Sam: Swing by here 1st. Got to run something past u

Me: What time?

Sam: Time is an illusion that disappears in the face of absolute being

Me: What?

Sam: Never mind. Come around 1

I IM-ed Abigail just once.

How do U feel?

She wrote back: Dyspeptic

128

I called my parents from the road Saturday, but neither of them answered their phones, and I didn't bother leaving messages. I just wanted to zip in and grab a different tie since I'd worn the same one to so many funerals. It was starting to kind of freak me out just looking at it. Like, this was my Waxy Corpse Tie. My Two Shovels of Dirt Tie. My Someone Else Has My Dog Tie.

I got to Forest Hills about 12:30 and texted Sam, who wasn't home yet, so I headed to my house first. Mom's car was in the garage. Dad's wasn't.

"Hey, it's me," I said, walking in the back door, where Mom and Sam's dad were hugging. And not just hugging. So much more than just hugging. It was close, intimate.

They pulled apart quickly.

Guess I surprised them.

Guess this is what Sam wanted to run past me.

Guess I was going to have to flatten his dad now.

129

"What the hell?" I asked, stepping between him and Mom.

"Briggs," Mr. Nguyen said, extending his hand to me.

"What's going on here?" I pushed his hand away.

"Briggs," Mom said. "You startled us."

"Obviously. What do you think you're doing?" I asked Mr. Nguyen.

"Briggs," he said, holding his palms out toward me.

"Briggs!" Mom said louder, and that's when I noticed her face was red and splotchy, and she had been crying.

My God. My mom was crying. Immediately, I felt sick, confused.

Weirder still—Sam's mom was there. Sitting at one of the stools at the kitchen island, her black hair twisted into a knot at the back of her head, which is how she wore it at work. She was my pediatrician when I was little. She motioned with her head to the stool next to her and said in a tone that was both serious and kind, "Why don't you sit there, Briggs."

I thought this must be how she looks when she gives bad news to her patients' families, but what was she doing here?

"I'm, uh—I'm good here," I said. I rubbed my hands over my face. "What?" I put my hand on my mom's elbow and asked, "What is going on?"

"The Nguyens are here helping," she said.

"Helping what?"

"Helping me," she said.

There were papers all over the counter. Bank statements. Spreadsheets. Canceled checks. There were legal pads, pens and pencils, and two calculators. There were lists in my mother's handwriting. One enumerated five items with the first three checked off.

- *Income tax returns*
- *Insurance policies*
- *Wills*
- *Property tax returns*
- *Business financial statement*

"What is this?" I asked. "Where's Dad?"

"At work," Mom said. "Where is he ever?"

"But what *is* this?"

"Briggs," she said, and the look on her face terrified me.

The last time I'd felt like this I was nine, and Mom and Dad were packing up the kitchen in the house on the thirteenth fairway, and no one was talking, and the dog was gone.

"I'm leaving your father."

130

Kennedy's car was in front of Sam's house when I got there. I didn't even remember the drive there. Or walking around his house. I just kind of materialized out back and watched as the basketball Sam threw me bounced past me into the neighbors' yard.

Kennedy ran after it.

"I just came from my house," I said, and Sam shook his head.

"I wanted to tell you before," he said, "but I wanted to do it in person."

"How did you find out?"

"Your mom's here a lot. Apparently it's a parental misconception that no one under the age of twenty-one can hear adults talking two rooms away."

"When did you find out?" I asked as Kennedy returned, dribbling the ball.

"You mean about your parents?" he asked.

"How do *you* know?"

"He told me," Kennedy said, pointing at Sam, who was making big sweeping Xs with his long arms and mouthing the word *no*.

He froze mid X when I looked at him. I grabbed the back of my neck with both hands and squeezed until it hurt.

"You told Kennedy before you told me?"

"Briggs, I'm sorry, but like I said, I wanted to tell you in person."

"Yeah, in person," Kennedy said as he sank the ball through the hoop. "That's how I told Taylor."

"You—you told *Taylor*?" Well, that explained those weird are-you-okay texts she'd been sending me. "So—what—everyone knows but me?"

"Hey, don't be mad at me," Sam said. "This isn't the kind of thing you text someone."

"It also isn't the kind of thing you tell everyone before you tell me," I said.

"We're your friends," Sam said.

"That makes it worse," I said, and I spit a sour taste out of my mouth. I grabbed my phone out of my back pocket. "One of you should have said something," I said as I quickly texted Taylor.

"When? You're never around," Sam said.

"What is that? My fault?"

"Well, maybe if you spent more time with your family, you'd have known before we did," Sam said as Kennedy's phone beeped.

"It's Taylor," he said, looking at his screen. "She's pissed at me."

I stared at Sam and felt sweat at my temples and weirdly light-headed. Detached.

I turned and headed back toward my car as Kennedy asked Sam, "You're just going to let him go like that?"

Sam didn't answer.

What was there to say?

131

I drove the sweltering hour back to South Haven with the windows open and music blaring. It was muggy out, and muggy inside, and I couldn't make sense of a single thought. They came too quickly. All I knew when I arrived at Mrs. B.'s was that I couldn't stay. I needed to be out of the house, so I went for a run, but every step, pounding against the pavement, pounded my anger up through my body, higher, bigger, like a hammer hitting hot steel against an anvil. And in a bizarre way, it felt good. Jarring and scorching and right.

I was still mad when I reached the lighthouse, still mad when I backtracked through town, still mad when I detoured through the burbs. Still mad when I met up with Ben and Brandon and everyone on North Beach for some killer games of volleyball. I took it all out on the ball, and my team won every game. And I was still mad.

I felt sharp inside. And dry. And worn out.

I flopped back on some towels and woke up forty minutes later to cool drops of water falling from Maddy's hair onto my face and chest. The cold against my skin felt harsh and raw.

"Briggs? Are you sleeping?" Maddy asked, then said to someone, "He is really out of it."

"Is Geri dead?" Brandon asked.

"I'm awake." I stretched and brushed off more drops of water when Maddy waved to someone across from me. I propped myself up on my elbows to see the bleached blond Dez wave back to her.

"That guy's still here?" I asked.

"He's throwing a big party on a friend's boat next Saturday, and I heard it's huge," she said.

"The party or the boat?" Brandon asked.

"The boat, the party, both, I guess," Maddy said.

She and Brandon were the only ones around. Didn't know where everyone else went.

"We should go," Maddy said.

"Thought you hated boaters," I said.

"We do," Brandon said. "But the boats are nice."

"I wouldn't mind having a yacht someday," Maddy said. "I'd name it—I'd name it— I don't know. What would I name it?"

"Not gonna happen on a vet tech's salary," I said, and sat up.

"Dude," Brandon kind of laughed.

Maddy just blinked at me.

"It's not," I said. "We used to have a boat. You want to own one someday, you've got to make more than a vet tech makes in ten years. You've got to pick the right field and work your ass off. That's how you get ahead. And then you wreck your family in the process, but, hey, at least you've got your boat."

"Uh—what the hell, Geri?"

"Everyone wants to be rich, right?" I said, and I wanted to spit again, but my mouth was dry. I looked at Maddy. "I'm just saying you should be a vet tech and be happy in the crappy shoebox you live in. Put a hundred flamingoes in the yard, 'cause, you know, why the hell not?" I started grabbing my stuff. "That's what we should have done."

And then I watched as Maddy's face melted, and big, round tears poured out of her big, brown eyes. And she wiped her face with her arm, and she said, "Excuse me." She actually said, "Excuse me," as she got up and ran for the bathroom at the snack bar.

"Maddy!" I called. "Maddy, wait!"

"Friggin' tourist," Brandon said, walking past me in Maddy's direction.

"Hey, man, I'm sorry!" I called, but Brandon jogged off.

132

I finished packing up my stuff and left North Beach without looking back. What was the point.

133

It was going on midnight a few nights later when I wandered out to the beach, down to the lake. I'd been avoiding most people and trying to avoid myself by working inside, sanding and refinishing doors and drawers, fixing running toilets, and painting the whole third floor Blue Hydrangea.

Now I dropped one of Mrs. B.'s beach towels on the sand and stretched out on it. It was scratchy. Or I was. The night air was warm and thick and damp. The lake was still. There was someone standing over me.

"Wha—" I shouted, and bolted upright. I spluttered as my eyes focused, and I saw and heard Abigail giggling out her apology and holding out a bag of Oreo cookies.

"Want one?"

"Oh my God. You scared the hell out of me."

"Sorry," she said, and bit a chunk off a cookie and sat down on my towel. I stood for another minute. Until the adrenaline subsided, and I was sure I wasn't having a heart attack.

Finally I sat and powered down three cookies.

"I heard about what you said to Maddy," she said.

"Yeah. I—I don't even have words for that. I'm sorry about the whole damn thing." I shook my head, shut my eyes tight for a second, felt sick.

"What's going on?"

"Well, my mom's leaving my dad, and all my friends knew about it before I did. He still doesn't know. He's just walking around oblivious, like everything's normal. How've you been?"

"Better than you." She leaned her shoulder into mine. "Better than Maddy's been for a couple days."

"Please do not give me grief about that. I feel bad enough."

"Yeah, okay."

"Sorry. I'm just—" I didn't finish.

Abigail placed her hand on my arm, and I flinched and said, "Man, your hand is cold."

She slid it under her leg, and I said, "Sorry, I just—I just need to sit here and think. I think."

"I hear this is the best place for it," she said. And she stayed there next to me, not saying a thing.

134

We had been out there for hours. Eating Oreos and listening to the slow, quiet rhythm of small waves turning to foam on the shore.

"The thing is, I get it," I finally said. "I mean, if I'm being honest, I get why my mom wants to leave him. She hasn't been happy for years. I'm not sure she ever was. Or we ever were. Except when we were here." I forced some kind of weak smile. "On vacation.

"My dad," I said, and shook my head. "My dad," I said again like I was sad for him and for Mom. And for me.

Like some kind of echo in my head, I heard Dad say, "Sixteen percent of twenty-three is twenty-three percent of sixteen."

Failure is not an option.

Do what I'm doing but do it backward.

What do ghosts eat for breakfast?

Ah, you need a haircut.

I think it would have crushed him to find out I never really found him all that funny. I just had a smile that let him think I did.

135

Back at K City Creative Paints, patient Chuck with the huge teeth took his break when we walked in, and Suzanne with normal-sized teeth helped us. I didn't bother learning the name of the color Mrs. B. chose. I knew she was going to hate it.

Mom sent me e-mail and texts every day. Short notes, which I hadn't returned, which made me feel guilty, so I called her from the parking lot while Mrs. B. checked out.

"Can you talk?" I asked.

"I can. Your father's not here. He's at work, of course."

"Yeah."

"I'm sorry you found out that way," she said. "I planned on telling you after you were settled in school so it wouldn't be too stressful for you. You'd be busy then."

"Yeah," I said again, and kicked at a few pebbles on the asphalt.

"I still plan on telling your father then for the same reason. He'll be upset. There's no good time for it, but at least you won't have to see it."

"Sounds to me like you were pulling a Grandma

Ruth," I said. "Leaving without saying good-bye. Never look back."

"I always thought there was something kind of admirable in that," Mom said.

"Yeah. And something kind of sad."

136

Every morning since last weekend, I stopped at Maddy's house on my run. Knocked on the door. Heard people inside, but no one ever answered.

I looked for her twice down at North Beach. Nicole never looked up from applying her sunscreen when she said, "Maddy's not here."

I thought I saw her, blended in among the hundreds of other beachgoers, though. In her flamingo-pink bikini.

Brandon had told everyone what a douche I'd been. They were sending a pretty clear *piss-off* vibe.

"Hey, do me a favor," I said to Ben when I saw him on North Beach, "and tell her I'm sorry."

"You could tell her yourself," he said.

"I've tried. *Am* trying," I said. "I've been to her house every day."

"Who's up for a game?" Brandon asked. Then he looked over my shoulder, jerked his head to shift those bangs, and called, "Dez, you wanna play?" He looked right at me when he said, "We're short a guy."

137

Sunday morning on my run I nodded to the few fishermen I had come to recognize by sight now. We still never
disturbed the silence with an actual "hi."

As I made my way back through town, I passed the
newspaper street boxes and nearly pulled a hamstring
when I stopped and turned back. This was the headline:

South Haven Celeb Drowns in Tragic Boating Accident

Underneath it was a full-color picture of Eddie "Dez"
DeZwaan taken the day he and his team won the volleyball tournament before the Fourth. Brandon, Maddy,
and I were in the background, clapping for the winners.

138

I sprinted back to Mrs. B.'s and saw Abigail climbing into the God Yacht with Dum.

"You heard?" I called as I jogged next door.

"We're just headed over to Maddy's now," Abigail said.

I raised a hand at Dum, who looked wrecked, worse than wrecked, and then pulled my eyes back to Abigail. "Hey, tell her I'm sorry."

"She knows," Abigail said. "She's seen you stop by every morning."

"Why won't she open the door?"

"She just wants to make you work a little harder."

"Tell her I'll make it my job."

139

After I picked Mrs. B. up from church, I sat with her at the kitchen table and read the article two more times. Third time, I read it out loud.

It began, "A boating accident last evening on Lake Michigan has claimed the life of a South Haven man and injured three others.

"Police say speed and alcohol were factors in the crash that caused the death of twenty-year-old Edward DeZwaan, who was knocked unconscious and fell overboard when the boat in which he was riding struck another vessel at approximately fifty miles an hour.

"'When you're going that fast, hitting the water is like hitting the ground,' said U.S. Coast Guard Officer Nick VandePels."

The names of the others who were injured followed. And then this:

"DeZwaan, a recent graduate of L. C. Mohr High School, moved to Los Angeles after graduation in the hopes of beginning a film career. Commercial work and bit parts led to screen tests, and DeZwaan was recently cast in a supporting role in a film starring and produced by Matt Damon, which was to begin filming next spring.

"DeZwaan was home for the month of July celebrating the news with his family.

"'He did what most people only dream about,' said his father, Joseph DeZwaan. 'He wanted to be an actor his whole life, and he was on his way to becoming a star. And he would have been. He would have been a big star.'"

I folded the paper and slid it away from me and stared out the kitchen window at the water. The sky was fuzzy that day, and the water was grayish blue. It was impossible to tell where one ended and the other began.

140

"His parents go to same *shursh,*" Mrs. B. said.

"Yours?"

"Yes. His funeral is there."

"At least it'll be short," I said, and before Mrs. B. could ask, I said, "We used to be Episcopalians. Like you."

"No, I am not the Episcopalian."

"Excuse me?" I asked after tearing at a piece of toast. I wasn't really hungry.

"No. I am Serbian. Most Serbs are Orthodox. So. I am Orthodox."

"Wait. You're not Jewish. I know that."

Mrs. B. scrunched up her entire face, drawing all her features around her nose, when she asked, "Why I am *goink* to Episcopalian *shursh* if I am Jewish person?"

"I have no idea."

"You never hear of Orthodox *Shursh?*"

"No."

She shrugged and said, "Ah. This is okay. Most Americans never hear of it."

"So what is it?"

"It is old. Very old religion. In Serbia, you are Orthodox or you are Catholic or you are Muslim."

"But you go to an Episcopal church?"

"Closest Orthodox *shursh* is *Kahlahmahzoo*, and the services there. Oh," she said, and tossed her hands in the air. "They are too *lonk*. Mr. B. and I go two times. Service starts at nine thirty. Service ends at three thirty."

"Six hours?"

"Yes, and it is too *lonk* to *leesen* to priest *talkink* and *talkink* and *talkink*. I start *prayink*, 'When will this end, God?' So. We find the closer *shursh*."

"Why Episcopalian?"

"They have the best *feesh* fry on the Friday nights *durink* the Lent. Orthodox are not supposed to eat the *feesh* or the meat *durink* the Lent, but"—she shrugged and grinned a little—"everyone cheats."

"So when it comes to—" I began, and couldn't believe I was actually asking this. "When it comes to—your— you know—funeral . . ."

"Ah." She raised that index finger and nearly smiled.

"Where will it be?"

"There are other Orthodox *shurshes* in *Grahnd Rahpids*. The priest will perform the service. But." Up went that finger again. "Memorial service happens here. In my house. Friends come. They tell to each other, 'She was nice lady.' And they eat and talk and have the good time. You will come."

"I will come, Mrs. B.," I said. "I just don't want to come too soon."

327

She shined those apple cheeks at me for a full five seconds before she got more serious and said, "It does not have to be soon, Briggs Baby, but I do not want to be the *seek* person for the *lonk* times."

Immediately I pictured Grandma Ruth, staring out the car window, saying nearly the same thing the night she twisted her ankle. I hadn't called her about Mom and Dad. I knew there was no way Mom had told her the news, and I didn't want to let it slip.

"No," I said. "It would be awful."

"It is lonely."

"Lonely," I repeated. "Hmm."

"Friends do not like to come around the *seek* person," she said. "No one wants to die alone, Briggs Baby."

"Is that why you wanted live-in help this summer? Just in case?" I asked, and she didn't answer. She just patted my knee three times and smiled until her cheeks turned red and bright as crabapples.

141

It was standing room only at St. Mark's Episcopal Church, which appeared to comfortably seat two hundred. No one sat comfortably. More than two hundred of us squished into the pews. Mrs. B. pressed against my right shoulder. Miss Mae pressed against my left. Mrs. Steiner crushed in next to her. They didn't say a word through most of the service.

Rev. Sharon Warner, who spoke like a really strict English teacher, officiated. She nodded at us between prayers and sometimes even between sentences.

"The Lord be with you," she said.

Mrs. B. and I and every other Episcopalian in the place knew to respond, "And also with you." But what I really meant was, "When will this end, God?"

Rev. Warner dragged the thing out much longer than I thought it would last, but the worst was yet to come. Dez's father rose to give the eulogy. He walked to the podium and bowed his head at the crowd like he was thanking us for being there. He set his notes in front of him and said quietly, "I can't. I can't. I can't do this." And he turned away and sobbed into a handkerchief he pulled from his pocket. Other sobs echoed around the church. Sniffling. Stuttered breath. Noses being blown.

I barely met Dez, so I suddenly felt embarrassed, like some kind of gawker, watching his father break down like that. I looked at my shoes just to be less intrusive, and I tried not to notice the man crying and losing his breath. But it was impossible. Finally, he pulled himself together enough to turn back to the congregation, apologize, and begin his eulogy.

"My boy," he said, and instantly started crying again, so heavily, I thought he might even throw up.

The woman I correctly supposed to be Dez's mom joined John Dumchak in helping the dad return to his seat, and Dez's mom took his place at the lectern. She spoke for only three minutes, pausing twice to swallow back her own tears. She called her son Eddie, not Dez, and described him as special, a good son, a good friend, a good person, a good man.

"But he wasn't a man, was he? He was twenty, and that's still a boy to me. A baby."

She called him kind and thoughtful and fun, and she gave us a breather when she said, "He was no Boy Scout, though. He had his faults. I swear that boy could not tell time, and I don't think he ever understood what hangers were for." Lots of people sighed out something resembling laughter.

Then she spoke of his big heart and how it never embarrassed him to say "I love you" to her or to his father or to his siblings or to his friends.

"But more important than that," she said, and her

voice cracked, "is that he knew we loved him. He knew. And that will be enough"—her voice got thick here—"to sustain me. It will have to be. And it will. I don't need to say it to him one more time for his sake." She cried and barely managed, "I only do for mine."

Dum and another guy helped Mr. DeZwaan, bent at the waist and shaking, out a side door. From different places in the church, a man and a woman shimmied out of their pews and followed.

"Dr. Williams and Dr. Singh," Miss Mae whispered to me. She even smiled, like she was relieved for something else to think about and dabbed at her eyes with the tissue I had given her earlier, my last one.

Mrs. B. handed me another just then, and I thanked her by tapping her knee three times.

142

Maddy and Abigail sat at the back of the church, along with Ben, Brandon, and their crowd. Nearly the same crowd at Pauline Ostrander's funeral a month and a half ago. I passed them on my way out. Only this time, no one whispered to each other. No one gave me a hard time about my phone. No one—not even Abigail—smiled into the distance.

143

It was chilly and overcast when I reached North Beach that evening, and pretty much everyone there—about sixty people in various-sized groups—wore sweatshirts and shorts. I liked cool days at the lake, but that one was impossible to enjoy.

Earlier, the DeZwaan family held a private interment, and Rev. Warner announced that they wouldn't be receiving visitors. Turned out reporters had been calling them, and they just wanted a few days of peace and quiet.

Abigail, Ben, Maddy, and their friends sat in a circle on a bunch of towels and one green-and-white-striped blanket. Maddy cried, and Brandon put an arm tight around her shoulder. Abigail sat next to Ben, talking quietly.

"Hey," I said as I walked up.

"Hi," Abigail said. Ben too.

"Geri," Brandon said, and looked at me like he was considering either hitting me or spitting in my face.

"We were all just talking about Dez," Abigail said, and moved closer to Ben to make room. "Want to join us?"

"Sure," I said, and sat as Brandon asked, "Why? You didn't know him."

"I met him," I said. "He seemed like a good guy."

"He was," Maddy said, without looking at me.

"Hey, hey, hey," Brandon said, sounding and looking excited. "You remember Alexis Brown?"

"Yeah, yeah."

"She's the one——"

"Right."

"Wait, who?"

"The chick he took to homecoming. When he won king," Brandon said.

"She was kind of odd," Abigail whispered to me. "And pathologically shy. She had never gone to a homecoming game or dance, and Dez thought she should. Just once. So he asked her to go with him."

"Nice," I said.

"I saw her today," Brandon said. "She looks great. Still hard to talk to, though."

"Wait, I saw her. Was she sitting next to Connor Cohen?"

"Oh, man!" Ben laughed. "Do you remember when Connor Cohen——"

"And Brittany Maier?!"

"Yes!" Ben laughed.

"In Dez's car?"

"His mom's car!"

They laughed again. Even Maddy, who wiped her face dry on her sleeves. They were all laughing and talking across each other, and I got up to go. Couple of them said see ya later. Abigail asked me to stay, but I just said nah.

"Maddy," I said, and most of the group quieted down.

She looked up at me with red, swollen eyes.

"I'm really sorry about what I said." And I handed her the tissue I had in my pocket.

She nodded, and I walked back to Mrs. B.'s thinking about Grandma Ruth, who left when she wanted and never looked back.

I looked back.

No one was looking my way.

144

I spent the next few days cleaning Mrs. B.'s gutters, unclogging one toilet and two sinks, and sealing the deck.

I wasn't so sure I wanted a place at the beach anymore. They were so much work to maintain.

145

I sprinted from the lighthouse back to Mrs. B.'s when she paged me during my run.

"You all right, Mrs. B.?" I had said into the walkie-talkie.

"Yes, yes. But come. You come home now."

Something was wrong. She didn't say *over and off*.

She waited for me on the front steps with her hands squeezed together. And her cheeks had no color in them at all.

"Mrs. B., are you okay?"

"I am fine. I am fine," she said, and patted my stomach. "Your father calls. Your grandma *Root* is in hospital."

"Did she fall again?"

"No, Briggs Baby. She has the stroke."

146

I made it to the hospital in record time. Talked to Dad on the way. Medicine. Anatomy. Practically everything in the body but the ileum was a mystery to me. All I knew from talking with Dad was that Grandma Ruth was in something called the Telemetry Unit, and her stroke was apparently mild.

"What's a mild stroke?" I asked.

"I'll find out more when I talk to her doctor," he said.

He sounded tired, and that was rare.

The Telemetry Unit looked like the deck of a spaceship with bedrooms off it. One central configuration housed doctors, nurses, desks, computers, and machines that beeped. The patients' rooms were quiet.

Grandma Ruth was asleep when I arrived, and judging from the wires traveling from the wall, over her shoulder, and down her nightgown to her chest, she wasn't going anywhere any time soon.

She was not going to like that.

A young, freckled nurse in navy scrubs tried to explain to me what was going on when I got there, but Dad talked over her, and she patiently smiled. I knew she would.

"Her cognition is fine," Dad said to me. "You'll see when she wakes up that she has a little facial droop and right-side weakness, and her speech is slow and a little slurred."

"It's making her angry," Mom said.

"I'm sure it is," I said.

"We're waiting on the results of tests," Dad said, and Mom listed them.

- MRI
- CT Scan
- Echocardiogram
- Neck ultrasound

"But it's not debilitating," Dad said. "She's going to need rehab, and I've got calls in to four places," he said as his phone vibrated, and he pulled it out of his pocket. "This is one of them."

"Sir," the nurse said. Her name tag read *Jenna*. "You can't use your phone in here."

Dad was already talking, so Mom guided him out of the room, down the hall. Away.

"Okay if I stay?" I asked Jenna.

"Sure. Can I get you a water?"

"No, I'm good, thanks."

"Your grandmother's probably just going to sleep for a while."

"I'd still like to stay."

"No problem," she said, and then pointed to a clicker connected to a cable on the table beside Grandma Ruth's bed. "That's the patient-call button. Let me know if you need anything or if Ruth does when she wakes up. I'm Jenna."

"Briggs," I said, too distracted to give her any kind of smile before she left.

"Please tell . . . her . . . that I am . . . *Mrs.* . . . Henry," Grandma Ruth said.

"Yes, Grandma Ruth," I said, and found my smile.

147

Grandma Ruth had not been sleeping. She had been waiting, she told me, with her eyes closed until my dad left.

"He annoys . . . all of us," she said.

Her speech was much slower than normal.

"Yes, he does, Grandma Ruth. He's just taking a call. I'll let you know when he's coming back."

"Hope he's not . . . talking to the under . . . taker."

"He's not," I said. "And anyway, you're going to out-live us all."

"Lord . . . I . . . hope . . . not."

She closed her eyes again. Waiting. And very quietly snoring.

Mom and Dad returned a few minutes later with the news that they'd found Grandma Ruth a good place for rehab. We stepped out of the room to talk.

"It's that new wing in Bluehair Court," Dad said.

"Bluestone," I said.

"Bet you're glad you're not working there now," he said. Heh-heh.

"Actually, I miss it."

"You do?" Mom asked.

"Yeah. I liked it there. They were the only adults in my life who never made me feel"—I looked at Dad, then Mom, then Dad again—"dyspeptic."

"Dys—what?" Dad rubbed my head and said, "Ah, you need a haircut."

I told them I'd wait there at the hospital and call when there was news. As Mom started to leave, she reached to squeeze my arm, but I stepped away before she got a grip.

148

I texted Abigail and Mrs. B. with the news and said I would be back tomorrow.

Abigail: Relieved to hear it. See you tomorrow

Mrs. B.: You are the good grandson. Drive carefully. Over and off.

149

Grandma Ruth woke up a little over four hours later. I was reading an article called "10 Qualities All Great Business Owners Share" in an old *Men's Health* magazine. Dad had all ten.

1. Vision
2. Optimism
3. Belief in One's Abilities
4. A Well-Conceived Plan
5. A Well-Conceived Backup Plan
6. Drive
7. Tirelessness
8. A Strong Work Ethic
9. Expertise in Your Field
10. Enjoyment in the Job

Too bad he didn't run our family the same way. As if it were a job.

"Briggs?" Grandma Ruth asked, and I walked to the side of her bed, which she patted.

"I'm not going to knock any of those wires loose, am I?"

"If you do . . . they'll have . . . a . . . crash cart here . . . in—"

"Ten seconds?"

"Three."

"You know you're going to be fine, right?" I said as I sat on the very edge of her bed.

She slid her hand next to my leg.

"I'm glad . . . you're here."

"Yeah, well, I need some Ficus care tips."

"Is that . . . sarcasm?"

"A little, and I have to tell you, Grandma Ruth, that some people find it funny."

She bumped her hand against my leg a couple times.

"I've been thinking about you lately," I said.

"Oh?"

"Yeah. I want you to tell me something," I said, and then added, "Please. How come you never say good-bye when you leave?"

"I hate . . . good-byes."

"Too hard?"

"Too . . . messy."

I grinned a little.

"How come you never look back?" I asked.

"How do you . . . know . . . I don't?"

"Because I always watch you go."

She closed her eyes. Tight. They looked a little watery when she opened them again, and I pulled a tissue out of my pocket and dabbed at the corners.

Then she bumped her hand against mine as if to say *That's enough, Briggs dear.*

"I never knew . . . anyone was . . . looking. That's why . . . I never . . . looked back."

"Well, you're going to have to from now on, aren't you?"

"If I . . . must." She moved her mouth kind of funny, like you do at the dentist after you're all numbed up, before she said, "I want you . . . to do something . . . for me now."

"Name it."

"Do . . . what . . . you . . . want."

"I am doing what I want," I said. "I promise. I want to be here."

"I don't," she said, and my grandmother, who had never laughed once in her life, chuckled. I've got to say it wasn't an easy sound to hear. In her condition, she sounded a little like she was drowning on air, but it was still a laugh, and it made me smile.

After a few seconds, she said, "Do what . . . makes you . . . happy."

"Have you had a happy life, Grandma Ruth?"

"No good to . . . complain."

I took a deep breath before saying, "You never really seem happy to me."

"I would have liked . . . to have been . . . a bot—bot—"

"Botanist?"

She bumped my leg. I guess that meant yes.

"Why didn't you?"

"I did what . . . was expected . . . of me."

"Marriage? Kids? Well, one kid."

"One was . . . enough."

That got another grin out of me.

"Your father . . . works . . . too hard."

"He does. I agree. No time for anything but work."

Bump.

"You work . . . hard . . . too."

"I'm a Henry," I said. "It's in my blood."

"Your mother's . . . not . . . happy . . . with . . . your f—father."

I wasn't sure how to answer for a couple seconds, so I finally just asked, "How do you know?"

"Takes one . . . to know one."

"Grandpa Richard? Same as Dad?"

Bump.

"I'm glad . . . you're not . . . Richard Gordon . . . Henry."

"The Third?"

Bump. Bump. Bump.

"You look really tired, Grandma Ruth."

Bump.

"I'm going to stay a little longer." I pointed to my chair. "Finish that magazine."

Bump.

"Briggs."

"Yes."

"I'm . . . happy . . . you're . . . here."

This time, I bumped my hand against hers.

150

I was reading an article called "Secret Foods That Fight Belly Bulge"—having read every other article in the only magazines available—when I heard a commotion in the hall. Raised voices. People moving quickly. Something unintelligible over a speaker.

I was just grinning a little that Grandma Ruth was sleeping through it when Jenna, the freckle-faced nurse, bolted into the room carrying what looked like a funky radio with paddles on the sides. I shot out of my chair, and she ordered me out of the room.

I stepped back, plastered against the wall as four people, all in scrubs, raced into the room pushing a cart loaded with boxes and bags of fluid and syringes, and they formed a ring around Grandma Ruth.

They moved rapidly but methodically. Talked all at once but communicated. Gave orders and followed them. It was chaos, and it wasn't.

"Briggs. Briggs."

I felt Jenna grip my arm, and I sort of snapped to look at her.

"You need to leave," she said. "Let's go."

She walked me out of the room, out of the unit to a nearby waiting room—brown and ugly and empty.

"I'm going to leave you here," she said. "I want you to stay here."

"What's—what's—"

"I'll find out, and I'll come and tell you. Okay?"

"Okay," I said, and stood like a statue and about as aware for ages after she left. Or minutes. Who knew? Who cared? I felt frozen and heavy and light-headed all at the same time, and I thought I might punch someone or break something if I could have moved, when Jenna opened the door again, and Sam and Kennedy walked in, looking serious and concerned.

"What—" was all I could manage to say.

"Your mom said you were here," Sam said, and we shook hands, kind of slapped shoulders. "We thought we'd come hang out. Keep you company."

"Yeah."

"What's going on?" Kennedy asked.

"I don't know," I said, and a square-shouldered, middle-aged woman in an ugly tan blazer entered the room and introduced herself as Kathy Kazlow, hospital chaplain.

151

Twenty-five minutes later, I had to call Dad to tell him Grandma Ruth died. He kept shouting *what* and *wait* and *wait, what* into the phone. I handed the thing to Sam and downed two bottles of water the chaplain brought me. She was a nice lady, and I hated the sight of her.

152

At home, I slept for sixteen hours and woke up to find forty-four text messages. Sam had told friends—only after asking me if I minded—and I texted Abigail and Mrs. B.

I could hear Dad on the phone in the family room when I finally dragged myself out of bed. I could tell from the tone and the rhythm—firm and relentless—that he was organizing something. Probably the funeral.

Grandma Ruth's priest didn't stand a chance.

Taylor texted me: SOOOOO SORRY BRIGGS!!!! CALL IF U NEED TO TALK

Mrs. B. texted: I am thinking of you, Briggs Baby. Over and off.

Abigail texted me a picture of her green-and-white beach blanket in front of the water. On the blanket was a package of Oreos. Underneath the pic she wrote:

A little mobile lake effect until you come back.

I planted myself at the kitchen counter and guzzled milk from the carton. Mom walked in and put a glass in front of me, which I ignored.

"Hungry?" she asked.

"Of course."

"Do you want a sandwich?" she asked.

"Sure," I said, and finished the milk and wiped a small drop of it off my chin.

"What kind?"

"How about peanut butter and grape jelly," I said, and Mom grinned at me.

"Is that sarcasm?"

"No one likes sarcasm," I said.

153

Dad gave the eulogy at Grandma Ruth's memorial service. Like he was giving a speech at a business meeting and bragging about an excellent employee. He spoke about Grandma Ruth's upbringing, education, and work ethic.

He said Grandma Ruth was committed to her family, her faith, and her church, and he even made some of the crowd, which numbered over a hundred and fifty, chuckle when he called her a "dogged crusader" for the rummage sale. I think two-thirds of the church turned out.

"It won't be the same without her," he said. "I see many of you nodding your heads. You all know. It really won't be. I can think of five other committees that won't be the same without her either. But neither will any of us who knew her and respected her and loved her."

He sat down. And because Grandma Ruth wouldn't have it any other way, this service followed the tradition of most Episcopal services and came to an end about thirty minutes after it started. I later learned from the priest that she had planned everything in advance and told him if the service went one minute too long, her lawyer would revoke the bequest she made.

Classic Grandma Ruth.

154

A big crowd had assembled at our house, where caterers set up lunch. People streamed in steadily. I shook warm and cold hands and thanked them for coming and appreciated it when anyone said, "She was a nice lady."

For all I knew a bunch of these people were crashers. I kind of hoped they were.

Within twenty minutes, our house was nearing shoulder-to-shoulder capacity. I ditched my coat and tie and found some relief in running out to the van in our driveway for supplies for the caterer.

Sam found me taking a break out there, leaning against the caterer's truck, enjoying the silence and the woody-perfume smell of boxwood. Grandma Ruth had planted them around the house just after we moved in.

"You okay?" Sam asked, and I nodded.

"You'll be happy to know that Grandma Ruth was not a robot. I found out right before she died."

"Cool," he said. "Was it a laugh or a fart?" he asked, and I punched his arm.

Kennedy eventually joined us there. Taylor too. And Emily. And Ashley. And Nishesh. He had never met

Grandma Ruth, but I appreciated that he came and was almost glad to see him. Almost.

We'd been outside only a few minutes when another crowd arrived. In front was Abigail, with Mrs. B. holding her arm. They both kissed my cheek. Behind them came Ben, Brandon, Zach, Josh, Danny, Lauren, Nicole, and Maddy.

"Uh-oh," Sam said quietly to me. "Gonna be a rumble."

"Nah," I said, and made the introductions like this. "Okay, listen up because I'm only doing this once." I pointed as I spoke. "Sam, Kennedy, Taylor, Nishesh, Emily, Ashley, Maddy, Lauren, Nicole, Danny, Zach, Josh, Brandon, Ben, Abigail, and the famous Mrs. B."

"Why I am famous?" she asked.

"Because I talk about you all the time," I said, and she smiled until her cheeks turned pink.

We walked inside. We hung out. We talked. We ate. My two groups of friends didn't mix, but Mrs. B. made the rounds.

I finally introduced her to Mom and Dad when they were free.

"He is the good boy," she told them. "He is the hard *wooker.* You are proud of *heem,* yes?"

"Well, I expect nothing less of him than that," Dad said.

"You are proud of *heem,* you say, 'I am proud of you,'" Mrs. B. said.

"Ah, he knows I am," Dad said, and he rubbed my head.

Abigail left early with Mrs. B. I told her I'd be back Saturday afternoon. We had to meet with Grandma Ruth's lawyer the next day and get something called the probate process going.

In the living room, semi crowded with chatty Episcopalians, I took Maddy's hand and said, "Again, Maddy, I am so sorry. I don't think I can say it enough. Am I forgiven?"

"Maybe," she said, and smiled huge in Sam's direction and stuck her tongue between her teeth. "You definitely will be if you bring *him* over here. He doesn't have a girlfriend, does he?"

"I know for a fact he doesn't."

I waved Sam over, and then left them to talk. Sam looked back at me, grinning and nodding like he was about to get laid. We both knew he wasn't.

The place cleared out about ninety minutes later. Ben, Brandon, and those guys were among the last to leave. We all stood talking in the front yard.

"Geri," Brandon said, extending his hand, which I shook. "Sorry about your grandma."

"Thanks, man. I appreciate you coming."

There were more handshakes. More condolences. Finally Ben said, "Okay, we gotta clear out. I'm sure Briggs is wrecked."

"Who the hell is Briggs?" Brandon asked, and Maddy slapped his shoulder, and Zach said, "Duh," and Ben pointed at me, and I just laughed, especially when I heard Brandon say, on the way to their cars, "I thought his name was Geri."

155

Grandma Ruth's lawyer came to the house Friday morning. We sat at the dining room table, which we only ever used for Christmas Eve, birthdays, and, apparently, readings of wills.

His name was Frank Hoekstra, and he looked like he should have owned polo ponies. His purple pocket square matched his tie. Dad had known him for years. They played golf at least once a month.

Frank Hoekstra explained the process of probate—that it took months but that Grandma Ruth's estate was not terribly complicated. She made small bequests to her church and to the Red Cross. Her home and its contents, minus her jewelry, she left to Dad. Her jewelry she left to Mom.

"Really?" she asked.

"She knew you sold the earrings she gave you, and didn't lose them."

"Did she," Mom said, like she wasn't at all surprised.

"And her stock portfolio she has left to Briggs," Frank Hoekstra said to seconds of silence.

"Her whole stock portfolio?" Dad asked.

"Yes," Frank said, and passed us each stapled copies of her records.

There were columns and columns of numbers. She seemed to have invested in tech stocks and dependable conglomerates like GE and Procter & Gamble. In the upper left corner was this: *Acct. Value (USD) $351,125.77.*

"This is held in trust?" Dad asked Frank.

"No. Free and clear after probate." Frank Hoekstra looked at me and said, "I tried to talk her into putting this into an irrevocable trust until you were thirty, but she wouldn't hear of it. She said it wasn't a gift if there were strings attached."

"Wha—" I said.

Frank and Dad talked a few minutes more before Frank said he'd be in touch. Dad showed him out, then returned to the dining room like his ass was on fire.

"Here's what we're going to do," he said as he sat and scooted his chair close to mine. He began talking with his hands, big gestures, like he was holding huge, invisible blocks and moving them around the table. "The property on Drumlin is worth four hundred K. We clean it out. Fresh coat of paint. You and I can do that in a week," he said to me. "We list it ourselves and save the commission."

"What about her things?" Mom asked.

"We keep the silver and the antiques. We sell the china. The rest, who cares? Salvation Army. Her church. Whoever wants to pick them up can have them."

"Dad."

"You don't want her clothes, do you?" he said with a near laugh. "Unless you think you might look pretty spiffy in that blazer. Heh-heh." He gripped my shoulder. "So listen, that's four hundred K in the bank. Briggs, you sign over the three fifty to me. We combine that with what I've got invested so far, and we buy Foam Works. Outright. Just buy it out from—"

"Dad."

"Or don't. You don't need to sign it over to me. I make you junior partner, and you buy in. You get dividends, profit sharing. You come to a stock meeting three times a year. We'll have them on weekends when you're home from school. We're a voting block. We still have control."

"Dad. Enough. Slow down."

"Now, listen, Briggs, you don't get ahead in this world by hesitating. You know that. We've got to seize the moment."

"Seize the moment? Dad," I said, and held the back of my neck for a few seconds. "Grandma Ruth just died."

"Yeah. We lost her. And I'm sad about that."

"We didn't *lose* her," I said, raising my voice a little. "She died. And you're not exactly acting like you're sad."

"Briggs," Mom said in a gentle, cautioning tone.

"Hey," my dad said, pointing at my face. "Don't tell me how I feel."

"I have no idea how you feel. You don't seem to feel anything." I pushed back in my chair. Dad copied the move. "All I see is a guy who's acting like a vulture over his dead mom's loot."

Dad slapped the table with both hands.

"Richard," Mom said.

"This is business, Briggs."

"This is your mom," I said. "This is Grandma Ruth."

"Don't expect me to cry like a baby over this to suit you," Dad said. "This is what it takes to run a business. I see an opportunity, and I take it. I'm looking out for this family."

"Oh, bullshit."

"What did you say to me?" Dad demanded, rising out of his chair and stepping close. I did the same.

"I said bullshit."

Dad opened his eyes wide and looked wild but didn't move.

"You're not looking out for us," I said. "You're looking out for your bottom line. That's not the same thing."

"I'm looking to the future. For you. For your mother. For us. For this family."

"There is no us," I said, stepping back, shoving the papers across the table. "There is no family."

"What?" he said. "What does that mean?"

"Briggs," Mom said.

"You gonna tell him or am I?" I asked.

"Briggs. Richard," Mom said as Dad, darting his eyes between her and me, asked, "Tell me what?"

"She's leaving you," I said. "Papers are drawn up. Sam's dad is her attorney."

"Don't be ridiculous," he said.

"It's true," I said.

Dad whipped his head toward Mom, and he stared at

her with his mouth hanging open. She folded her hands together and rested them on the table.

"Is it?" he asked. *"Is it?"*

She drew a long breath and let it out before saying, "It is."

"Now?" He was mad. "After everything I've done? After everything we've worked for?"

"Everything we've worked for was everything but us," she said.

"That doesn't make any sense," he said. "We'll talk when you make sense."

"That's just it, Richard," Mom said as she stood. "We don't talk."

She left the room after a particularly icy stare at me that made my stomach cramp.

156

I couldn't sleep. An earlier rainstorm blew a nice breeze across the lake, and Mrs. B.'s house was cool and dry with the slider and windows open, but I couldn't sleep.

It was after midnight when I threw on shorts and an old blue sweatshirt and took a towel down to the lake. It was early August, and the moon was nearly full. Bright. Reflecting off the rippled black surface of the lake. The sand was cool under my feet.

I just sat there listening to the sound of water swishing onto the shore and trickling back out again. And I let that lake have its full effect on me, giving in to every uninterrupted thought, every memory, as they came, as they were. Not how I thought they were. Not how I wanted them to be.

Like Abigail had said, there was no place better to just sit and think.

I drew my knees up and dropped my head onto them and cried. For myself, for Grandma Ruth, for Pauline Ostrander, for Maria Santos, for Dorothy D. Webb, for Jonathan Carroll, for Howard Levy, for Eddie DeZwaan. I cried for seeing my old dog and wanting him back and for Abigail and bathrooms. I cried for Mom's stupid lists and Dad's stupid puns and the way they never, ever talked. I cried that they were splitting up, that Mrs. B.'s knees still *squicked,* that I was going to have to say goodbye to her in a little over a week and that I might never see Abigail again. And I cried that no matter how hard I worked, I couldn't change a single thing that happened that summer. All I could do was offer someone a tissue, pat their knee, and give them a smile.

It was Abigail's cool hand on my back. I knew it without looking up. She sat next to me and pressed up close and stroked my head while I sniffed and sobbed. She smoothed her hand across my back, squeezed my arm, kissed my shoulder, and stayed close and quiet until I was a wrecked, wet mess.

I dried my face on my sleeves and looked at her, wanting to say something, but I was too exhausted for words. With her thumbs, she pushed the remaining tears off my face and said, barely above a whisper, "It's nice to meet you."

157

Sam: **Did u hear Taylor and Nishesh broke up?**

Me: **Nope. What happened?**

Sam: **She dumped him**

Me: **Why?**

Sam: **She said he was too available for her. Whatever that means**

Me: **It means she's fine**

I walked out of the bathroom at Pickler Funeral Home—the bathroom with the fake palm tree in the maroon urn—smiling until I saw Mrs. B. frowning at me, her strong, little fists shoved on her hips.

"Why you are in there so *lonk*?" she asked.

"Well, apart from the obvious, I was also checking my texts."

"Phone? You use the phone?"

"Yeah." I pointed. "In there."

"No. This is my funeral. You do not use the phone at my funeral."

"This isn't your funeral. It hasn't even started yet."

"No. We are in the funeral home. It is like the *shursh*. You do not use the phone here. Give. Give to me," she said, and I handed it over. "You are *goink beck* on the probe . . . the probe—"

"Probation?"

"Yes."

"You know you're leaving for Arizona in a week, right?"

"Yes."

"So I'm on probation for my last week here?"

"You want the job? You do what I say."

"I want the job, Mrs. B.," I said, and held my arm out for her to take.

"Good," she said as we walked toward the room where the service would be. "Maybe you want the job next *sahmmer* too?"

"I definitely want the job next summer too," I said.

"Good. I hire you now," she said, smiling up at me. She looked at the program that the usher in a black pinstripe suit handed her and grinned until her cheeks turned shiny red. "Ah," she said to me. "You will like this one."

158

I spent the next week helping Mrs. B. pack and getting the house ready to close up. Mostly I cleaned. I kept the kitchen floor spotless. You could eat off that floor. Or lie down on it if you wanted.

159

A couple nights later Abigail and I polished off a bag of Oreos watching the sunset over the water that was clear aqua by then. Even at that hour, you could see the rippled, sandy lakebed for yards offshore.

"So what about you?" I asked.

"What about me?" she said.

"What's your plan?"

"I don't have one."

There was a steady breeze that night. Abigail fought her fly-away hair for a minute before pulling it back into a ponytail, exposing those pointy elf ears I loved.

"You want to know what I think?" I asked.

"I have a feeling I'm going to hear it."

"Well, that's your fault. My beach activities never used to include thinking."

She leaned back, propping herself up on those long, thin arms, and she said, "Let's hear it."

"I think the two of us can sit here feeling sorry for ourselves because of the sucky big changes in our lives, or we can get off our butts and do something."

"I can't change having Crohn's disease."

"I can't change my parents splitting up."

"Weren't you the kind of guy who said life is what you make it?"

I slid a few stray strands of her hair behind her ear.

"I'm still that kind of guy," I said. "I just figured out that sometimes plans change. But you still have to have them. And you still have to work at them."

We were quiet a few seconds. I copied Abigail's pose. We stretched out our legs. We crossed our ankles.

"I have no idea what I want to do," she said.

"Neither do I."

We tipped our chins into the wind coming across the water and pressed our shoulders close.

160

"I don't think I'm all that interested in law school anymore," I said the next night.

"Were you ever?" Abigail asked.

"Not really."

She and I strolled up the beach, past a bunch of dark cottages. Closed up for the summer. Only a few little kids played in the water, and the wind was louder than their laughs.

"What about gerontology?" Abigail suggested.

"I can rule out law school, medical school, nursing school, vet tech school, or any career that involves body fluids. What about you?"

"I'm going to have to second the no-body-fluids career path since I produce enough of my own."

"You know that's completely disgusting."

She tipped her head back and laughed.

I was still interested in getting my MBA. And construction management sounded interesting too.

Abigail enrolled as a commuter at Kalamazoo College in the education department but wasn't sold on a teaching career. She still wanted to travel the world and still hated that she couldn't.

Together we ruled out firefighter, cop, postal worker, UPS driver, bank teller, investment broker, computer programmer, telemarketer, talk show host, game show host, funeral home cosmetologist, puppeteer, and guy on TV who sells crap no one needs.

Our plans were works in progress.

"At least one plan is concrete," I said, sloshing shin-deep in warm water. I reached for Abigail's hand, and she let me take it. "I'm working here for Mrs. B. next summer." I shrugged, smiled. "Guess she and I will have to do the long-distance thing till then."

Abigail laughed and tightened her fingers around mine. "I hope to be in Spain next summer," she said. "But I know you'll be happy here."

"Mostly," I said. "Just not looking forward to dealing with the tourists."

161

Abigail and I drove Mrs. B. to the airport in Grand Rapids on the morning of August twelfth. She gave us hugs and kisses and told us we were good babies.

"Let me know you landed safely, okay, Mrs. B.?" I said at the sign reading *Ticketed passengers only beyond this point*. I really hated that sign. "Just send me a text."

"Yes. And you let me know the way how you are *doink* at the school."

"We'll check in with each other every now and then," I said, and I leaned closer to her. "You know, if you want the relationship to work, you have to treat it like a job."

She grinned until her eyes all but disappeared, and she raised those shoulders when she asked, "We are the job now, Briggs Baby?"

"We are the job now, Mrs. B."

162

We were pulling out of the airport parking lot when Abigail said, "She's your girlfriend," through that self-satisfied smile, lips closed but stretched wide, and handed me a tissue. "It's always hard to say good-bye to someone you love."

"Then no good-byes for you," I said, my voice thick, and my eyes sticky with tissue dust.

She lowered her eyes for a second before saying, "Okay. No good-byes."

I pulled a clean tissue from my pocket and handed it to her.

"It's a Serbian thing," I said. "The gentleman always carries the tissue."

163

Mrs. B. let me stay in her house that night. In the morning, I'd turn off the water, drain the faucets, unplug everything but the few lamps she left on timers. The Howes had her keys and checked on the place all winter.

That night, Abigail and I sat by the water in front of Mrs. B.'s and watched a patchy sunset. Rain was predicted tomorrow, and flat, gray clouds dotted the sky. But they parted often enough that we got to watch the red-orange sun's descent behind the lake.

I stood and offered Abigail my hand as she got up. I pulled her close and reached to move a piece of her hair behind her ear.

"I got it," she whispered, and I kissed her, feeling every lush bit of her lips against mine, tasting her, breathing her lake scent into me, feeling her hands on my skin under my shirt. I smiled against her mouth. "Man, your hands are cold."

She started to pull them away, but I stopped her with, "No, I love your cold hands," and we kissed again, sweet and slow. She pressed her hands against my back again and rested her cheek against my neck. I wrapped my arms around her, and we stayed like that, eyes closed and barely breathing.

Finally, she stepped back.

"I've got to go in," she said in a way that let me know she *had* to go in. Right then.

"I know," I said, and we kissed once more, and she jogged toward her house.

I turned for a last view of the sunset.

When I looked back—and I did look back—she was standing on her deck, looking my way and waving. And smiling a smile that did not need a name.

164

The Ficus was the last thing I put in my car before locking up the house. Then I walked around back and inhaled my last breath of lake air for the year. Cool and slatey and just as unspoiled as it was in June and would be again next summer. Some things—thank God—never changed.

I was just walking back to my car when I saw the God Yacht slowly cruising past, and I shouted, "Dum!"

He rolled down his window and called, "You ready, Briggs? Are you ready?"

"Not remotely, man!" I laughed.

165

Dad moved into Grandma Ruth's house on Drumlin Court. He and Mom agreed to a trial separation.

I spent my first week home, mid-August, helping him move. It was a Friday afternoon when he and I finally unloaded the last of the boxes. We carried them up to Grandma Ruth's bedroom, which was a dull orangish pink. Kind of the color of an ileum. I saw pictures online.

"I've been looking over Grandma Ruth's stocks," I said. "I figured I'd just leave the account where it is right now. Not touch it for a while."

"You should set up a meeting with the broker. Make sure you can work with him," Dad said. "I can introduce you to a couple others if you want."

"I know four from the club. They wanted me to meet their daughters."

"Well, now they really will."

We kind of nodded at each other.

"This room would look much better in a neutral color," Dad said. "Maybe eggshell."

"We could take up the rug. See what the floor looks like underneath."

"You busy tomorrow?"

"Nope. You?"

"No."

166

I arrived at the Drumlin Court house at ten a.m. Dad had already bought the paint and supplies, and without much more than "good morning," we got to work, taping the trim.

The silence was comfortable enough. In any case, we were used to it.

167

Jason Hirsch had a party the next weekend. There were forty-two people there. Roughly twelve percent of our graduating class.

Jason greeted me with a big handshake and, "Briggs Henry."

"Hey, Jason," I said. "How's it going?"

Sam and Kennedy were there. Taylor too. Without Nishesh. We were all talking about roommates and how many days until each of us left for school.

Taylor and I didn't wander off for a private conversation underneath the crabapple trees, which were loaded with clusters of shiny fruit that made me think of Mrs. B.'s cheeks, of course.

I pulled out my phone.

Checking in Mrs. B. All's well here. How r u?

I deleted "r u" and wrote "are you."

Ten minutes later she texted back.

I am fine, Briggs Baby. Having the nice time with my sisters. Over and off.

Me: **Over and off, Mrs. B**

168

Abigail and I texted each other regularly. Mostly at night.

Abigail: How are things with your parents?

Me: No one's talking

Abigail: Could be worse

Me: How?

Abigail: They could be talking only thru attorneys

Me: I hate attorneys

Uh . . .

Me: Except your parents

Abigail: Nice save. They hate most attorneys too

Other times I got texts like these out of the blue.

Abigail: Political lobbyist?

Me: No. Anatomy prof?

Abigail: No. Pharmacist?

Me: Too much like med school. Professional bike walker?

Abigail: Hilarious. Undertaker?

Me: Now you're just being gross

Abigail: I'm used to gross

Me: No ur not

Abigail: I'm GETTING used to it

Me: Big changes take time to get used to

Abigail: Big changes suck

Me: Did u actually say suck???

Abigail: It's a word

169

Mom offered to help me move into my dorm room, but I told her I wanted to go alone. Dad didn't even offer. He said he had a meeting with a Subaru rep that day that could lead to a big contract.

"You understand, don't you?" he asked.

"Of course," I said, and meant it.

In the driveway, Mom recited her list, which began with *drive carefully* and ended with her giving me five twenties. Apparently, she expected me to face a higher number of emergencies than usual.

"I'm sorry about . . . blurting it out like that," I told her. "You leaving Dad."

"I know you are," she said, and did that mom-thing of putting both hands on my cheeks for a couple seconds.

"There aren't any more secrets, right?" I asked.

"Like what?"

"Like, I don't know. Sam's my half brother?"

"Sam Nguyen is not your half brother," she said evenly. "Chris Kennedy is."

We shared a little laugh, and we hugged, and she said, "Now go," before walking inside.

I texted her from the car:

Take care of my ficus please

Mom: You're not taking it?

Me: Not this semester. I dont want anything to happen to it

I honked as I backed out, and she waved from the kitchen window. I just wanted to make sure she was looking.

170

A crowd of student volunteers in yellow T-shirts swarmed me and my car the moment I pulled up near my dorm. They welcomed me to campus, grabbed my stuff, and moved me in.

It took two trips and fifteen minutes.

My room looked like a prison cell and smelled like ammonia and old leather shoes. Bunk beds, tile floor, beige cinderblock walls. But it was bigger than my room in the shoebox, and I figured I'd get used to it soon enough.

I didn't have a yellow shirt, but after I registered, I spent the day helping people unload their cars. I hauled boxes of vinyl records, mattresses into rooms that already had beds, giant pillows, giant rubber balls, couple cases of toilet paper, foam chairs, messes of Christmas lights, three hamster cages, eight or nine bundles of rope, and, weirdest of all, a four-foot-long dinosaur made entirely of LEGO.

That weekend there were parties—called socials—every night, and I said "Nice to meet you" over a hundred times and meant it but wondered if, in weeks or months to come, I'd regret a few of those. Probably.

I found space in the room for all my stuff and hung up posters of vintage Oldsmobiles Dad had by the boxful in our basement. I found them when he moved into Grandma Ruth's.

I dived into my classes and by the end of September a bunch of new friends suggested I run for Central Student Government, but I'd done the class president thing in high school, and politics wasn't for me. I did decide to pledge. I was a Phi Psi legacy, twice over. Dad and Grandpa Richard. I liked the SigEp guys better, so I went with them.

It would have been nice to share these things with Dad, but he and I still weren't talking much. I told Mom about them via texts.

She said she and Dad started marriage counseling.

Me: Hows it going?

Mom: We're both finding it very difficult.

Me: Think youll work it out?

Mom: One way or another. How are classes?

Me: I got a 98 on my last calculus quiz

Mom: Of course you did.

This was my family. The Henrys. We had expectations. We achieved. We catalogued our successes, but sometimes we needed our hair cut.

171

Me: I really like my Construction Materials and Method class

Abigail: I'm loving Spanish. You should hear me roll my Rs

Me: I'm free this weekend. Maybe I'll head in to SH for a lesson

Abigail: Te echo de menos

Me: Remind me

Abigail: I miss you

Me: U do?

Abigail: It's from a dialog in the book. Along with Me tomas el pelo. Roughly "You're kidding me"

Me: Got it

Abigail: We're learning idioms this week

Me: Right. Idioms

Abigail: I've got to run

Me: Sure

Abigail: Hey, Briggs

Me: Yes?

Abigail: Te echo de menos

172

It was a Friday afternoon in October when I ran back to my dorm room in search of props. Mainly a black T-shirt and sunglasses. One of my SigEp buddies was organizing a contest. We were going to re-create iconic movie scenes in pics. *The Shining. Titanic. Forest Gump. The Matrix.*

I heard a knock on my door and called out, "It's open."

I shut my dresser drawer and turned to see my dad. Standing in my room. Holding a Ficus and looking like he didn't know what the hell to say or even, exactly, where he was. I'm pretty sure I looked just like him.

Seconds passed before he finally said, "You forgot this."

I took the plant from him and set it by my desk.

"Thought it might . . . spruce up the place," he said.

My roommate and I kept the room pretty neat, but neither of us had made a bed since we got there, and we opted for the stack method of organization—stacks of books, stacks of papers, stacks of clothes that didn't fit in drawers and that we just couldn't bother to hang up.

"Thanks," I said. "I actually left it home on purpose. I was worried I'd forget to water it or something."

"Sure. Well. I can take it home."

"No, it's good," I said. "It'll be fine here."

"So everything's good? Settling in?"

I nodded and shrugged at the same time and said, "It's a process."

"If you want to feel like you belong," he said in that game show host voice, hoping I'd finish the sentence for him. *Act like you belong.* But instead I just gave him a halfhearted, "Yeah," and he gave me one right back.

"Yeah."

"Do you want to sit down?" I offered.

"Uh, no. Maybe we could go somewhere and talk."

"Talk?"

He sighed out a long breath and said, "Talk."

"Sure. You want to see the campus?"

"I'd like that."

On our way outside he told me, "Mom sends her love. You know, she and I are in therapy."

"Yeah, she mentioned it. Uh. How's it going? Not that I need many details."

"Uh, not great," he said. "Hard." He scrunched his eyebrows down like he was completely confused when he said, "Apparently she doesn't find me very funny."

"You? No," I said as we stepped outside in the sky-blue cool of the day.

"Is that sarcasm?" he asked in a way that let me know he finally understood that it was.

"Look, I wanted to tell you in person that we've filed the papers," he said. "Divorce." He nodded a couple times, like he was just now agreeing to it. "It's for the best."

"Yeah. Uh. I'm sorry."

"Me too. Me too. We'll stay in counseling through the process, but after that . . ."

He shrugged. He ran his hand over his head. I scratched at the back of my neck.

"Hey, I pledged SigEp," I said.

"Well, why not Phi Psi? You're a legacy. Did you tell them that?"

"Yeah. I like SigEp better."

"But what's wrong with—"

"Dad," I said. "Why don't you ask me why I like the SigEp house better?"

A trace of a smile appeared on his face, and he said, "Okay. Why do you like the SigEp House better?"

I listed my reasons, and he said *uh-huh* after each, and I could tell he wished I had joined Phi Psi.

He asked me how classes were going, and I said, "Good. I really like my construction management classes."

"Construction management. Uh-huh. Nothing wrong with throwing a pre-law class in there."

"No," I agreed. "Nothing wrong with it." My phone chimed, and I pulled it out of my pocket. "Nothing wrong with drafting classes either."

"Do you know what the starting salary of a general contractor is?"

"I'm sure you'll tell me," I said, smiling at him *and* at my phone.

It was this text: **Thinking of you. Just checking in.**

Me: **Everything's good. Everything okay there?**

"Who's that?" Dad asked.

"My girlfriend," I said.

"You have time for a girlfriend?"

"I'm making the time," I said. "It's long-distance."

She texted back:

Everything is fine.

"Those relationships can be tricky," Dad said.

"Relationships take work."

"So the marriage counselor tells me."

"So about contractors and their salaries," I said.

"Thirty to fifty thousand. In a good year."

"That's not bad."

My phone chimed with one more text.

"No, it's not bad," Dad said. "But do you know the average starting salary of someone with a JD-MBA?"

I glanced at my phone while Dad kept talking. And I thought, of all the changes in my life since I was nine, the one thing that stayed the same was him. There was something kind of admirable about that. And something kind of odd.

I read the text to myself: **Over and off.**

Me: **Over and off, Mrs. B.**

ACKNOWLEDGMENTS

I am so grateful for my agent, Faye Bender, and my editor, Jess Dandino Garrison. Thank you, Faye, for your enthusiasm for this book and your support of it and me. And thank you, Jess, for your invaluable guidance, suggestions, brainstorming sessions—and patience—that helped Briggs find his story.

Thank you, David McCahan, my brother, for your earnest and thoughtful descriptions of life with Crohn's. I hate that you have this horrible disease, but only you could make the word *ileum* funny.

OHYA! Warmest thanks and big hugs to my talented and fabulous author friends: Rae, Jody, Julia, Linda (whose name is Linda and not Lisa), Lisa, Edie, Margaret, and Natalie, who understand this challenging business and always keep me laughing.

Thank you, Rich Vandepels, my cousin, for teaching me about boating safety and the Coast Guard, and thank you, too, for your service in the Coast Guard and to this country.

And thank you, Tim, my husband, who loves the lake as much as I do and makes every book I write possible.

ERIN McCAHAN is a native Michigander who grew up on the beaches of Grand Haven and Macatawa. Now a resident of landlocked New Albany, Ohio, she and her husband return every summer to North Beach in South Haven, on the shores of Lake Michigan. Look for them under the red-and-white-striped umbrella.

Learn more about Erin at ERINMCCAHAN.COM, and connect with her on Facebook at @AUTHORERINMCCAHAN and on Twitter @ERINMCCAHAN.